KiTTEN

CONSTRUCTION COMPANY

Meet the House Kittens

3 1526 05213403 5

KITTEN
CONSTRUCTION · COMPANY
Meet the House Kittens

John Patrick Green
with color by Cat Caro

First Second
New York

For the builders

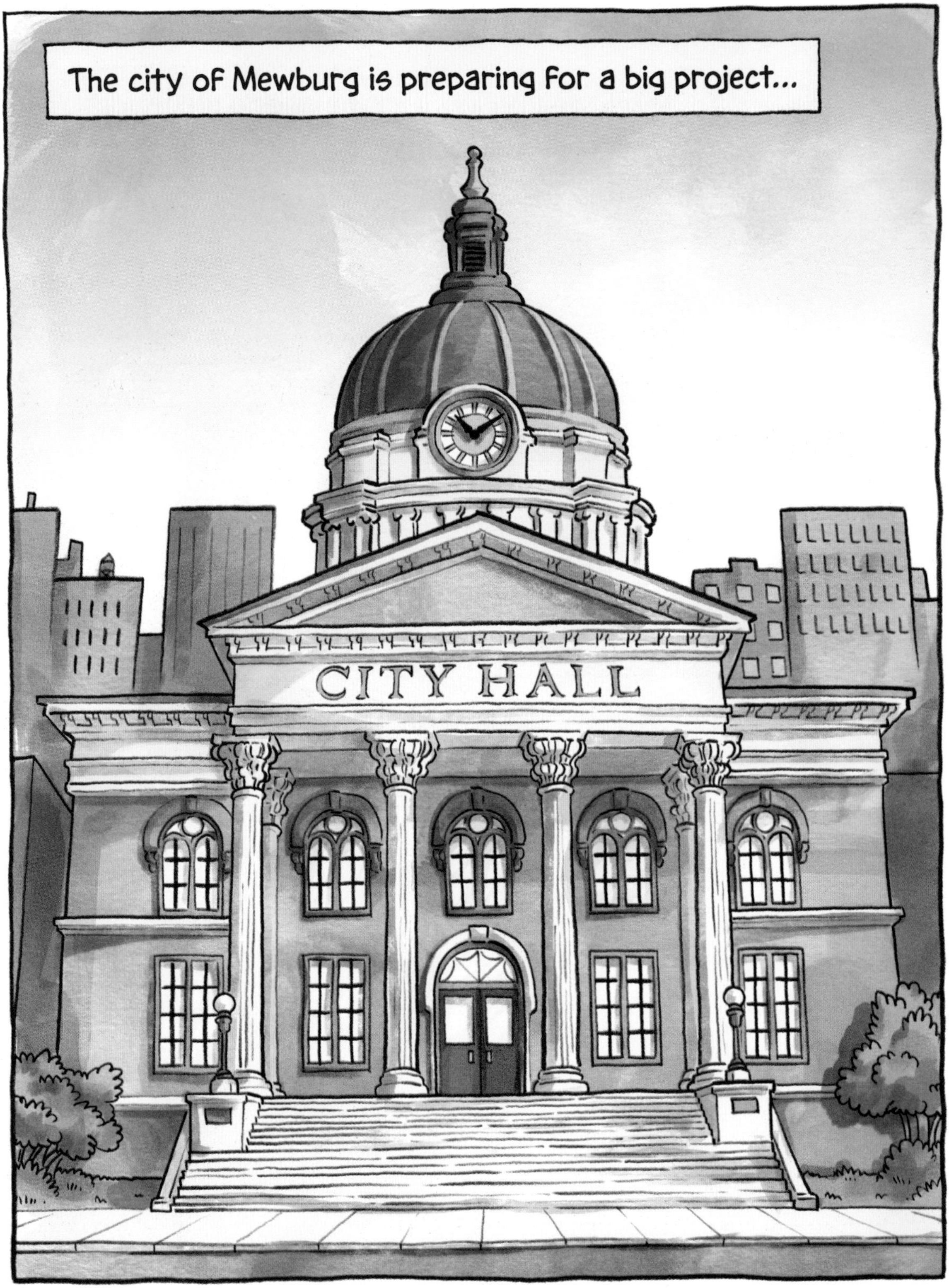

The city of Mewburg is preparing for a big project...
CITY HALL

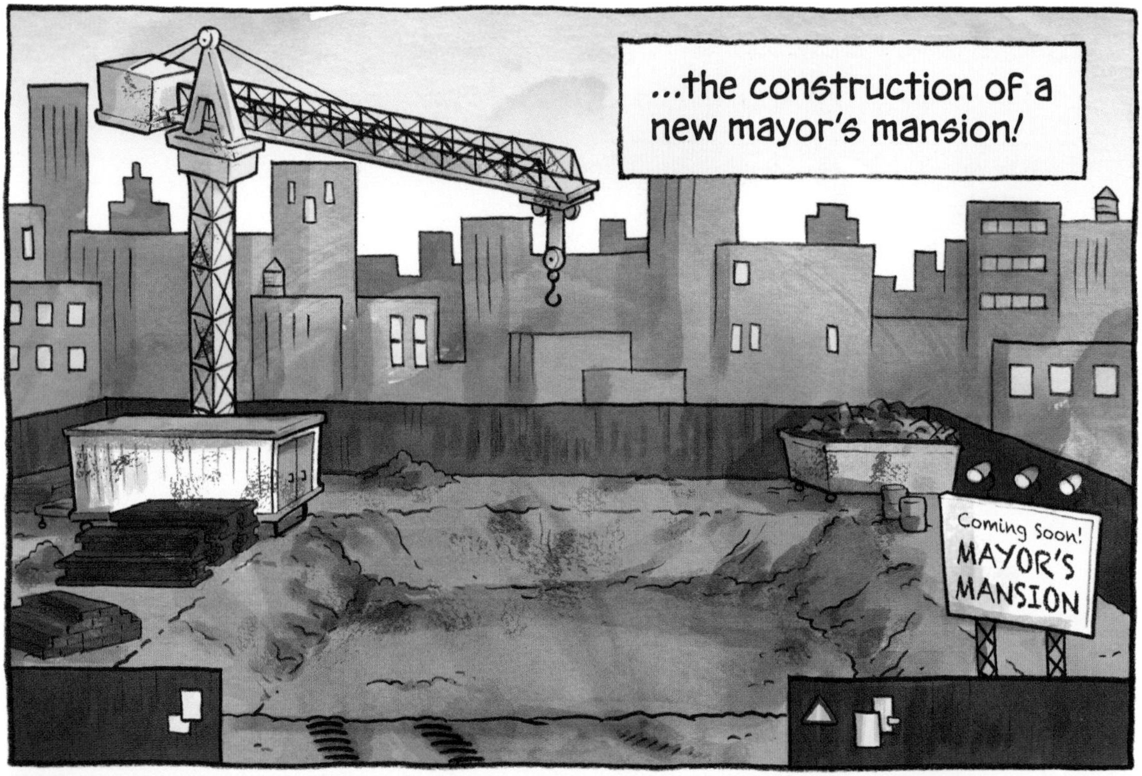
...the construction of a new mayor's mansion!
Coming Soon! MAYOR'S MANSION

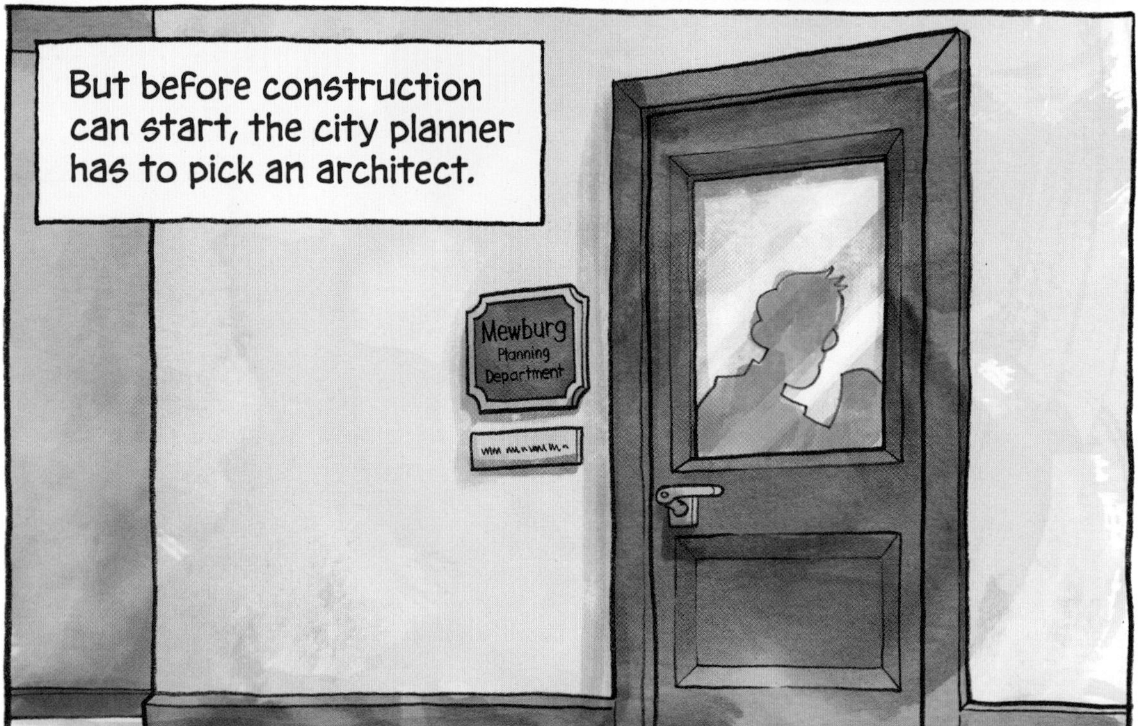
But before construction can start, the city planner has to pick an architect.
Mewburg Planning Department

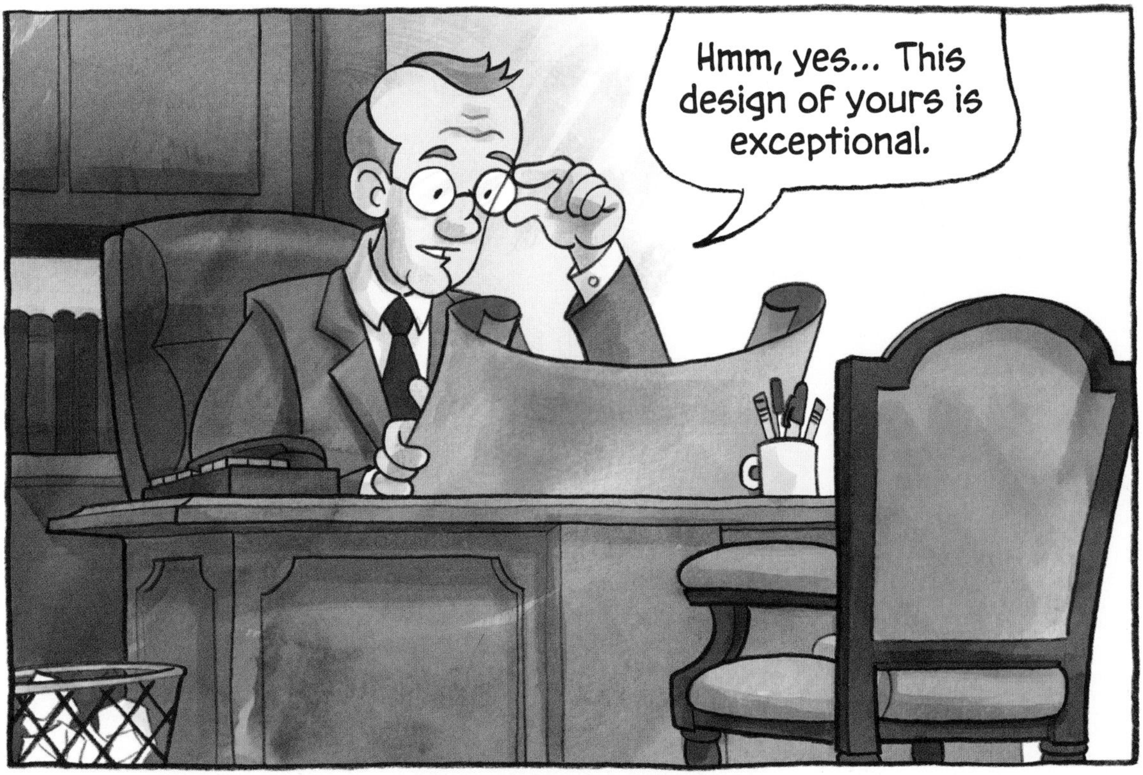
Hmm, yes... This design of yours is exceptional.

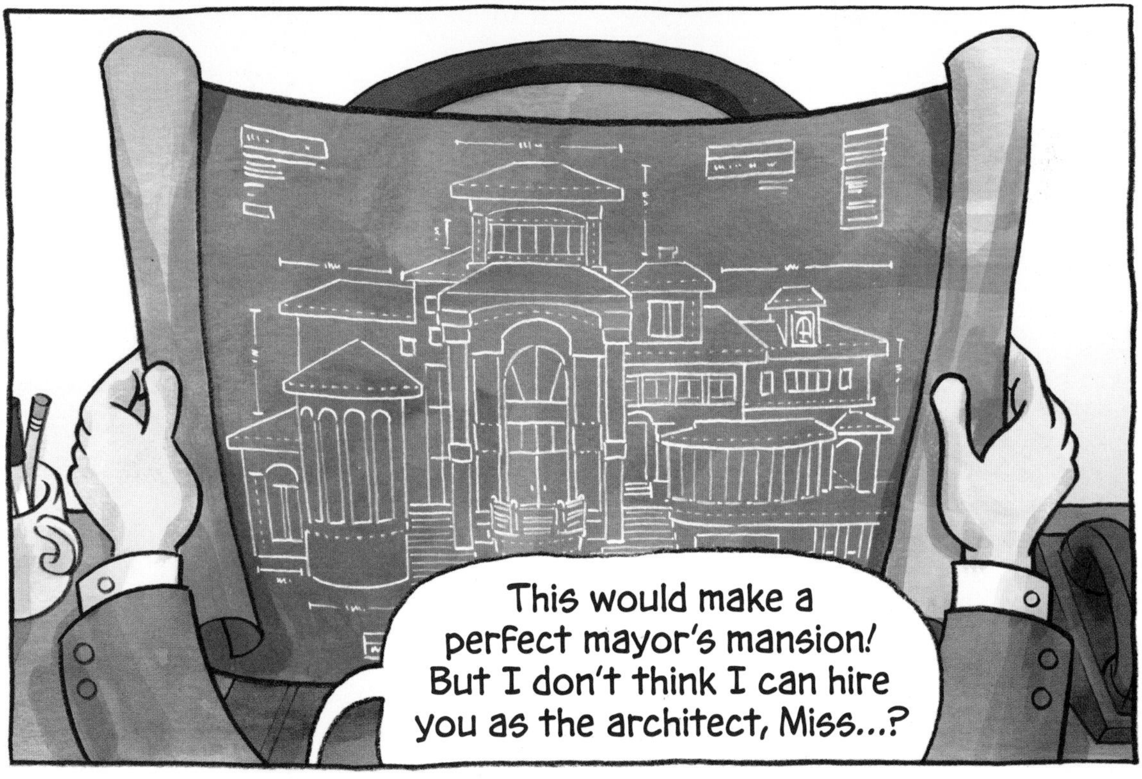
This would make a perfect mayor's mansion! But I don't think I can hire you as the architect, Miss...?

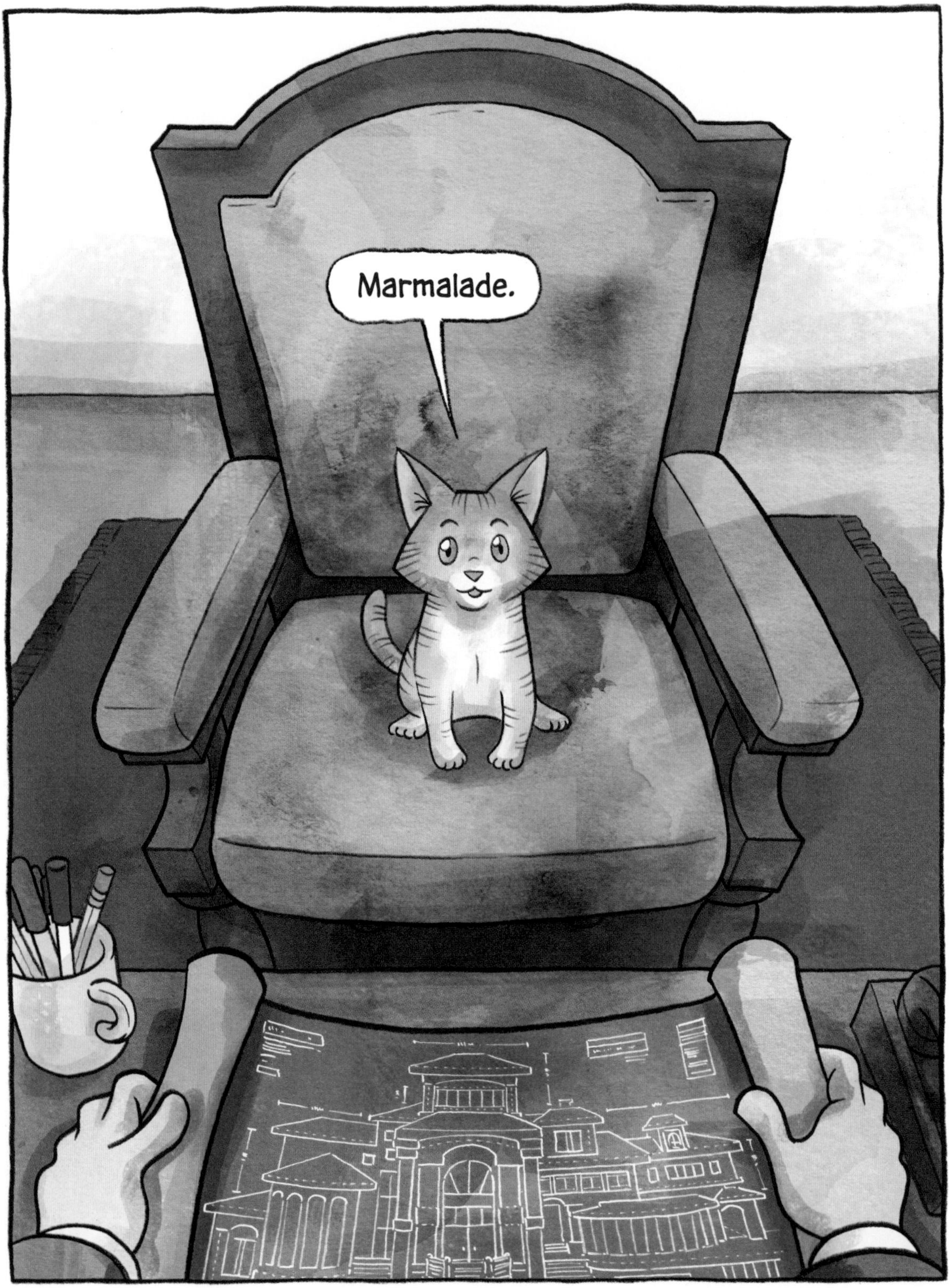
Marmalade.

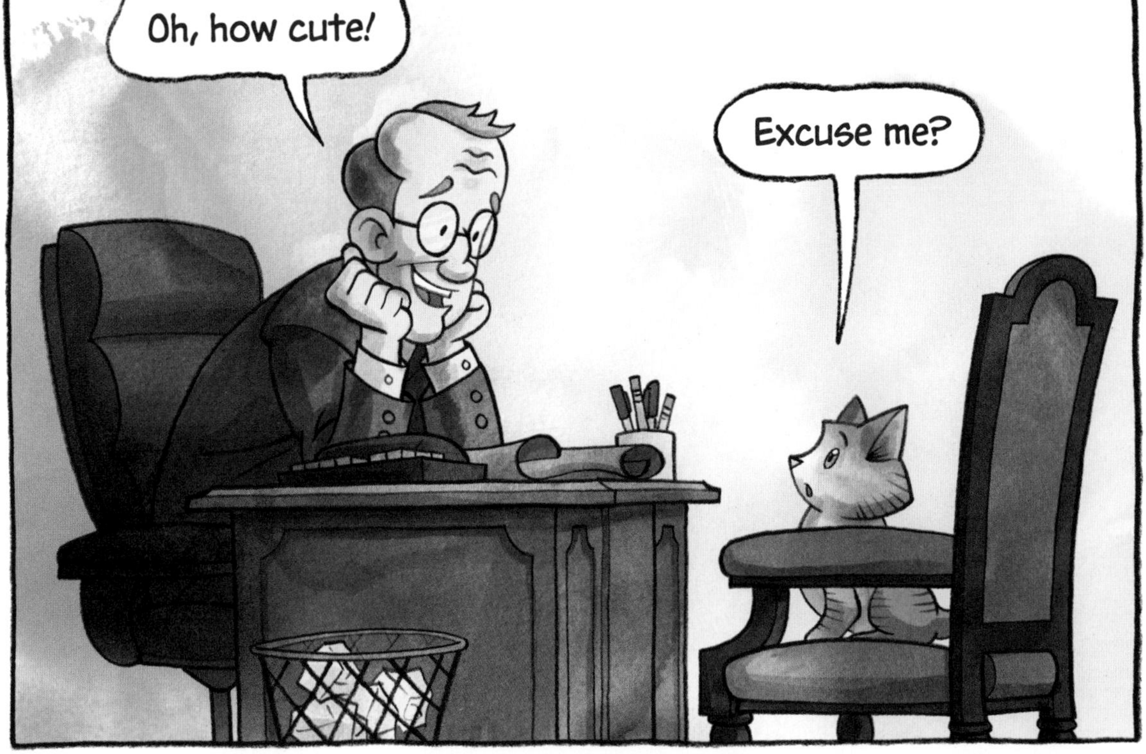
Oh, how cute!
Excuse me?

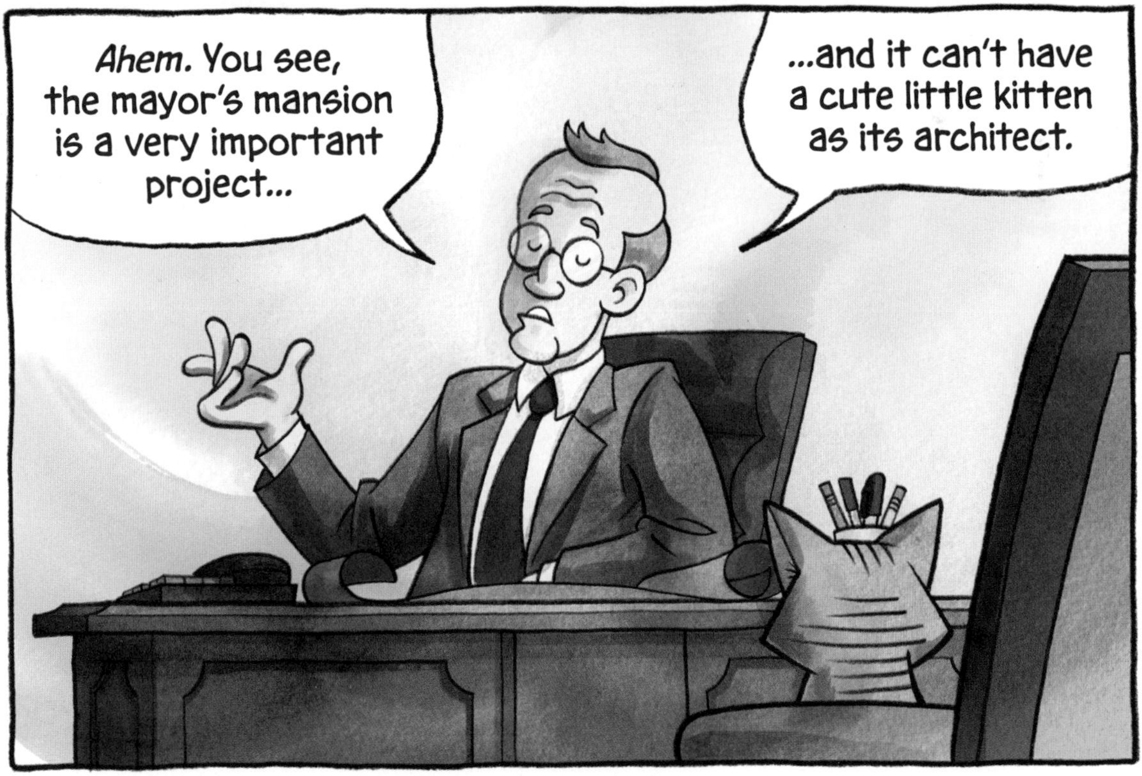
Ahem. You see, the mayor's mansion is a very important project...
...and it can't have a cute little kitten as its architect.

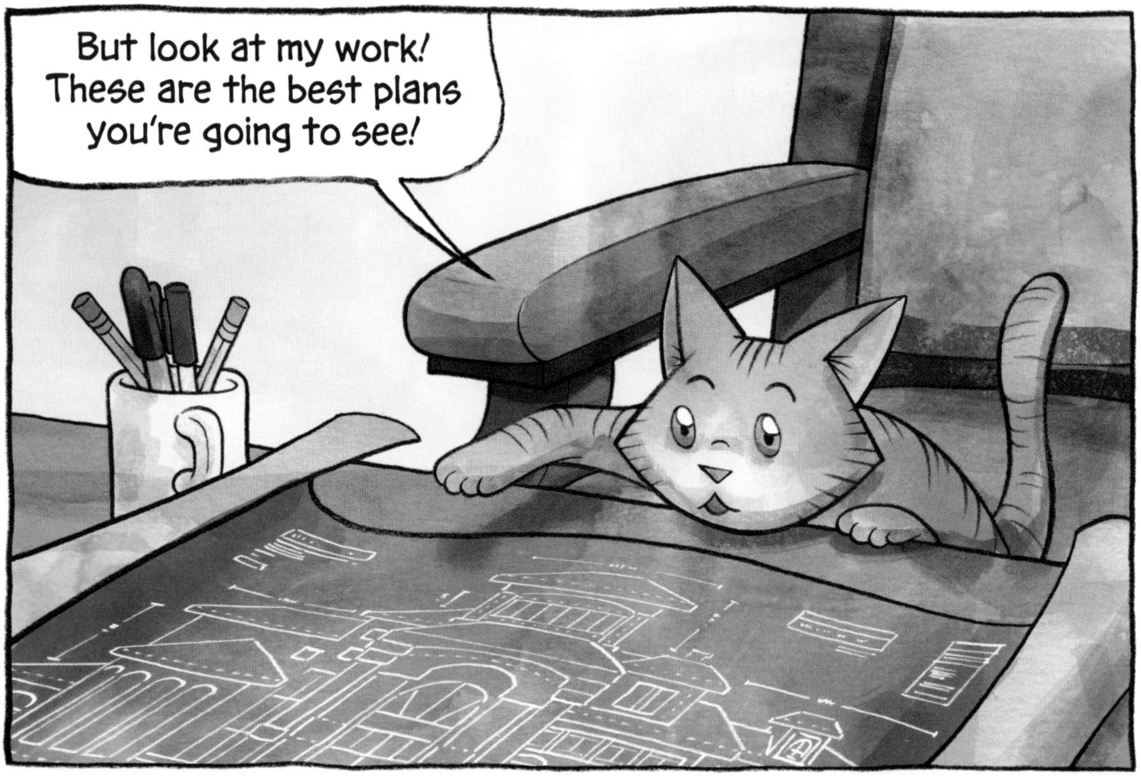
But look at my work! These are the best plans you're going to see!

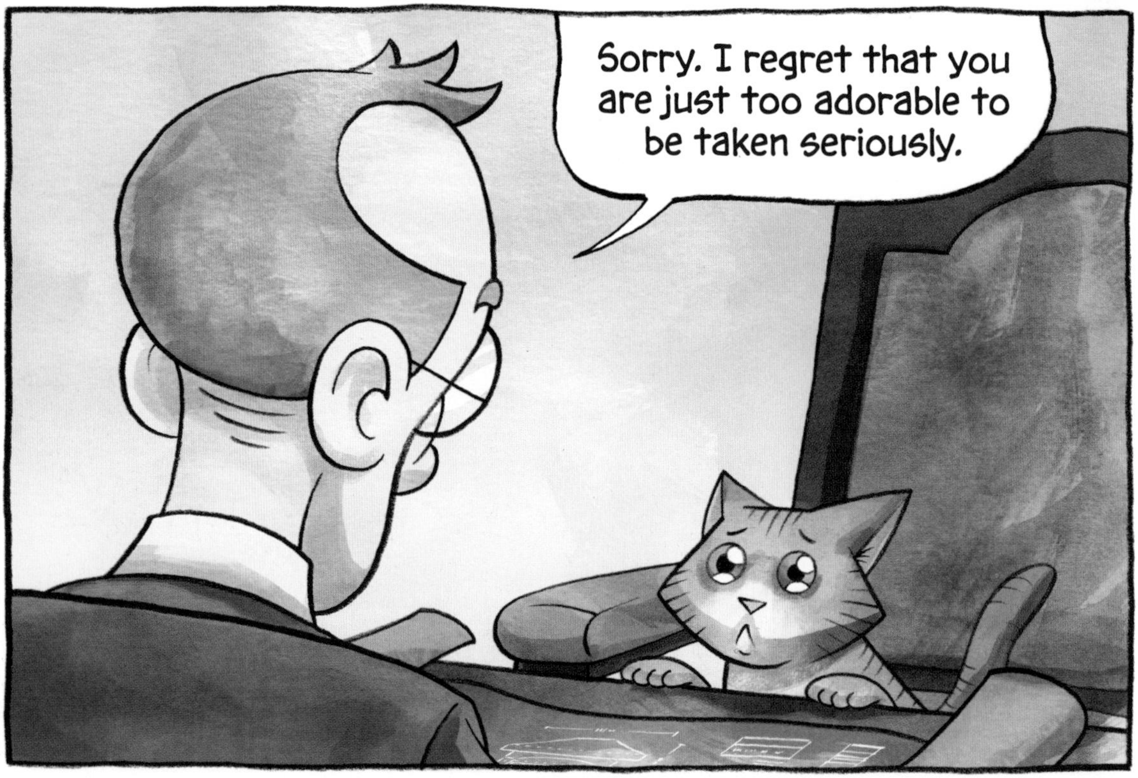
Sorry. I regret that you are just too adorable to be taken seriously.

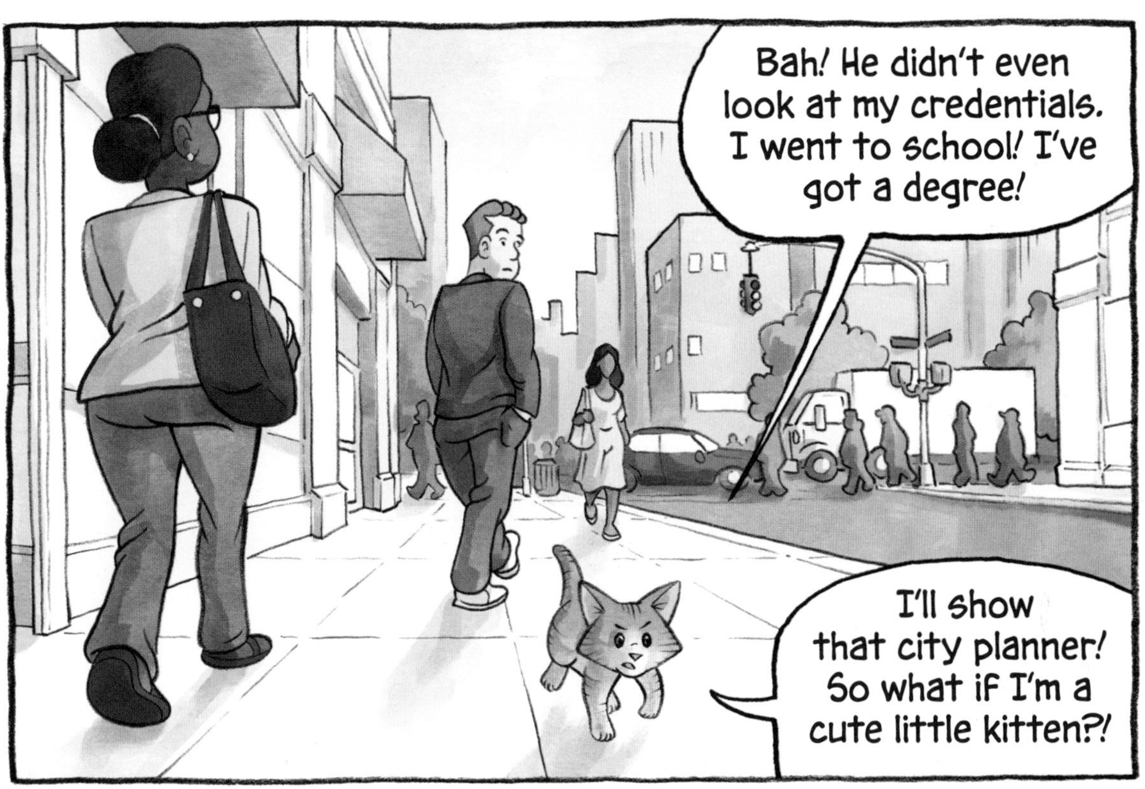
Bah! He didn't even look at my credentials. I went to school! I've got a degree!
I'll show that city planner! So what if I'm a cute little kitten?!

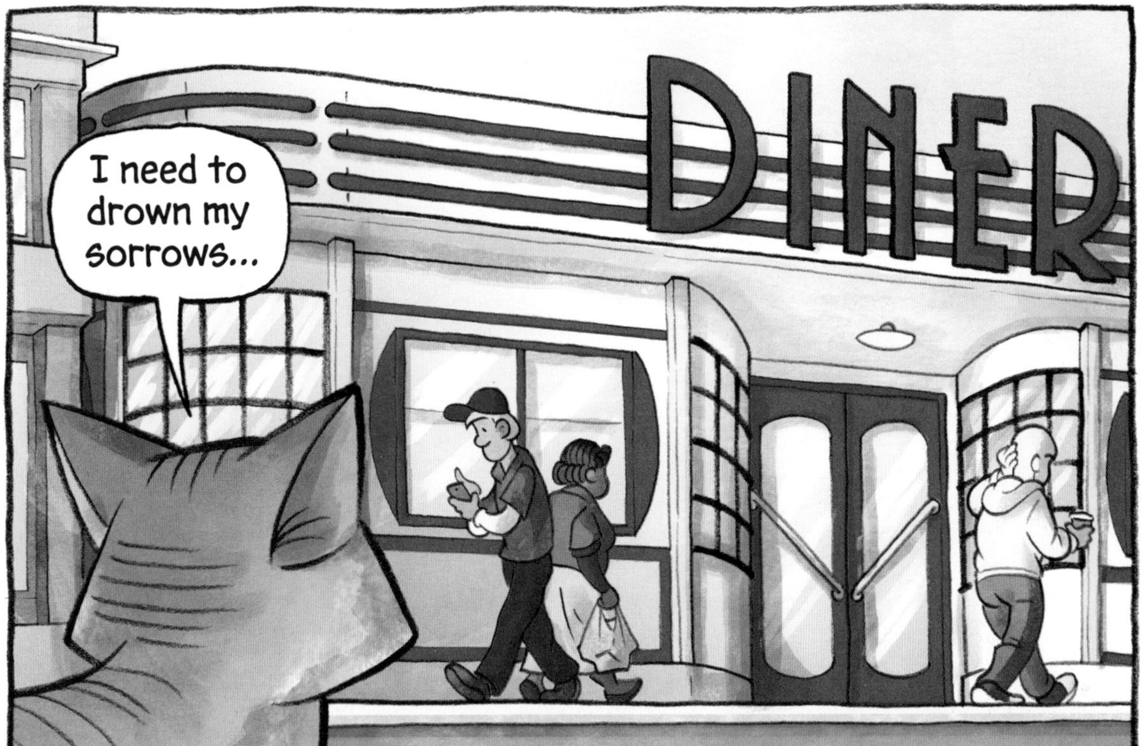
DINER
I need to drown my sorrows...

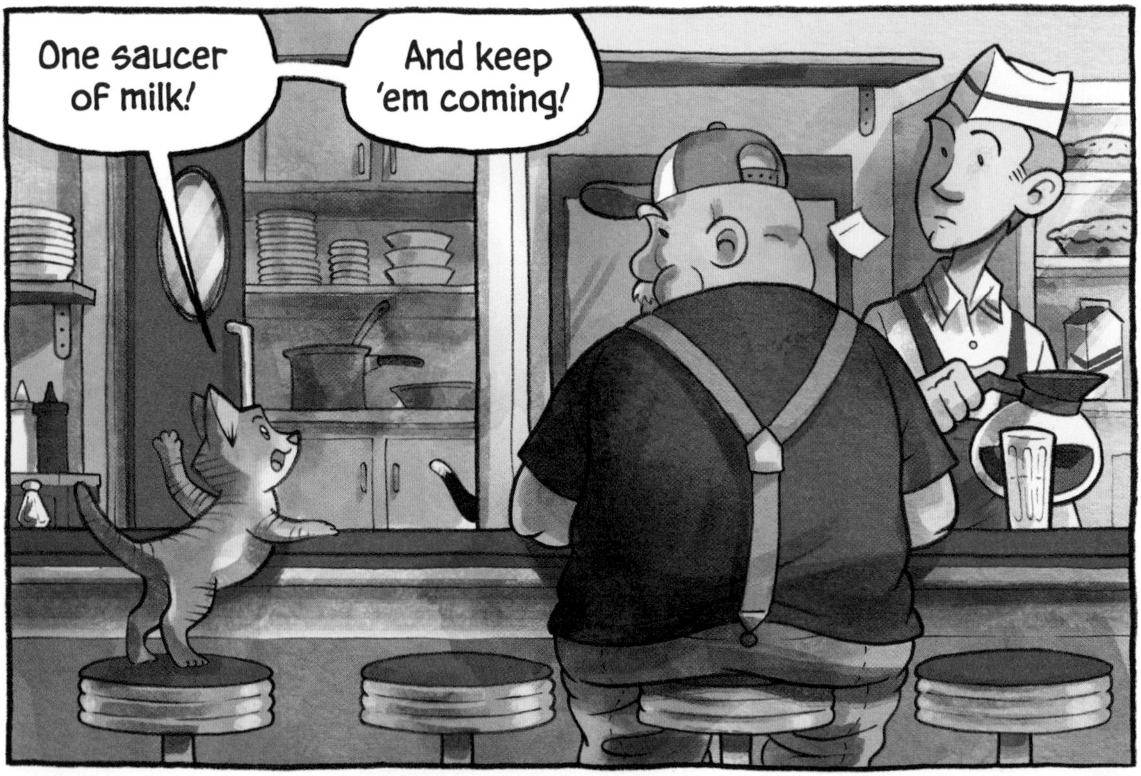
One saucer of milk!
And keep 'em coming!

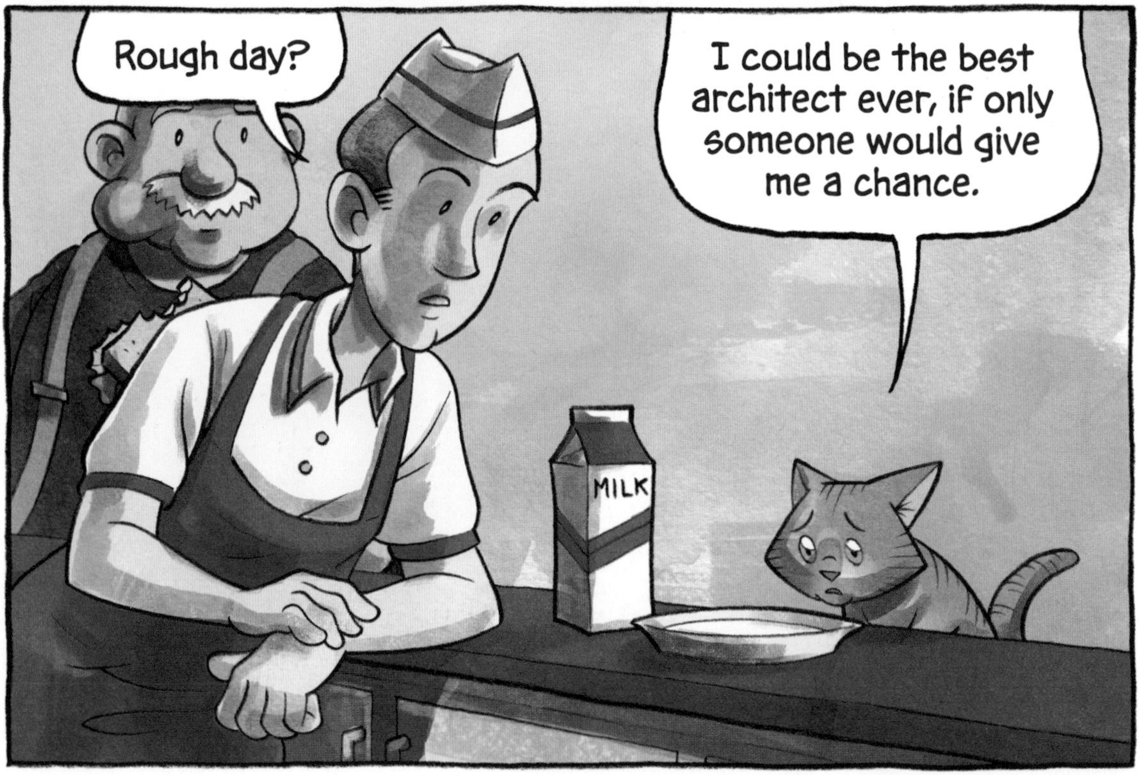
Rough day?
I could be the best architect ever, if only someone would give me a chance.
MILK

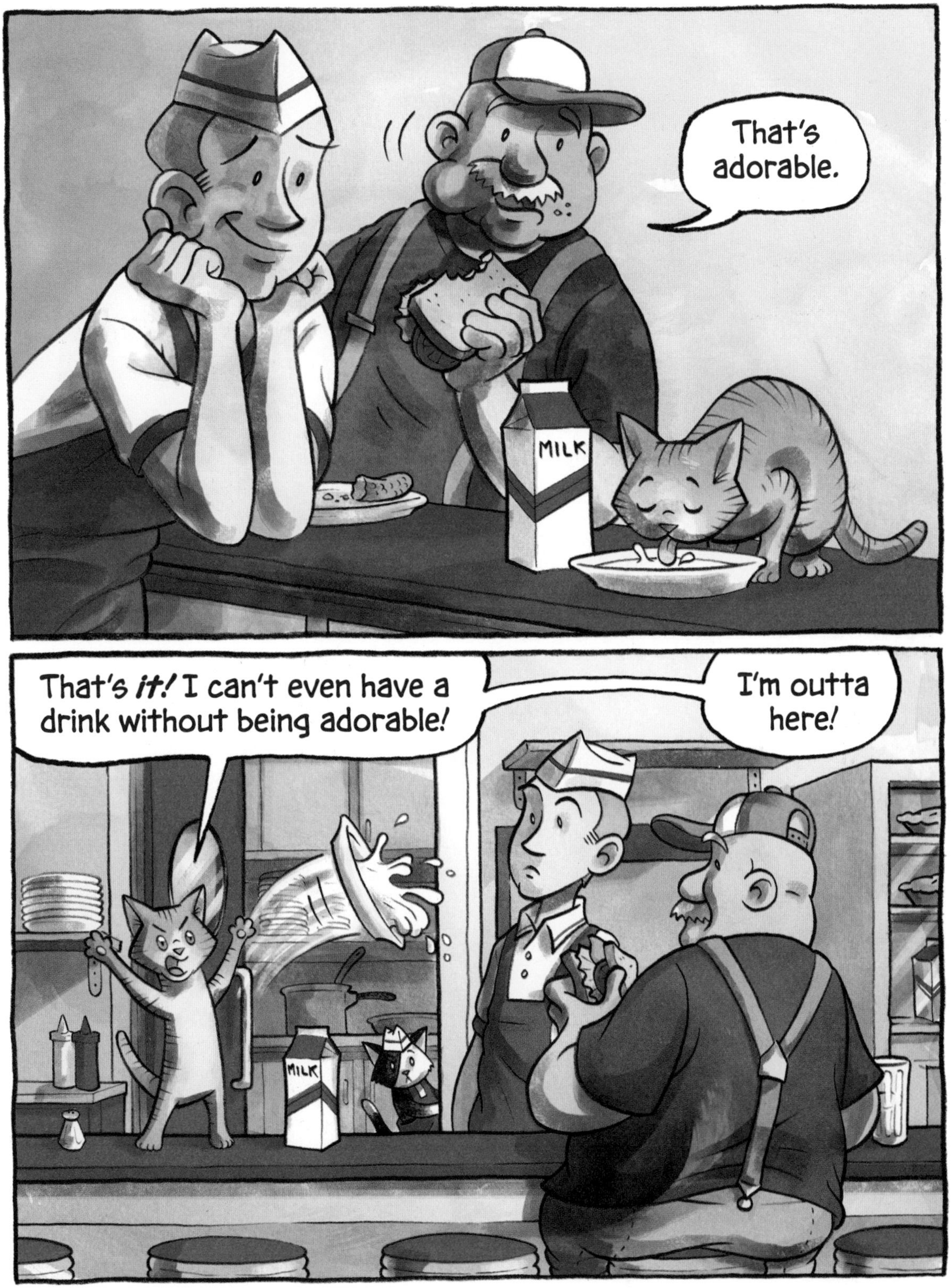
That's adorable.
MILK
That's *it!* I can't even have a drink without being adorable!
I'm outta here!
MILK

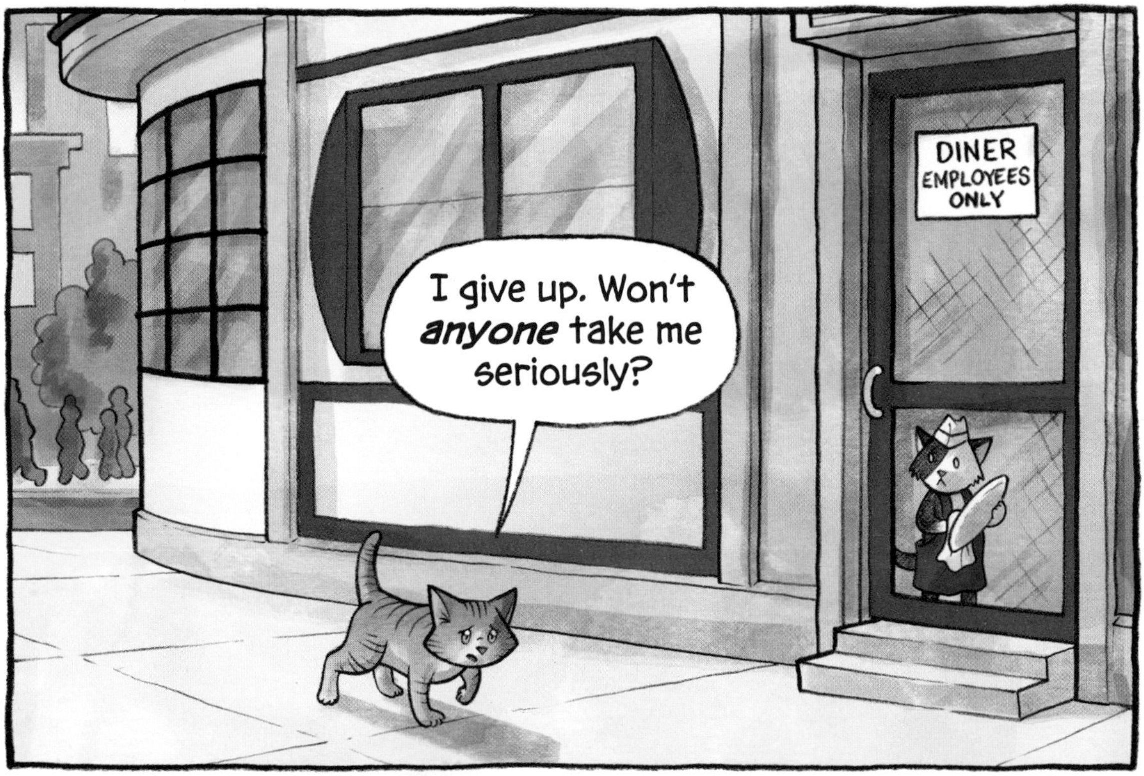
DINER EMPLOYEES ONLY
I give up. Won't **anyone** take me seriously?

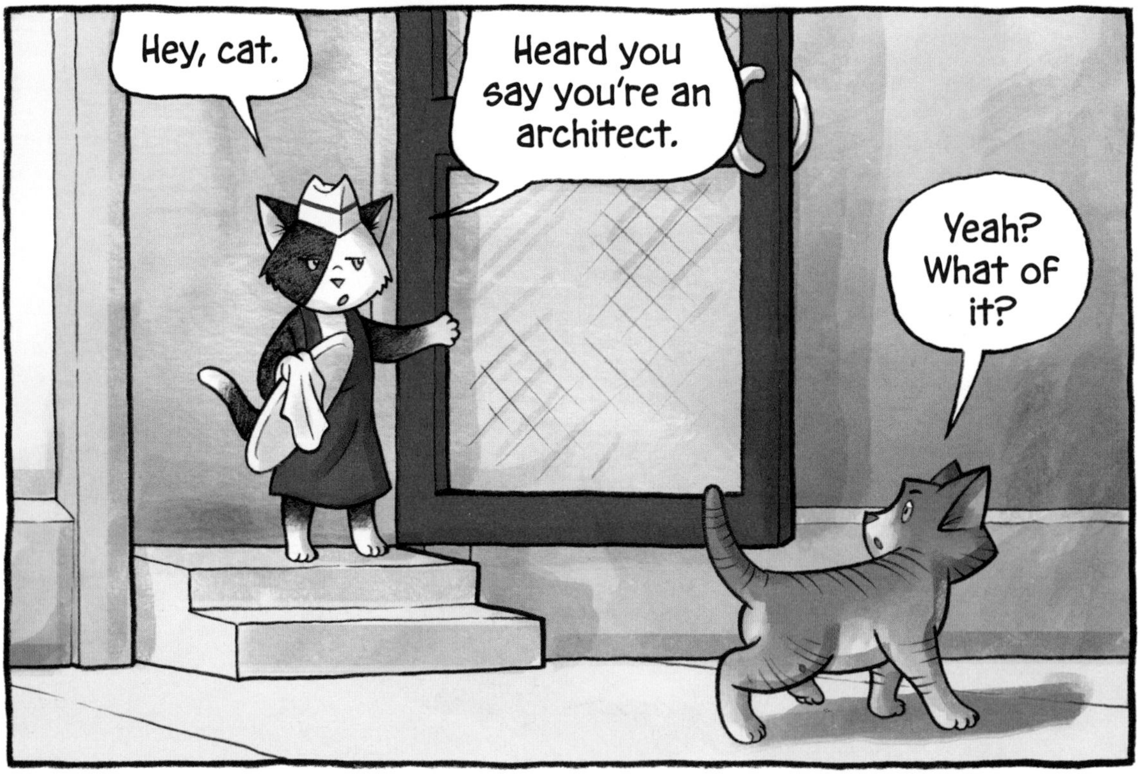
Hey, cat.
Heard you say you're an architect.
Yeah? What of it?

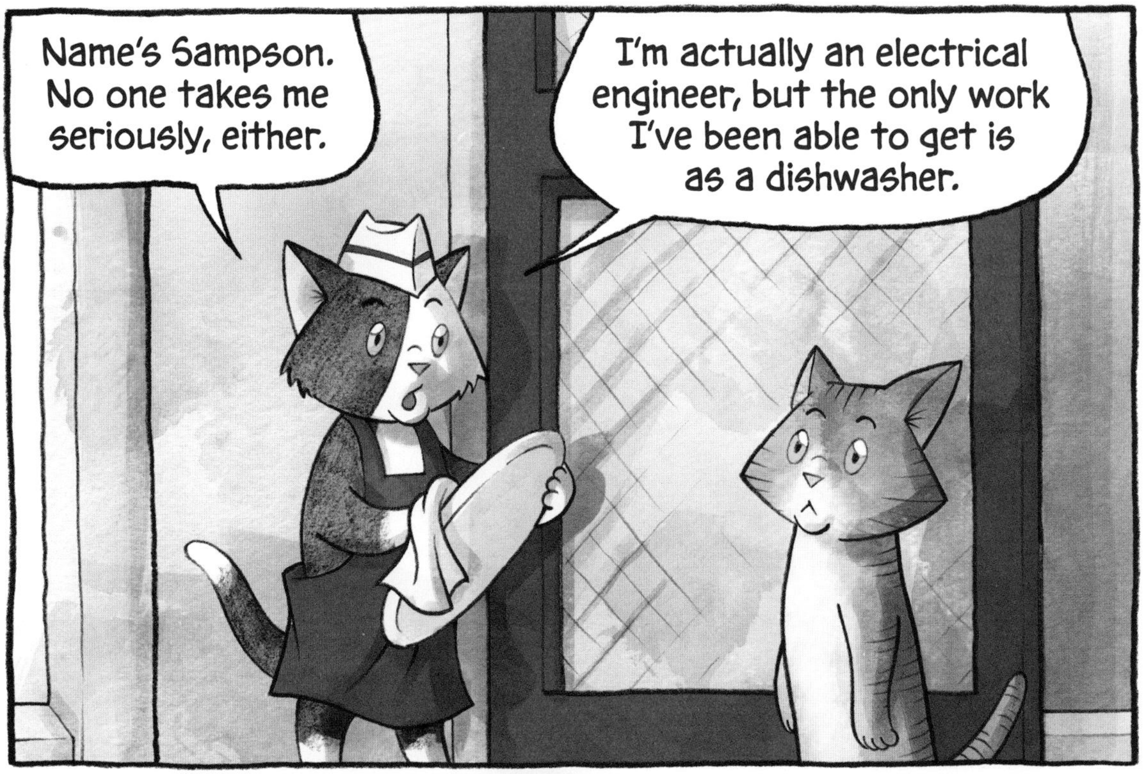
Name's Sampson. No one takes me seriously, either.
I'm actually an electrical engineer, but the only work I've been able to get is as a dishwasher.

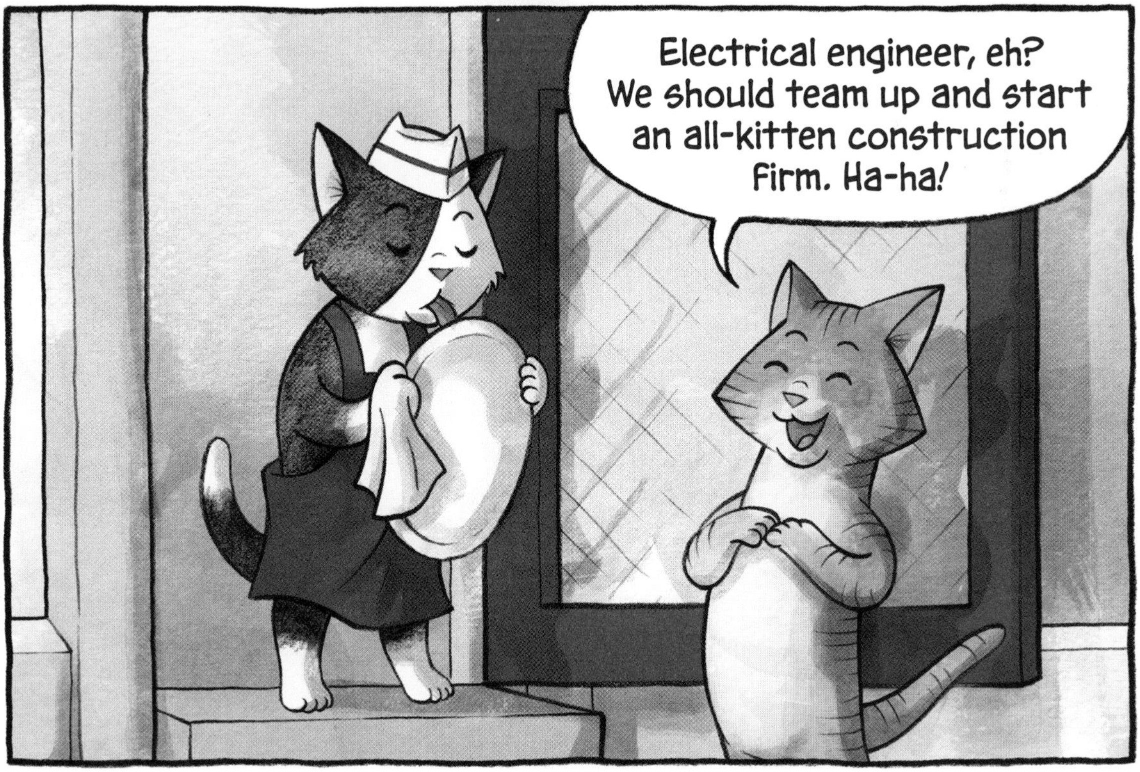
Electrical engineer, eh? We should team up and start an all-kitten construction firm. Ha-ha!

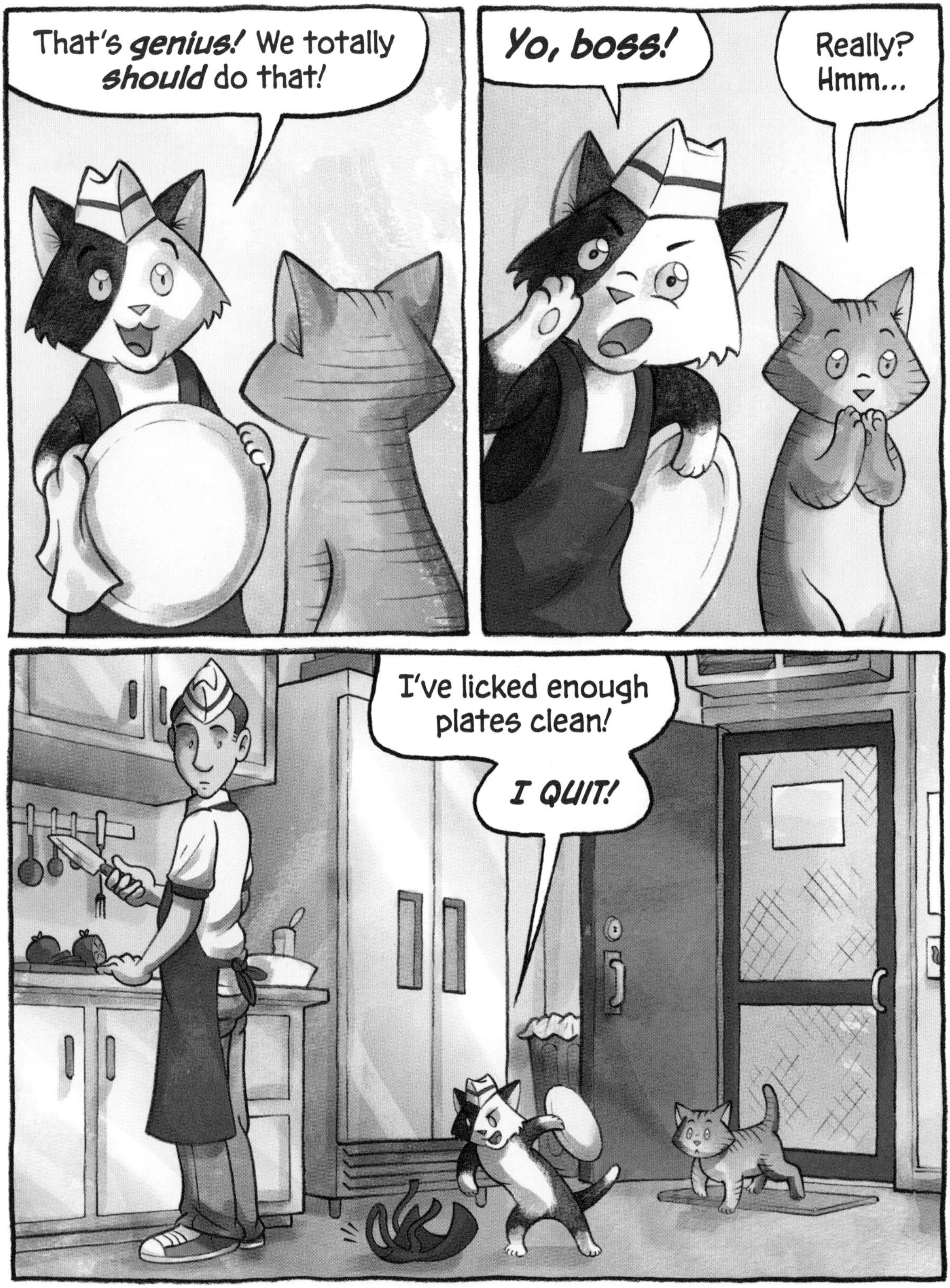
That's *genius!* We totally *should* do that!
Yo, boss!
Really? Hmm...
I've licked enough plates clean!
I QUIT!

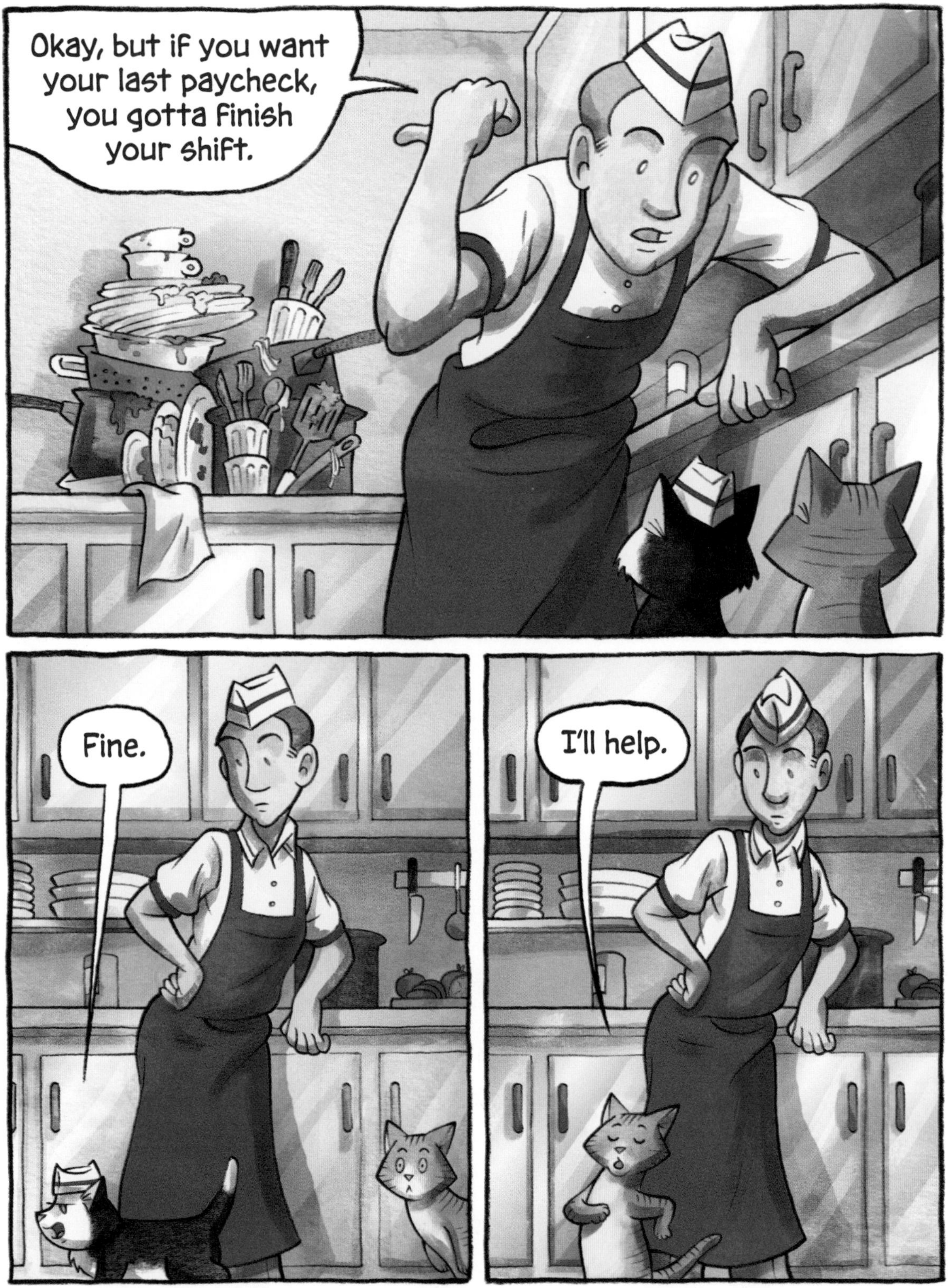
Okay, but if you want your last paycheck, you gotta finish your shift.
Fine.
I'll help.

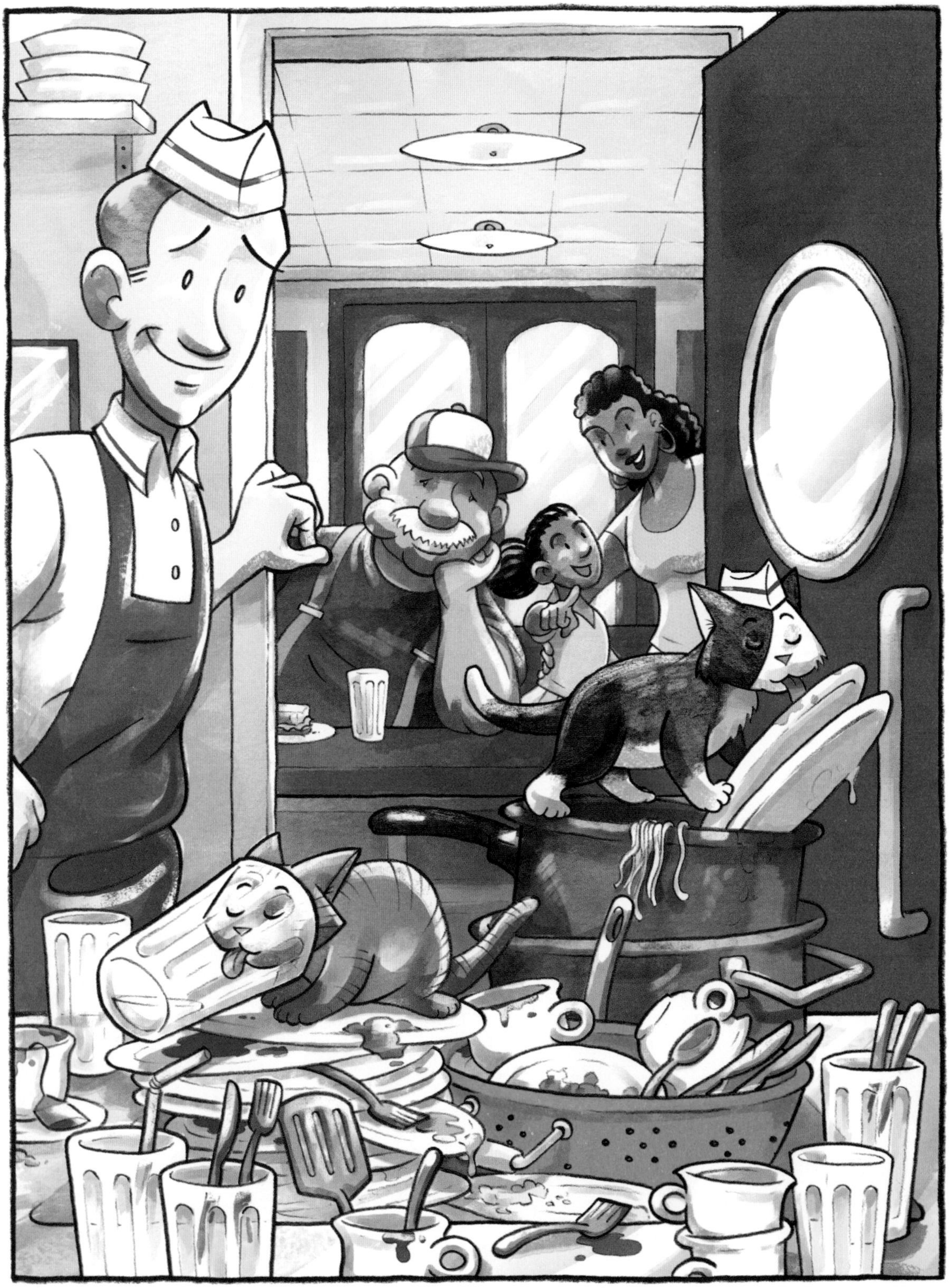

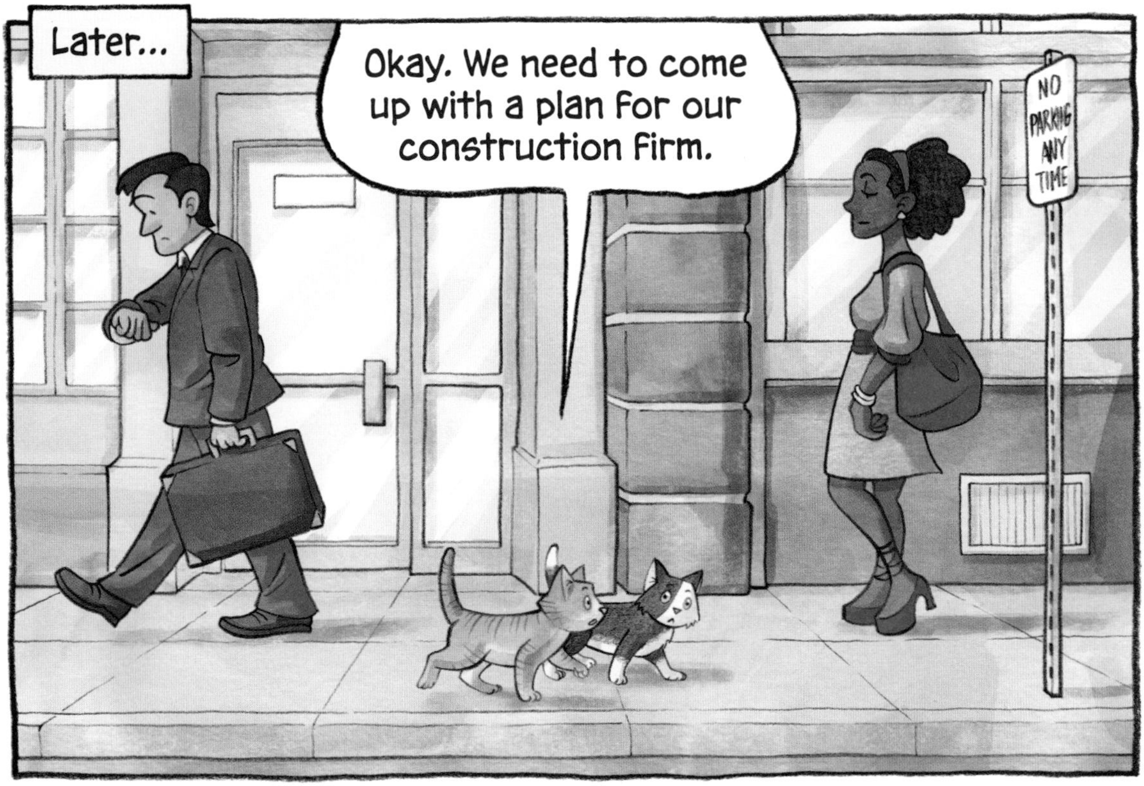
Later...
Okay. We need to come up with a plan for our construction firm.
NO PARKING ANY TIME

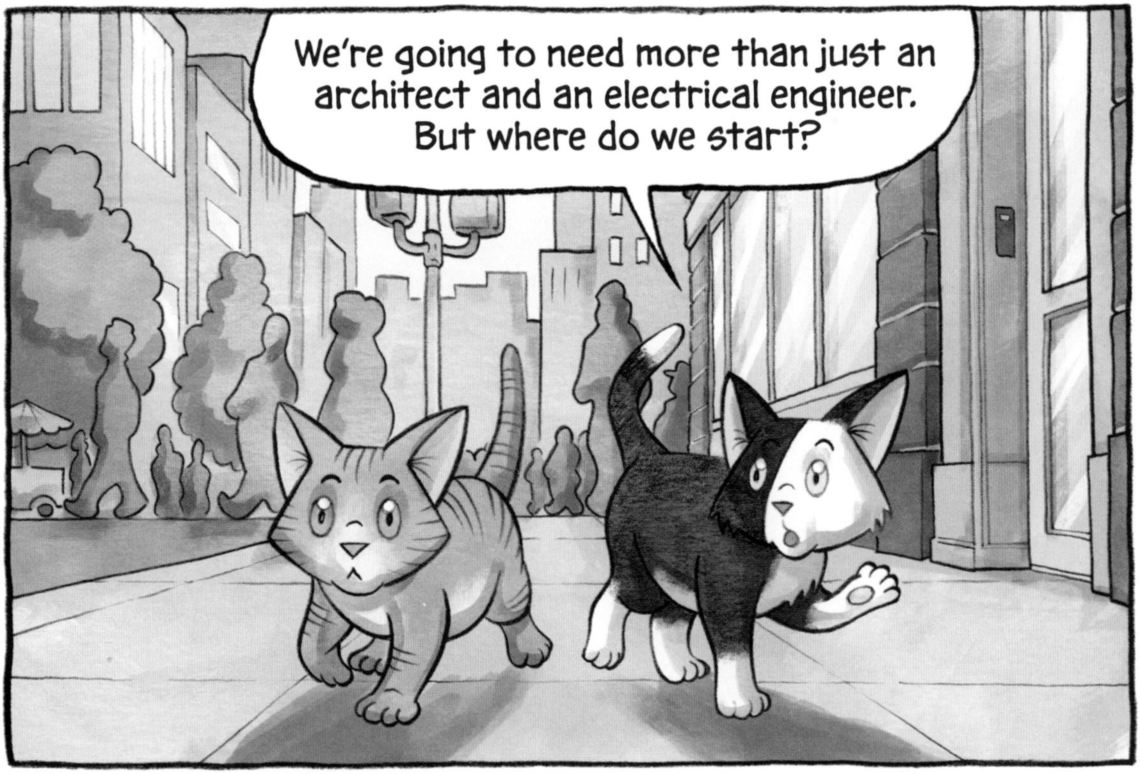
We're going to need more than just an architect and an electrical engineer. But where do we start?

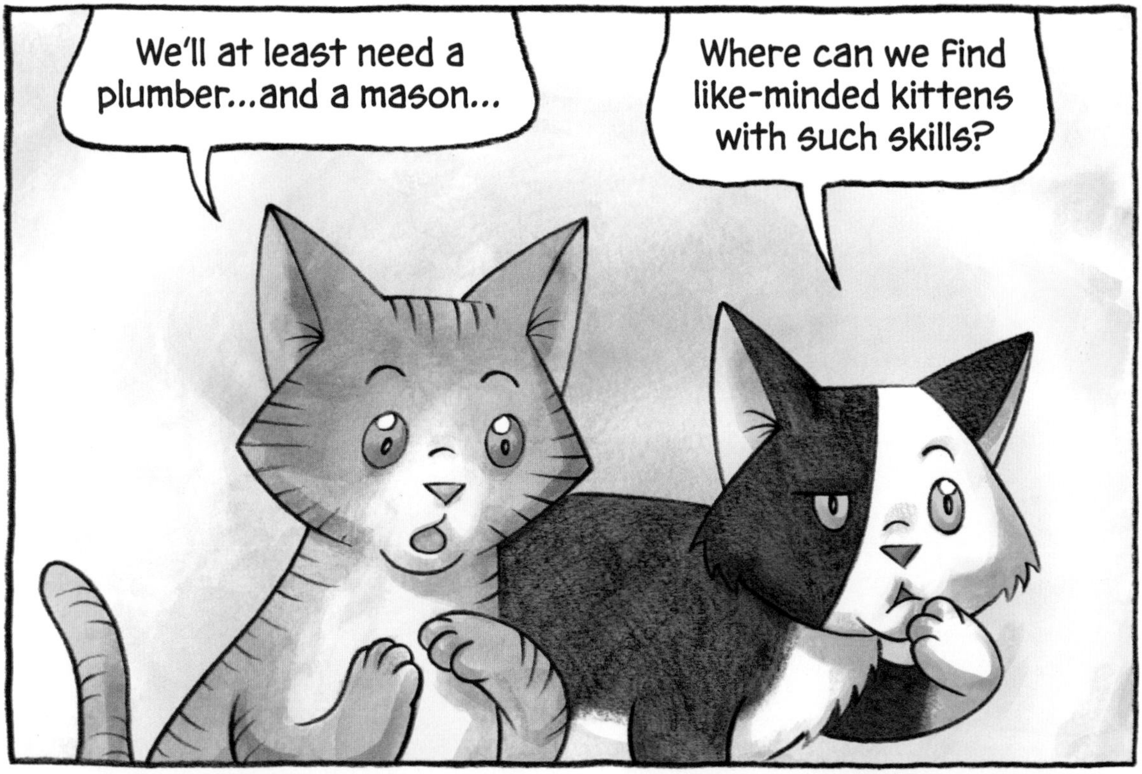
We'll at least need a plumber...and a mason...
Where can we find like-minded kittens with such skills?

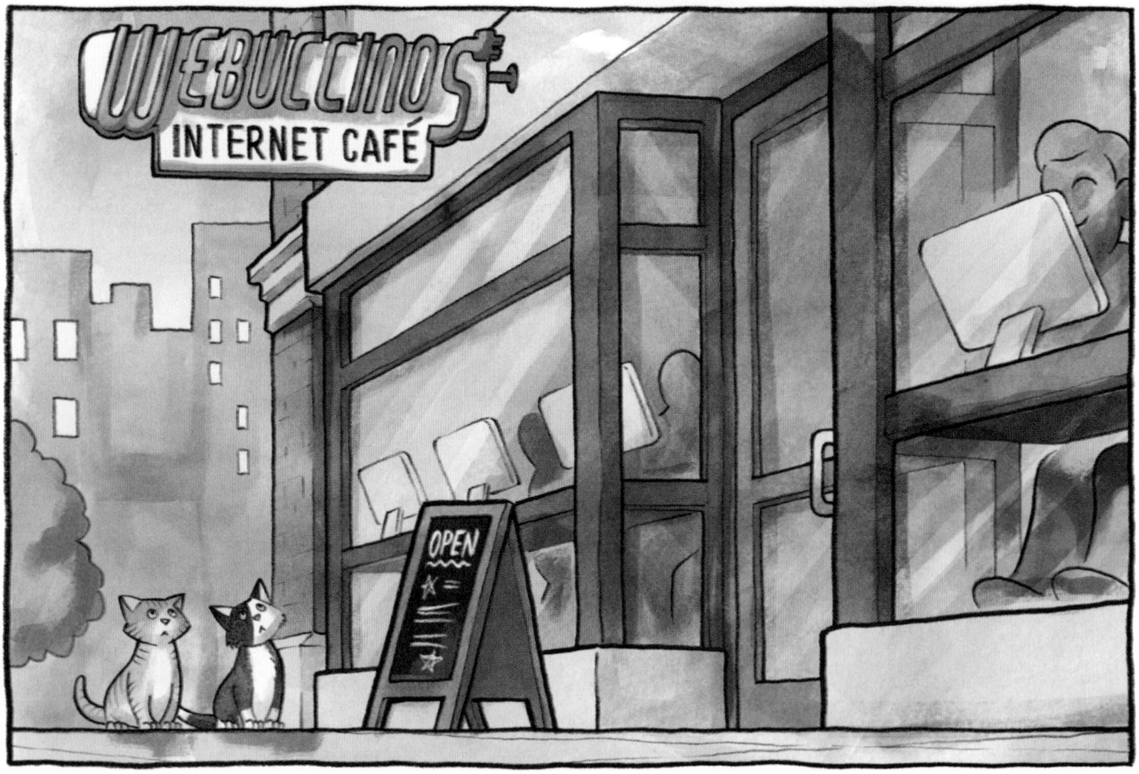
WEBUCCINOS
INTERNET CAFÉ
OPEN

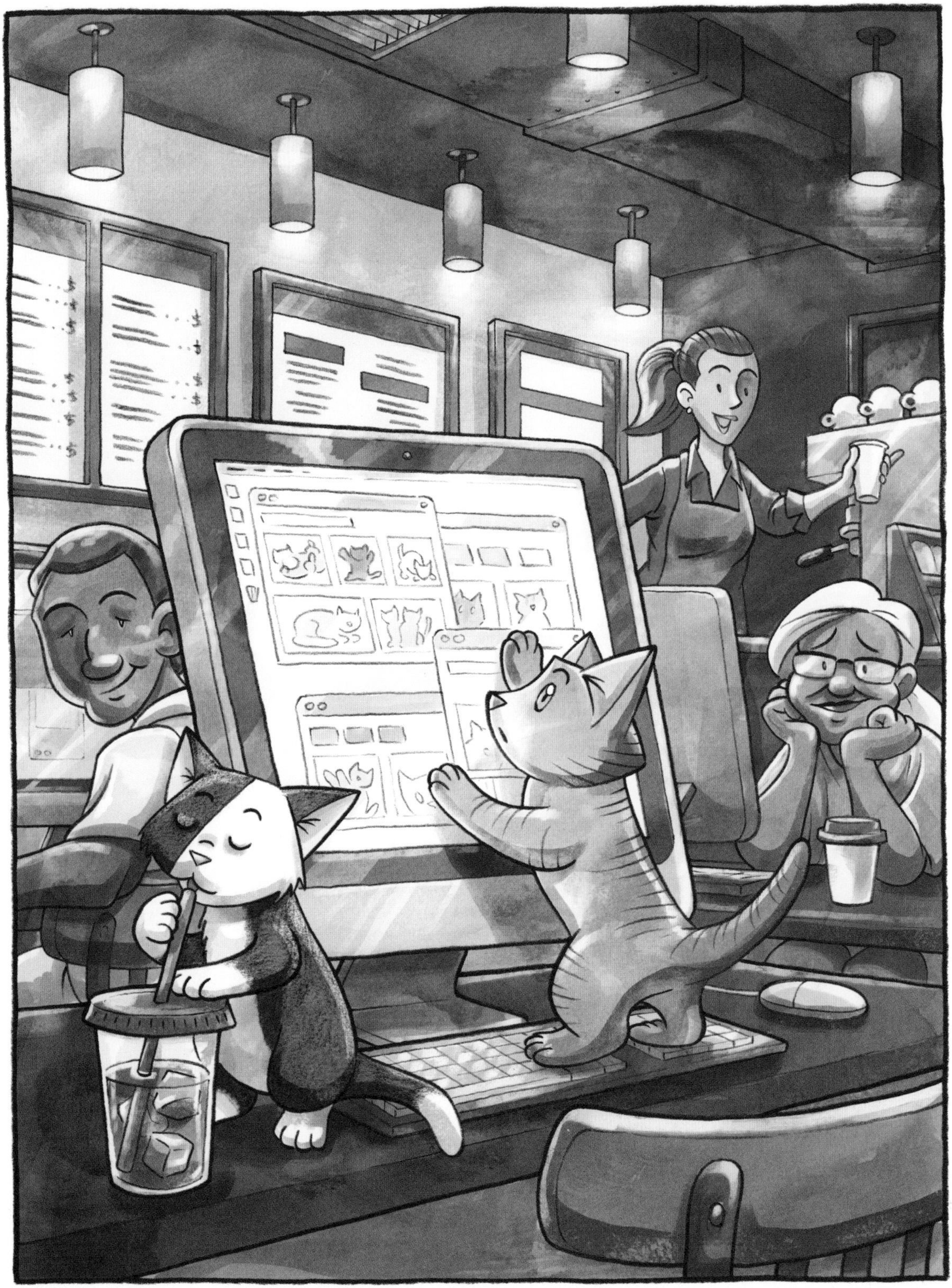

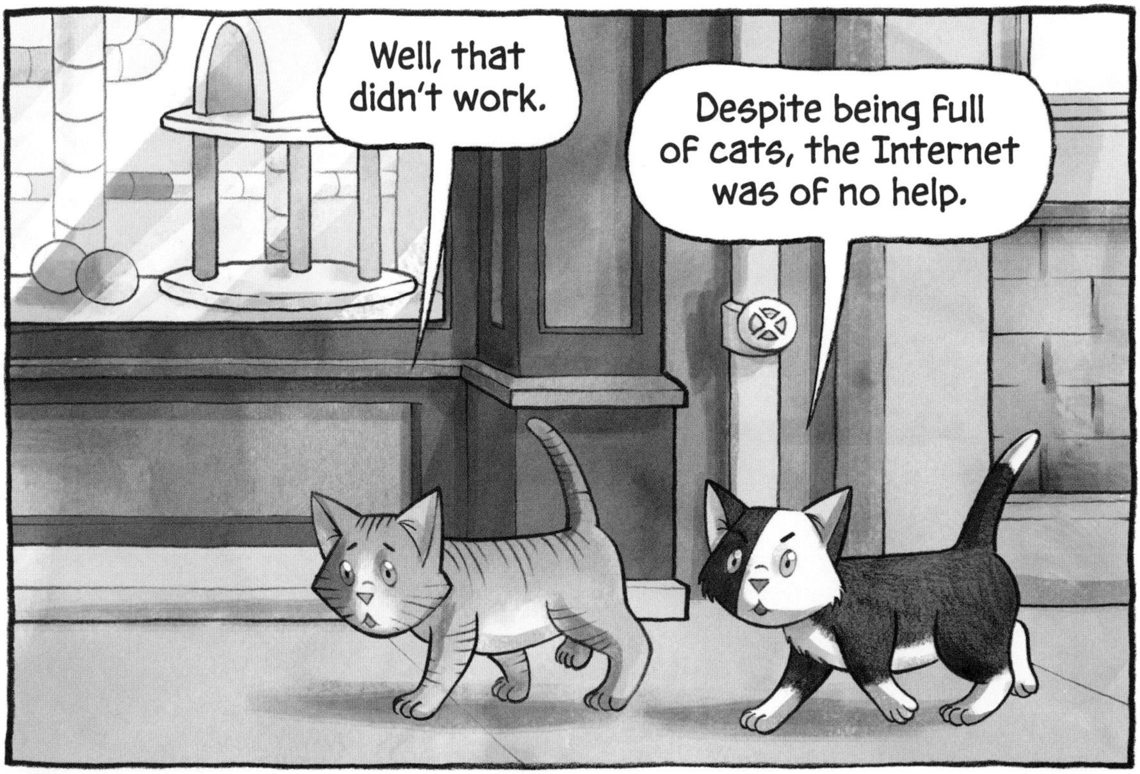
Well, that didn't work.
Despite being full of cats, the Internet was of no help.

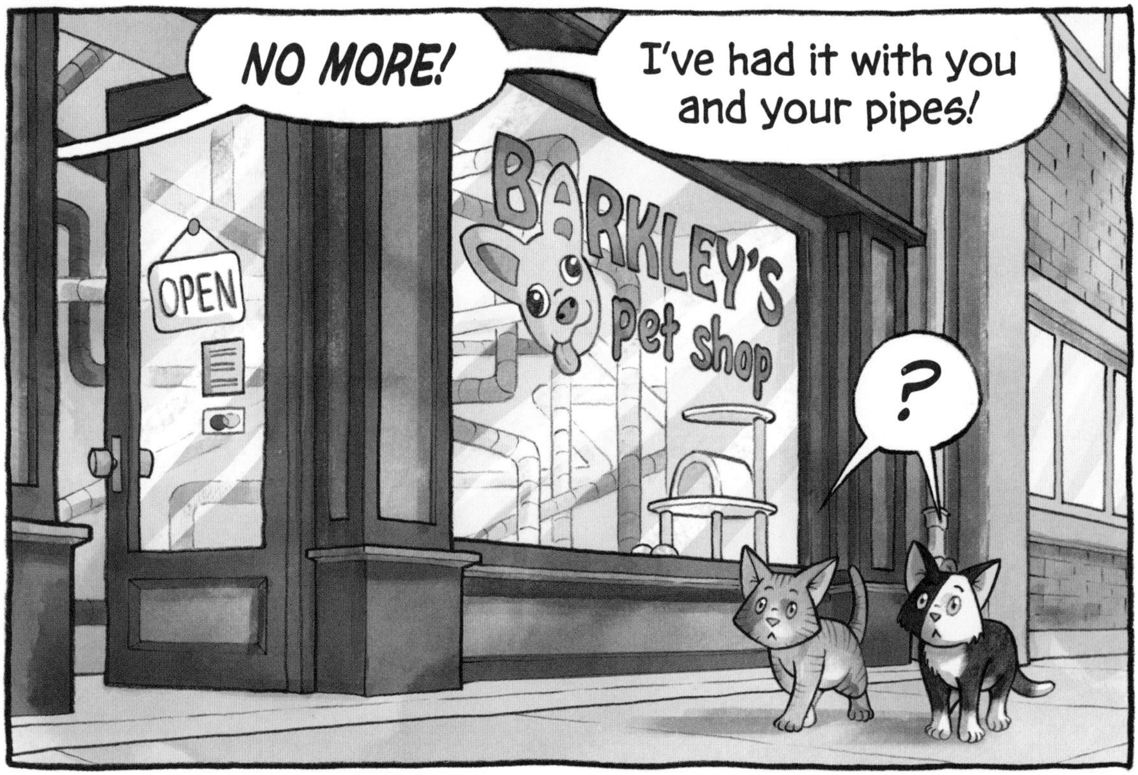
NO MORE!
I've had it with you and your pipes!
BARKLEY'S pet shop
OPEN
?

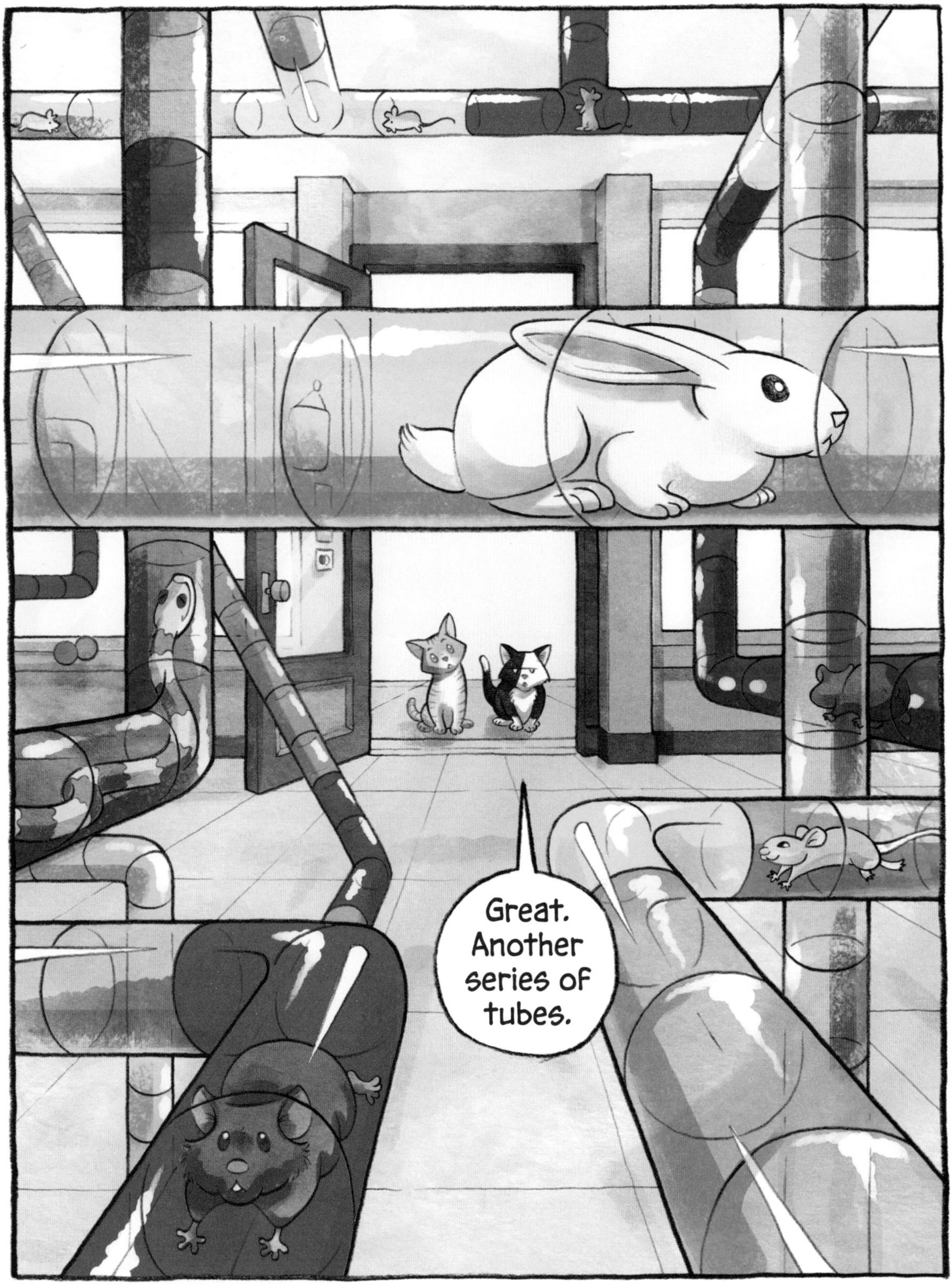
Great. Another series of tubes.

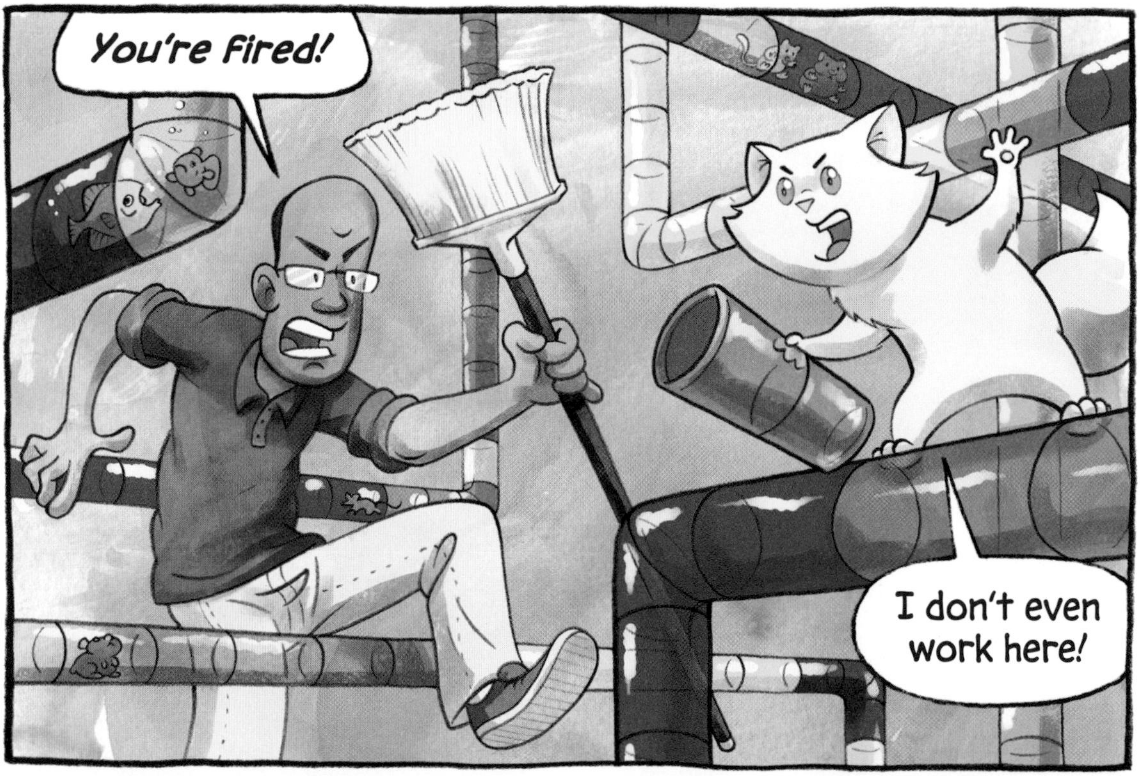
You're fired!
I don't even work here!

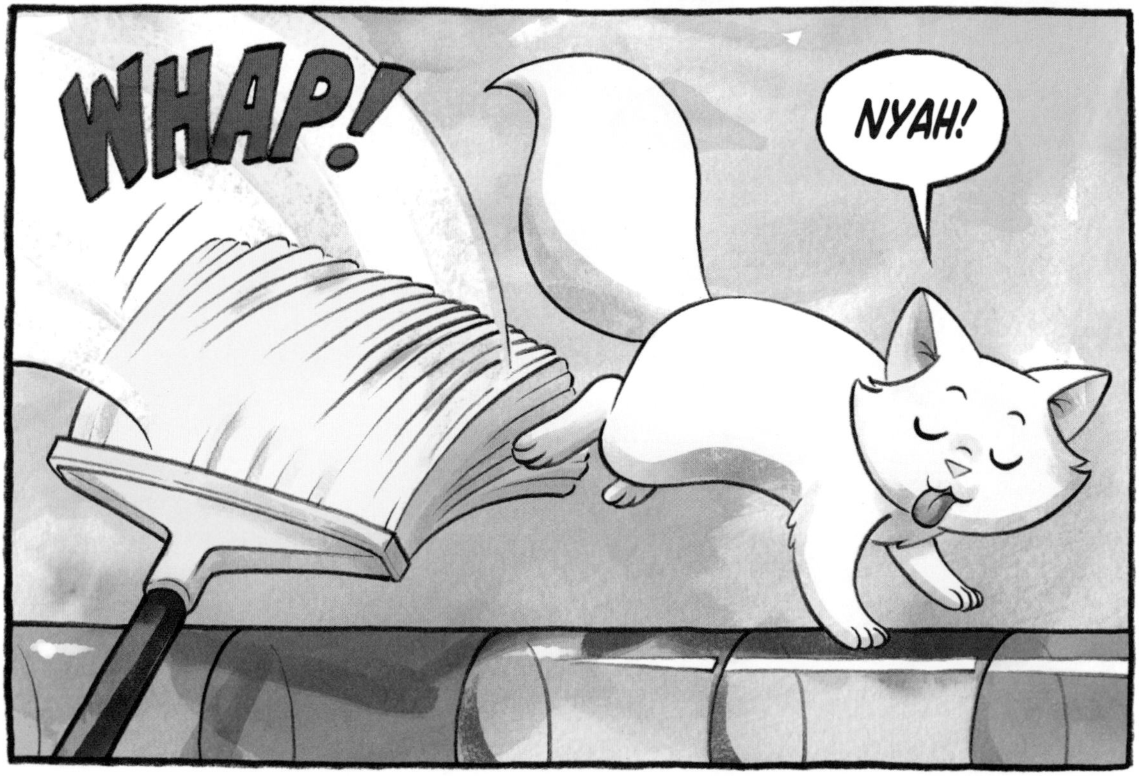
WHAP!
NYAH!

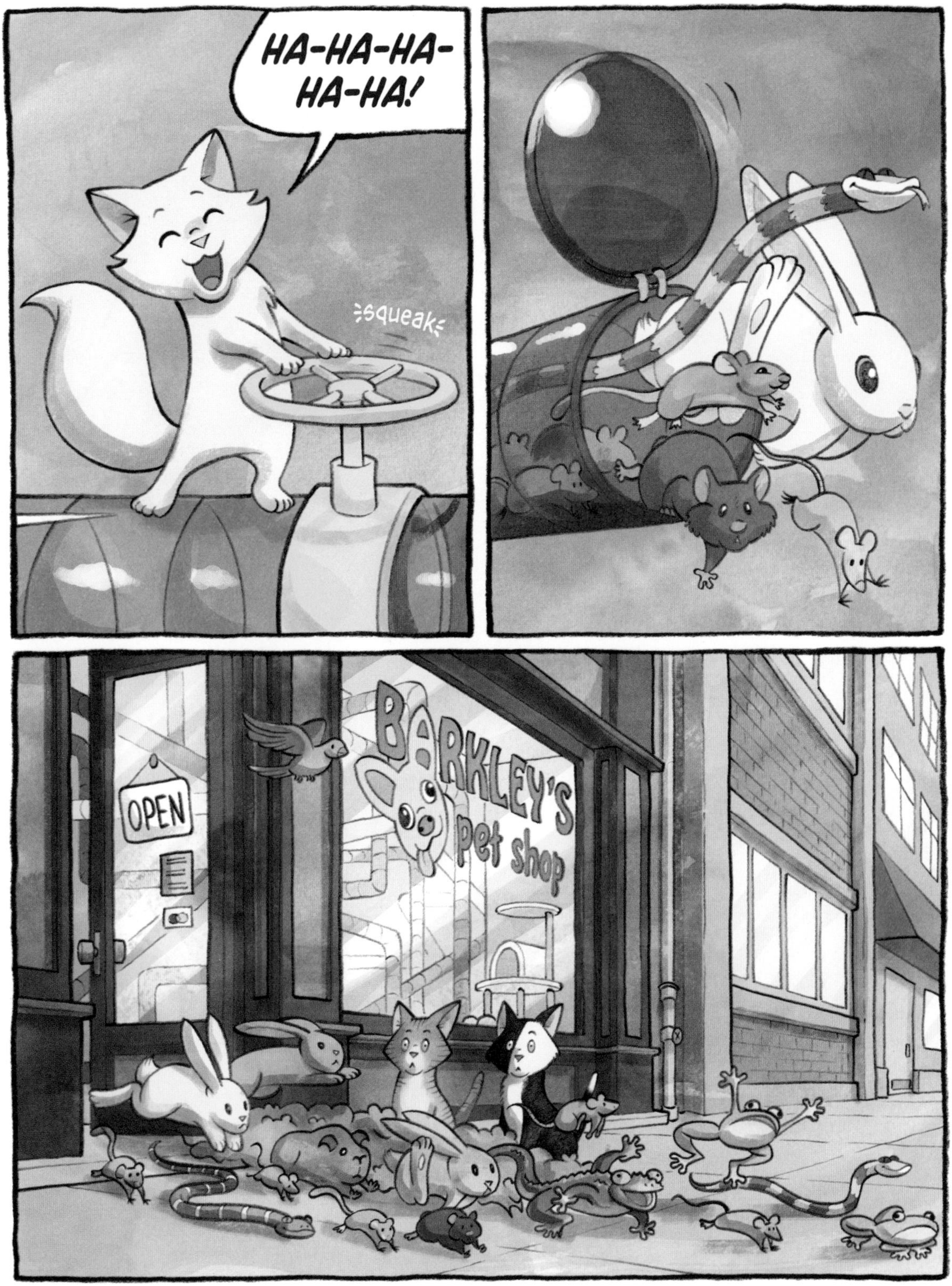
HA-HA-HA-
HA-HA!
squeak
OPEN
BARKLEY'S
pet shop

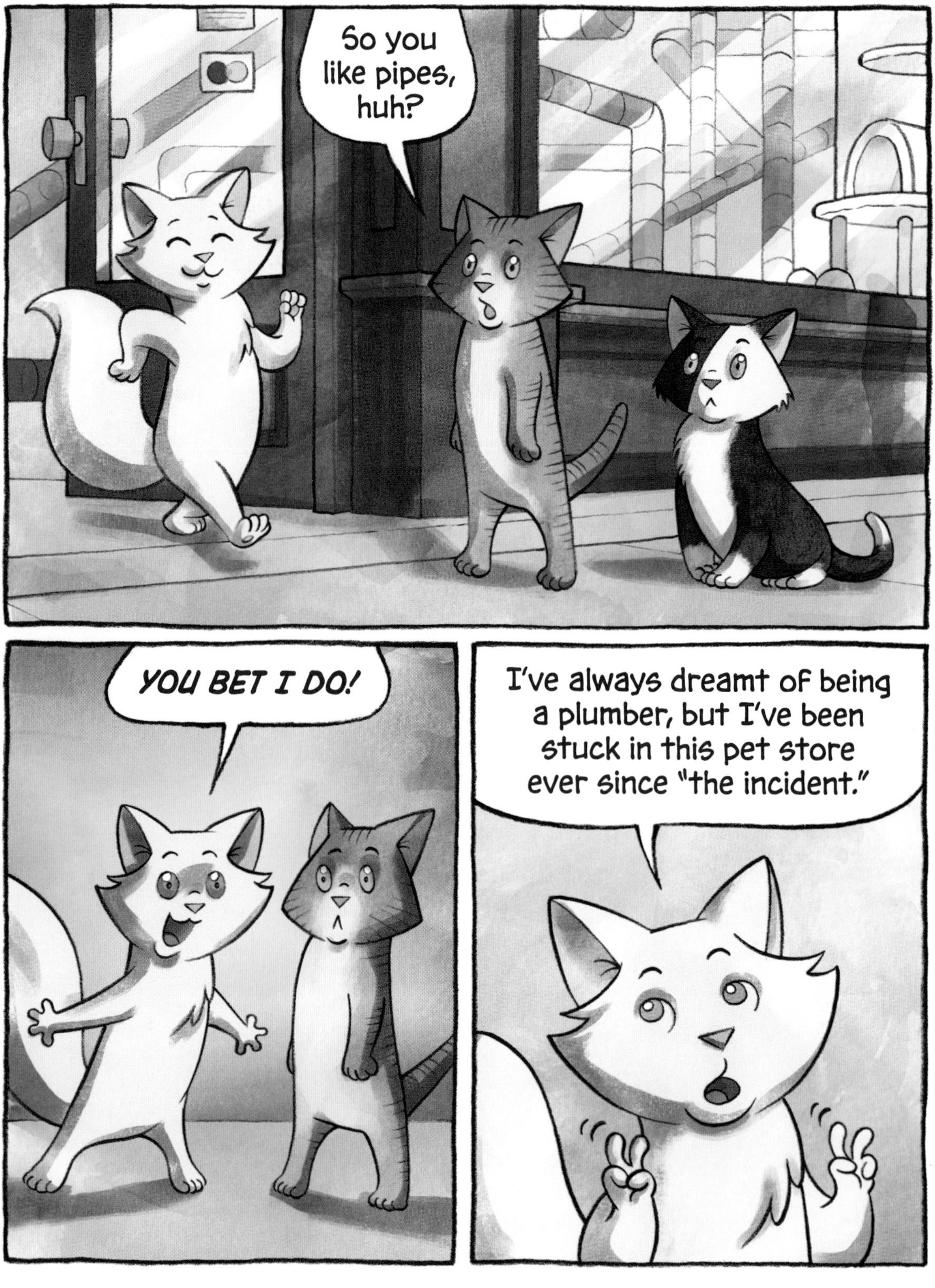

So you like pipes, huh?
YOU BET I DO!
I've always dreamt of being a plumber, but I've been stuck in this pet store ever since "the incident."

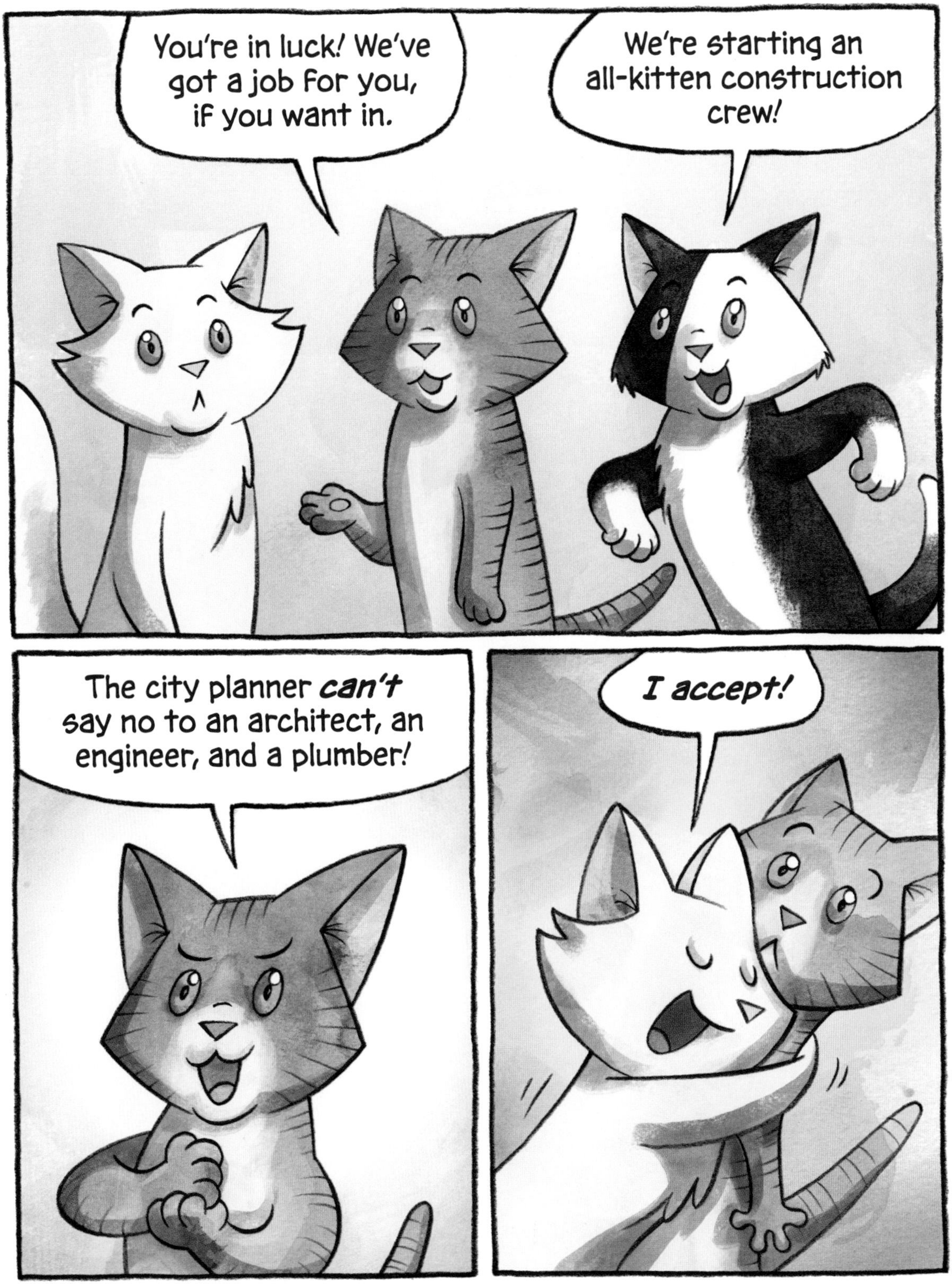
You're in luck! We've got a job for you, if you want in.
We're starting an all-kitten construction crew!
The city planner ***can't*** say no to an architect, an engineer, and a plumber!
I accept!

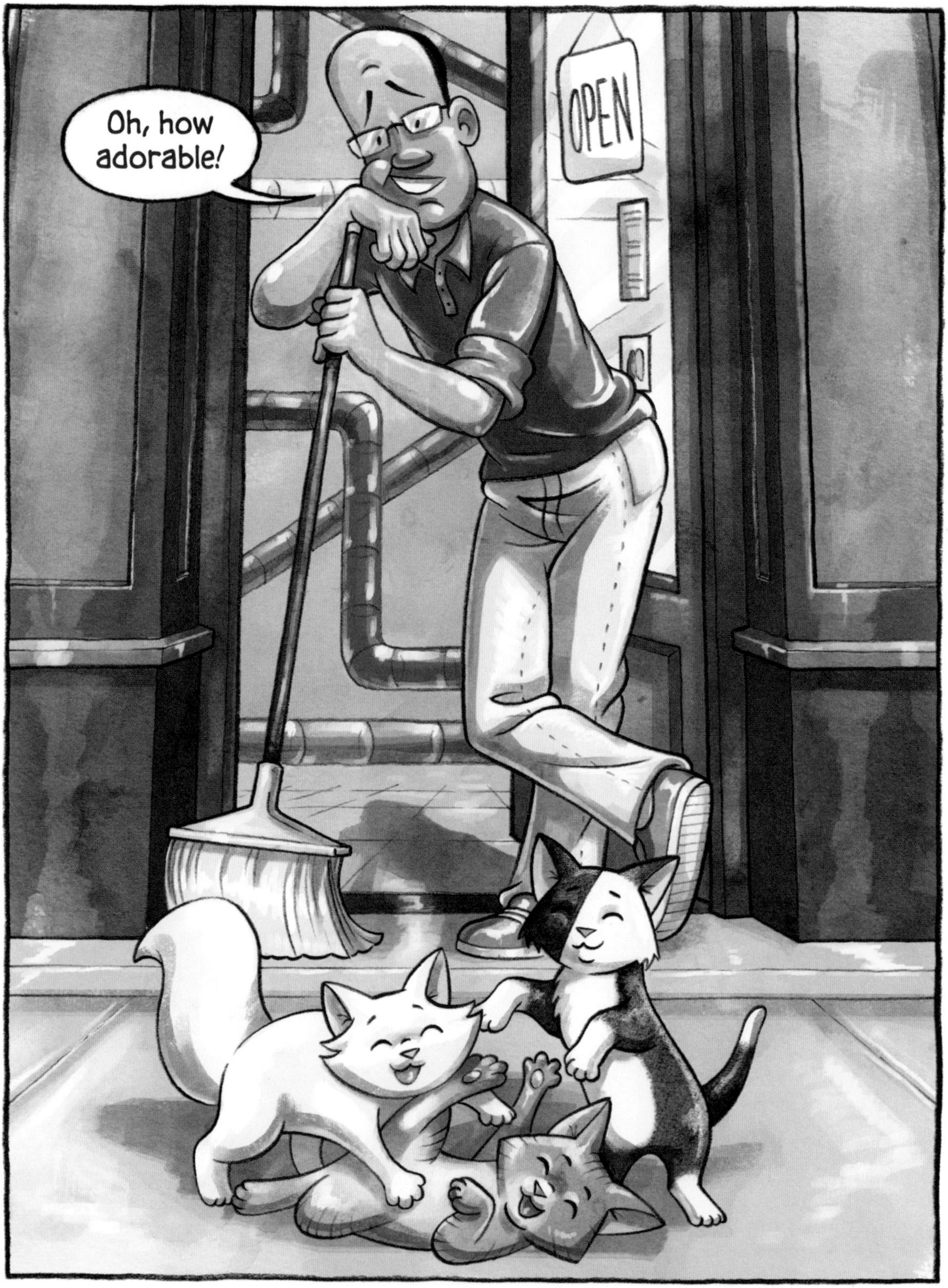
Oh, how adorable!
OPEN

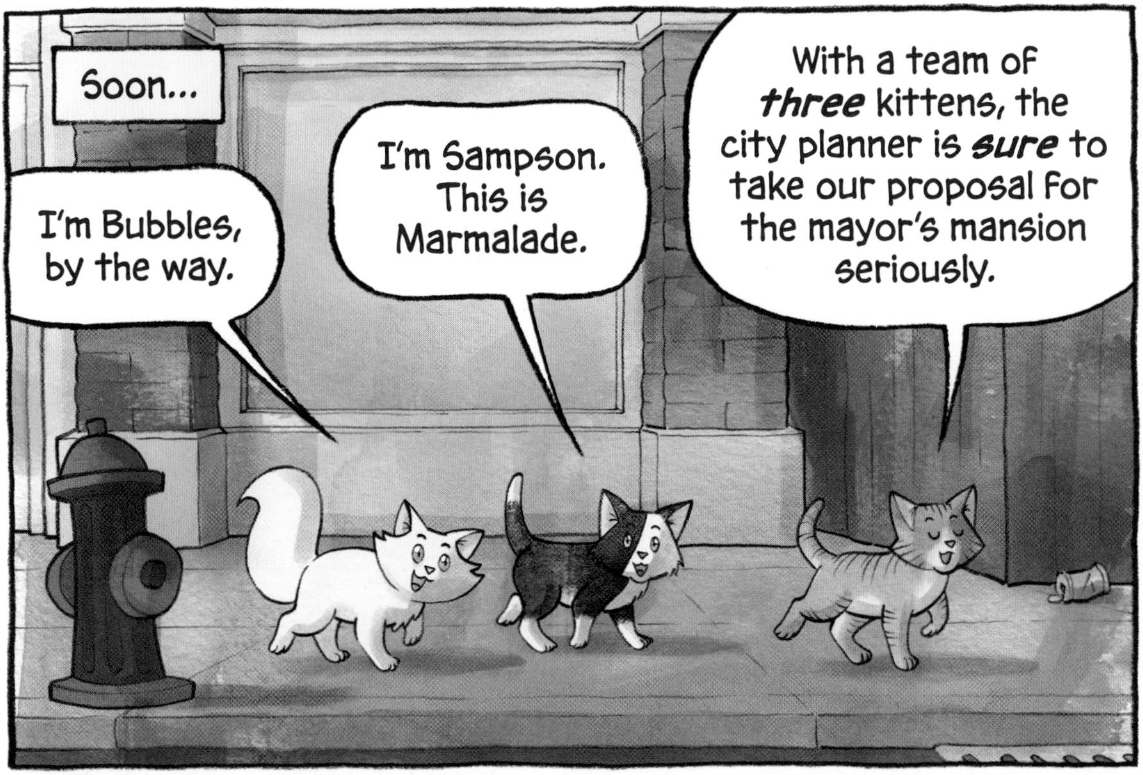
Soon...
I'm Bubbles, by the way.
I'm Sampson. This is Marmalade.
With a team of *three* kittens, the city planner is *sure* to take our proposal for the mayor's mansion seriously.

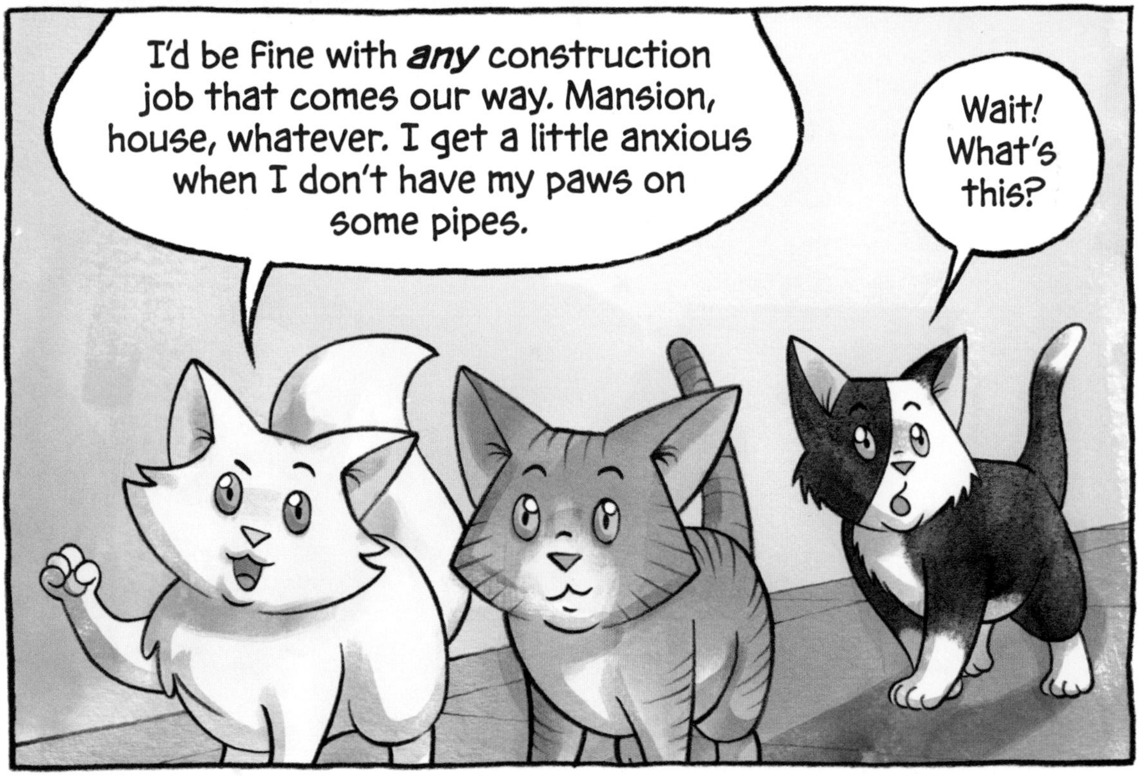
I'd be fine with *any* construction job that comes our way. Mansion, house, whatever. I get a little anxious when I don't have my paws on some pipes.
Wait! What's this?

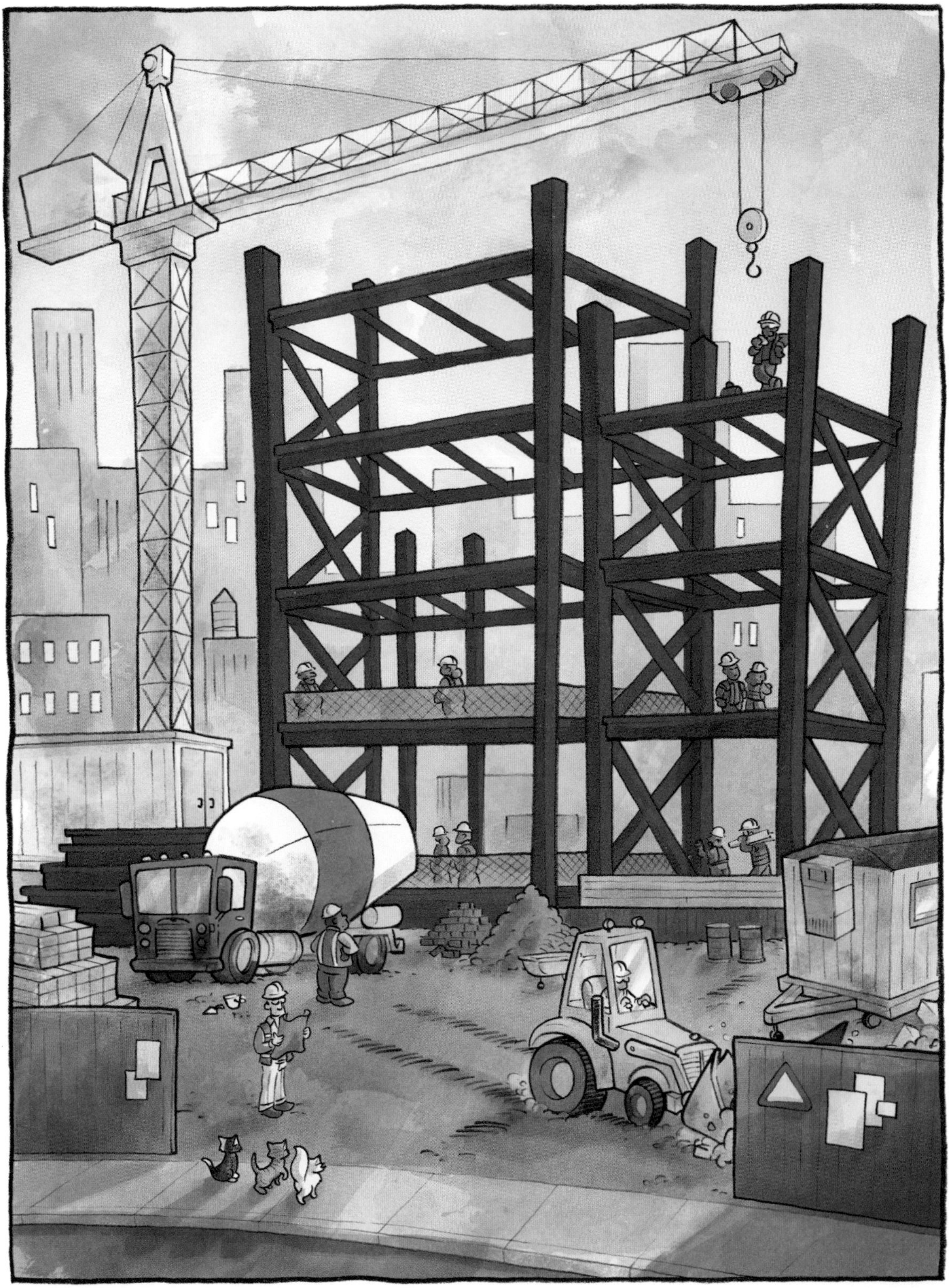

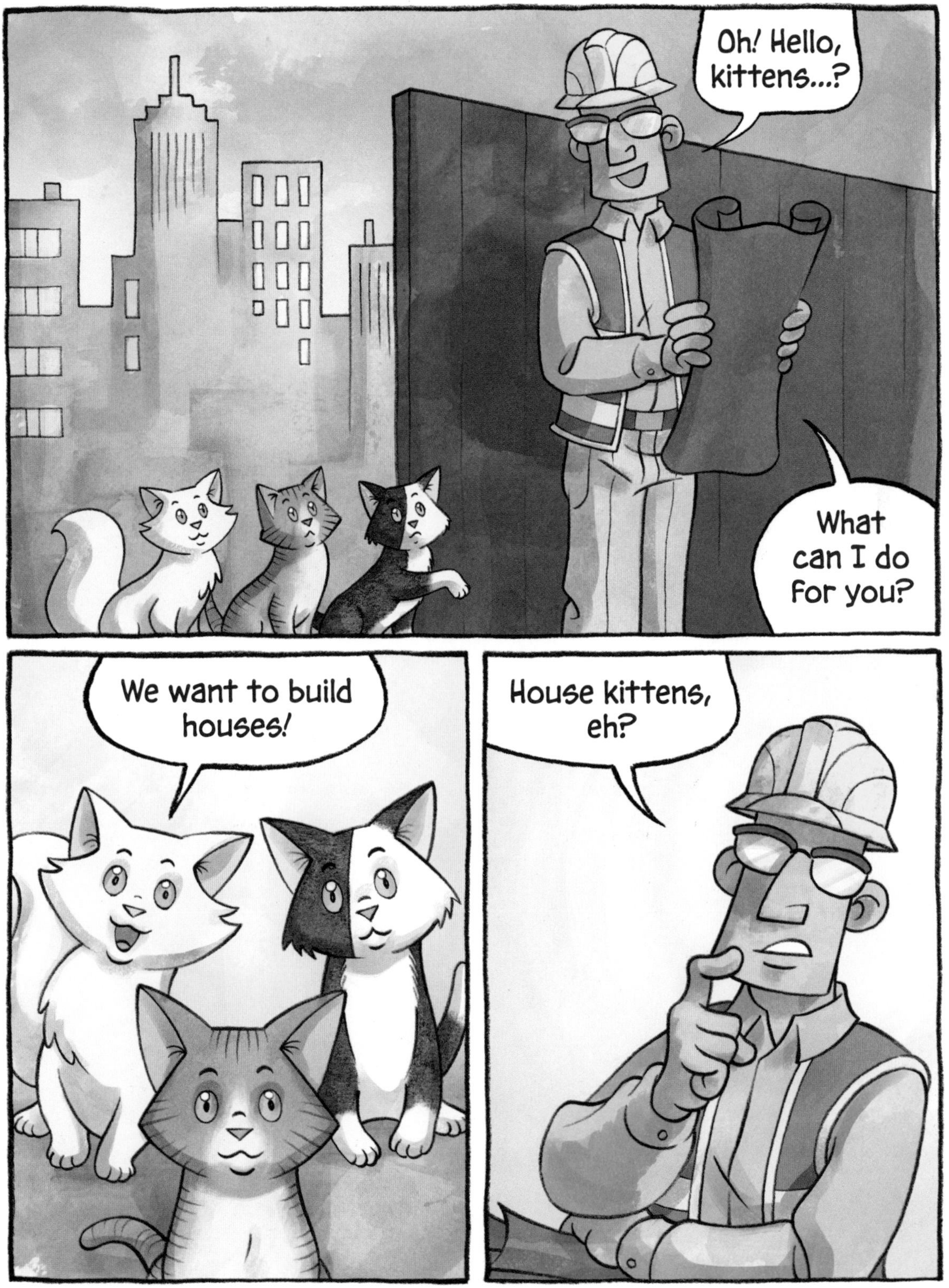
Oh! Hello, kittens...?
What can I do for you?
We want to build houses!
House kittens, eh?

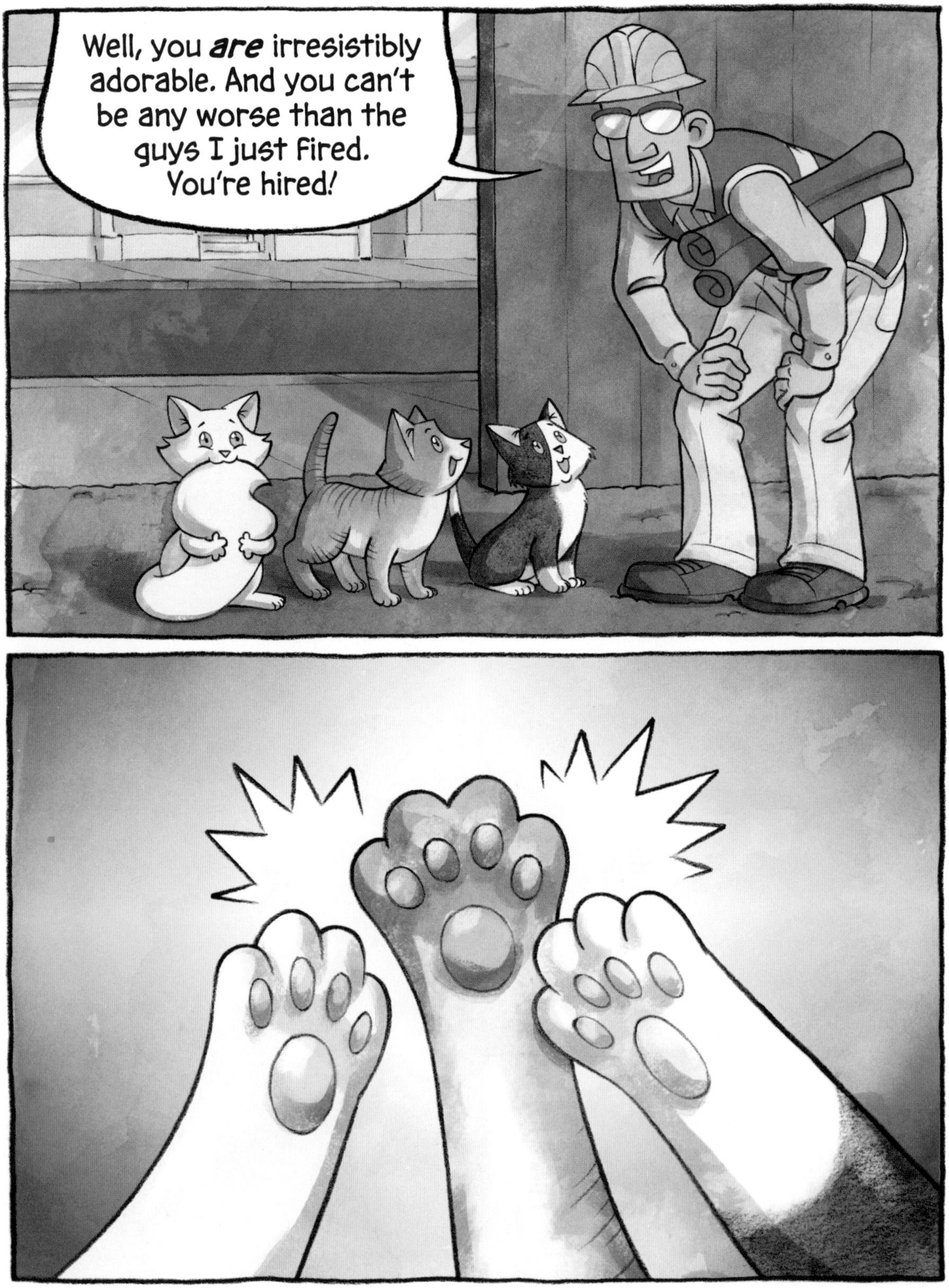
Well, you *are* irresistibly adorable. And you can't be any worse than the guys I just fired. You're hired!

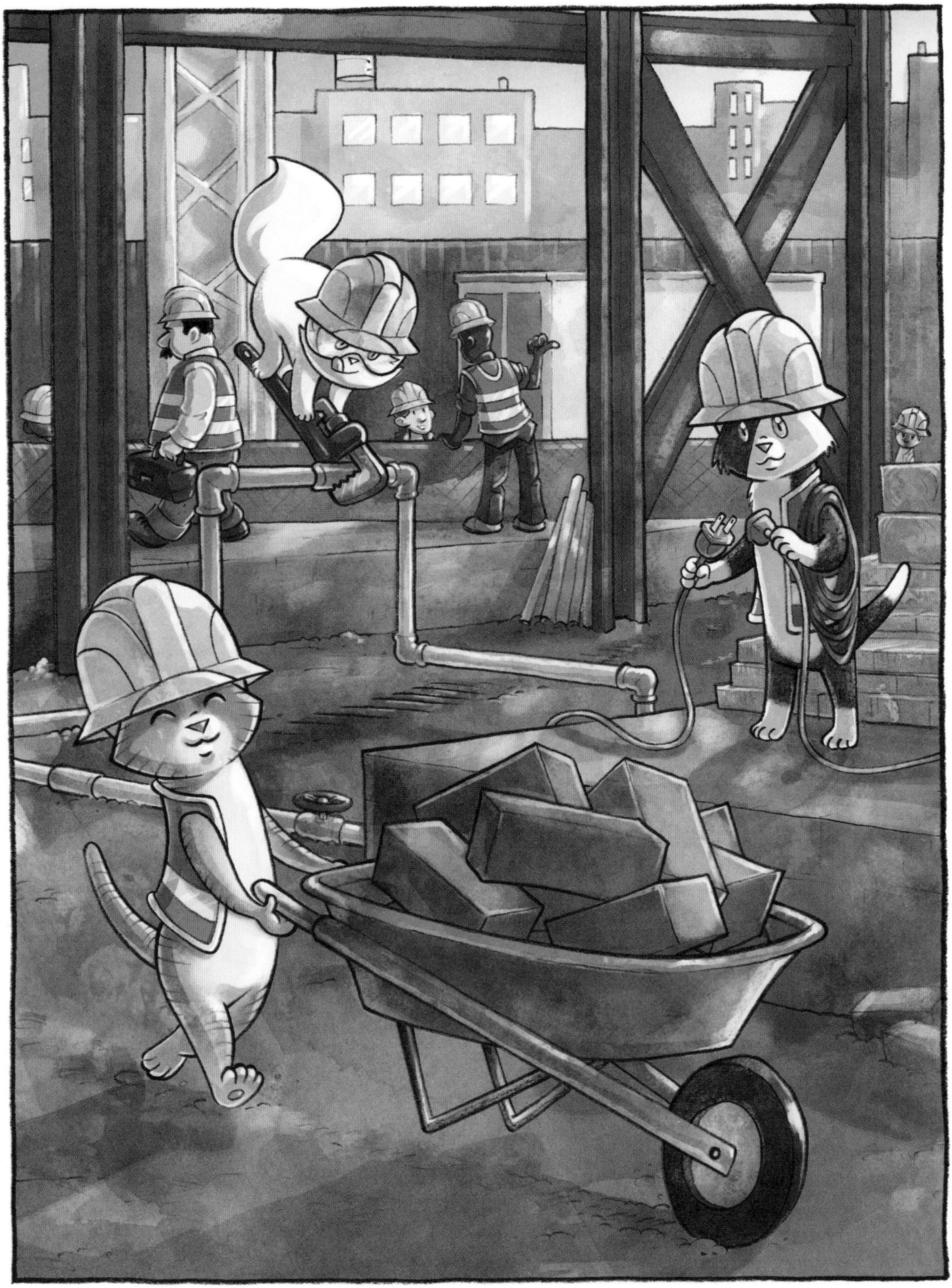

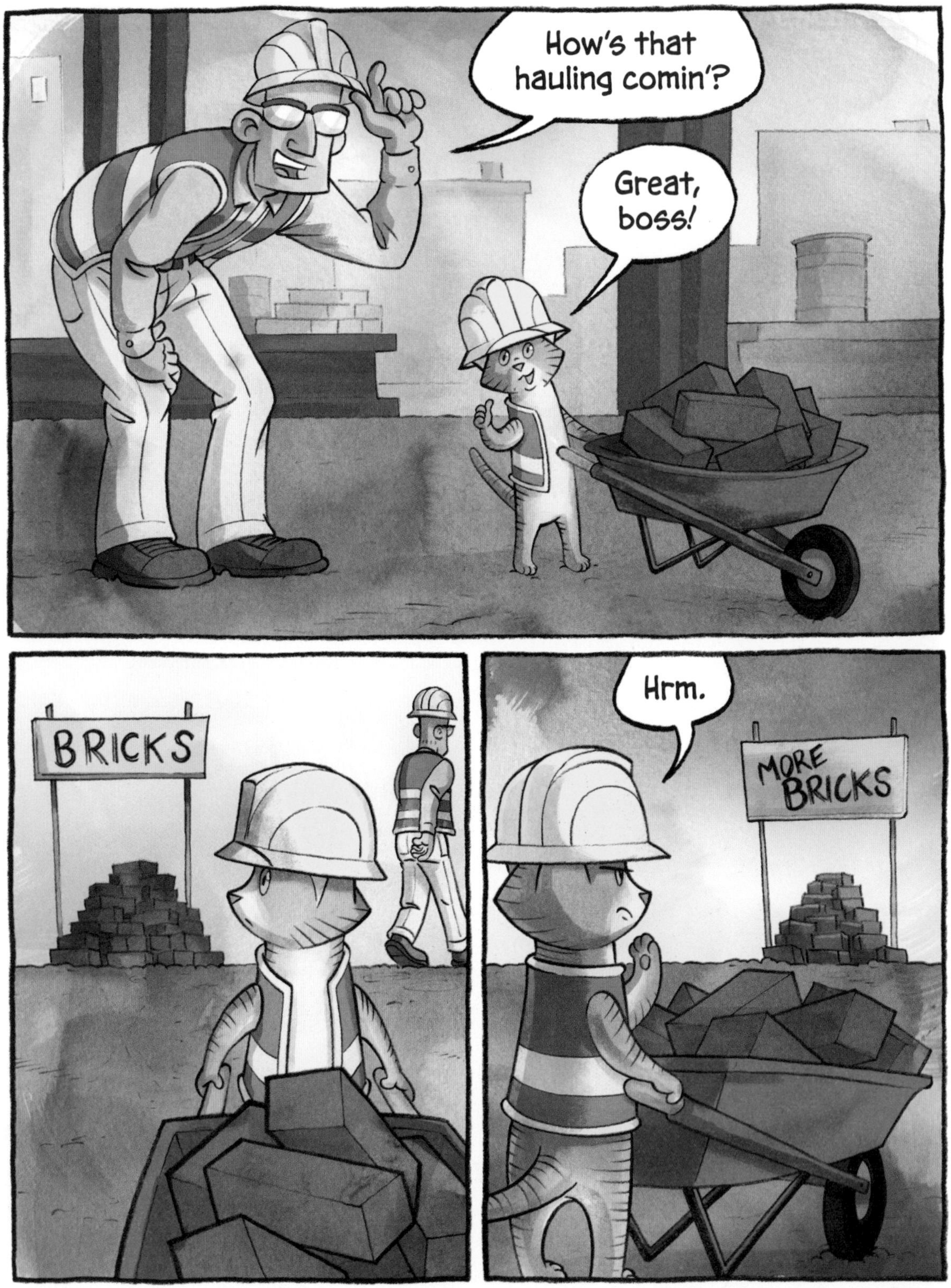
How's that hauling comin'?
Great, boss!
BRICKS
Hrm.
MORE BRICKS

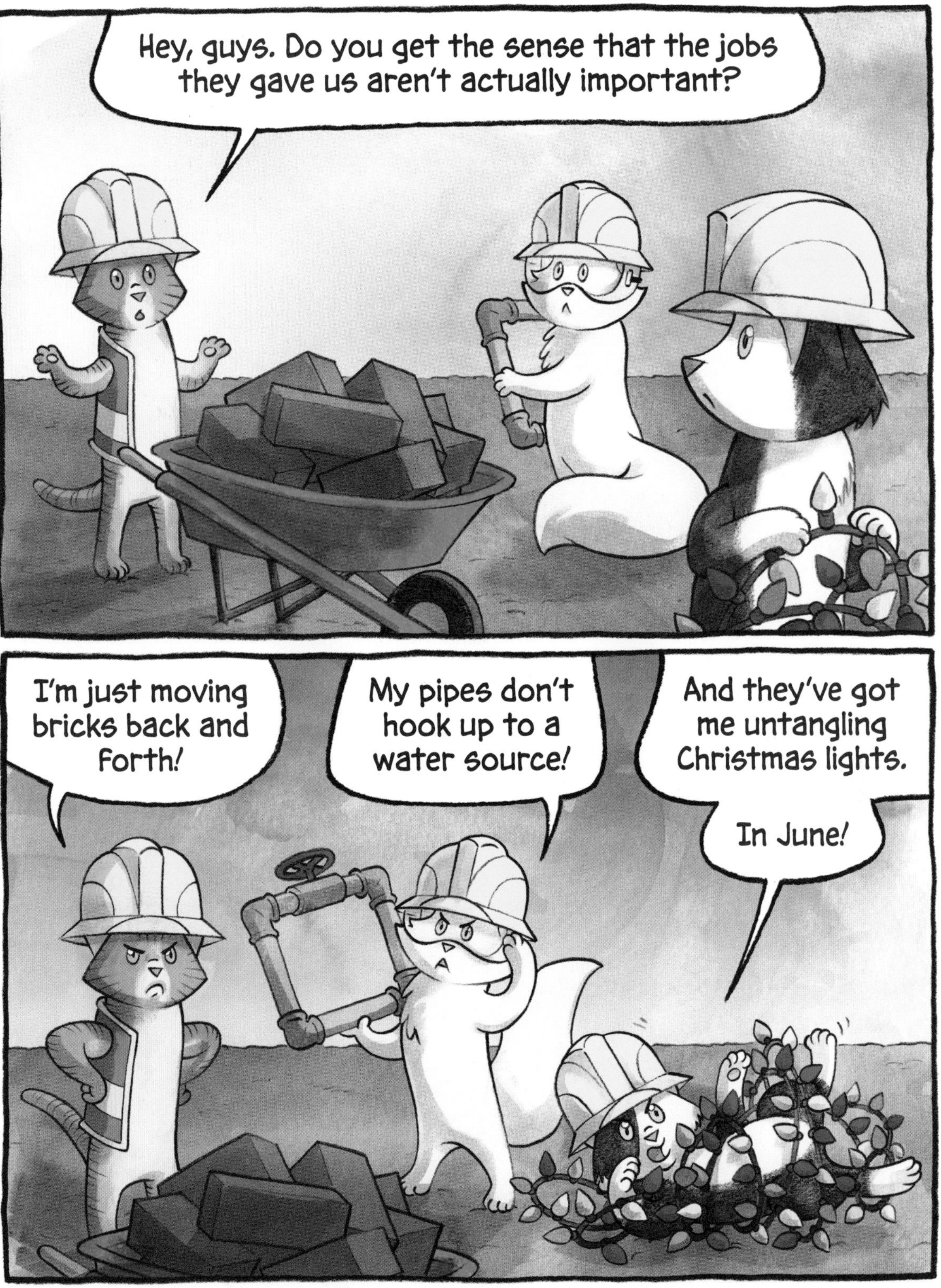
Hey, guys. Do you get the sense that the jobs they gave us aren't actually important?
I'm just moving bricks back and forth!
My pipes don't hook up to a water source!
And they've got me untangling Christmas lights.
In June!

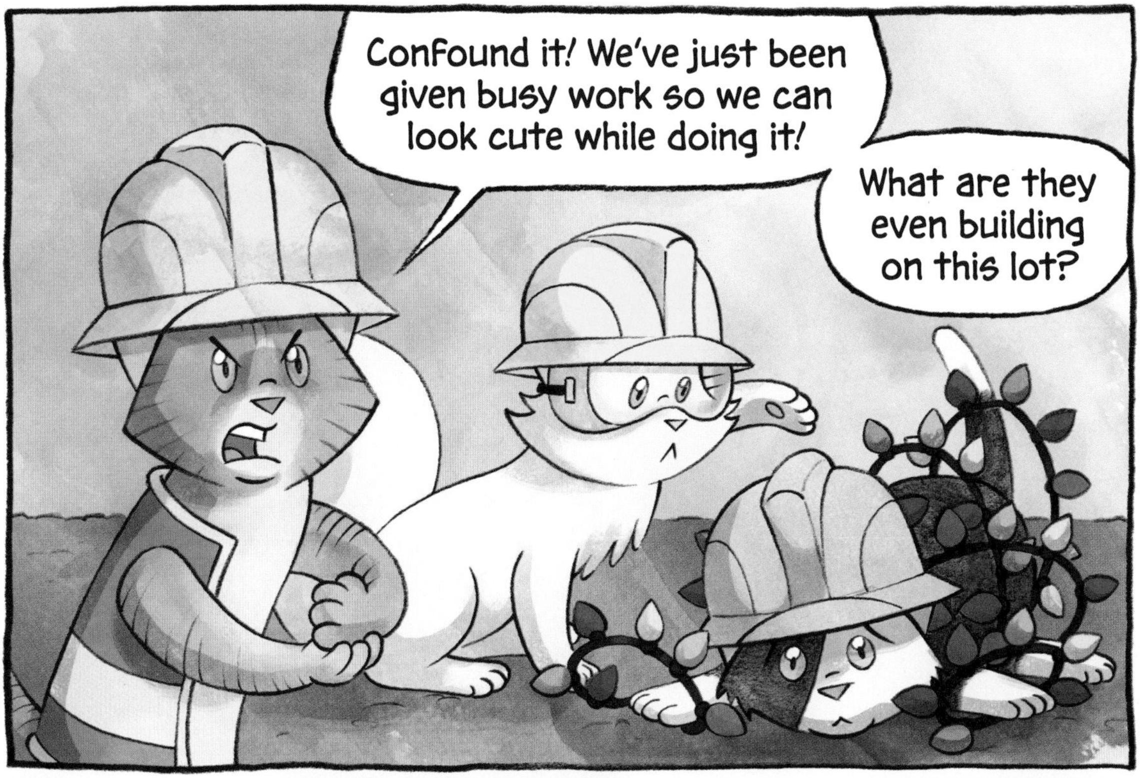
Confound it! We've just been given busy work so we can look cute while doing it!
What are they even building on this lot?

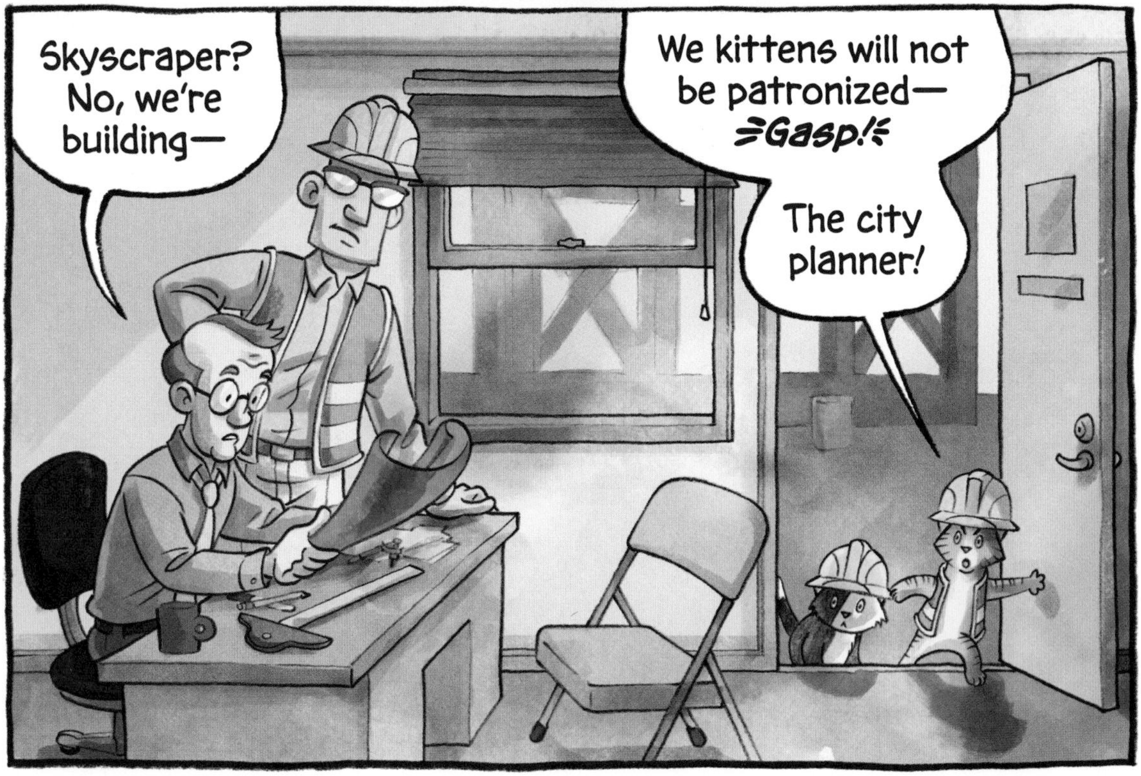
Skyscraper? No, we're building—
We kittens will not be patronized—
Gasp!
The city planner!

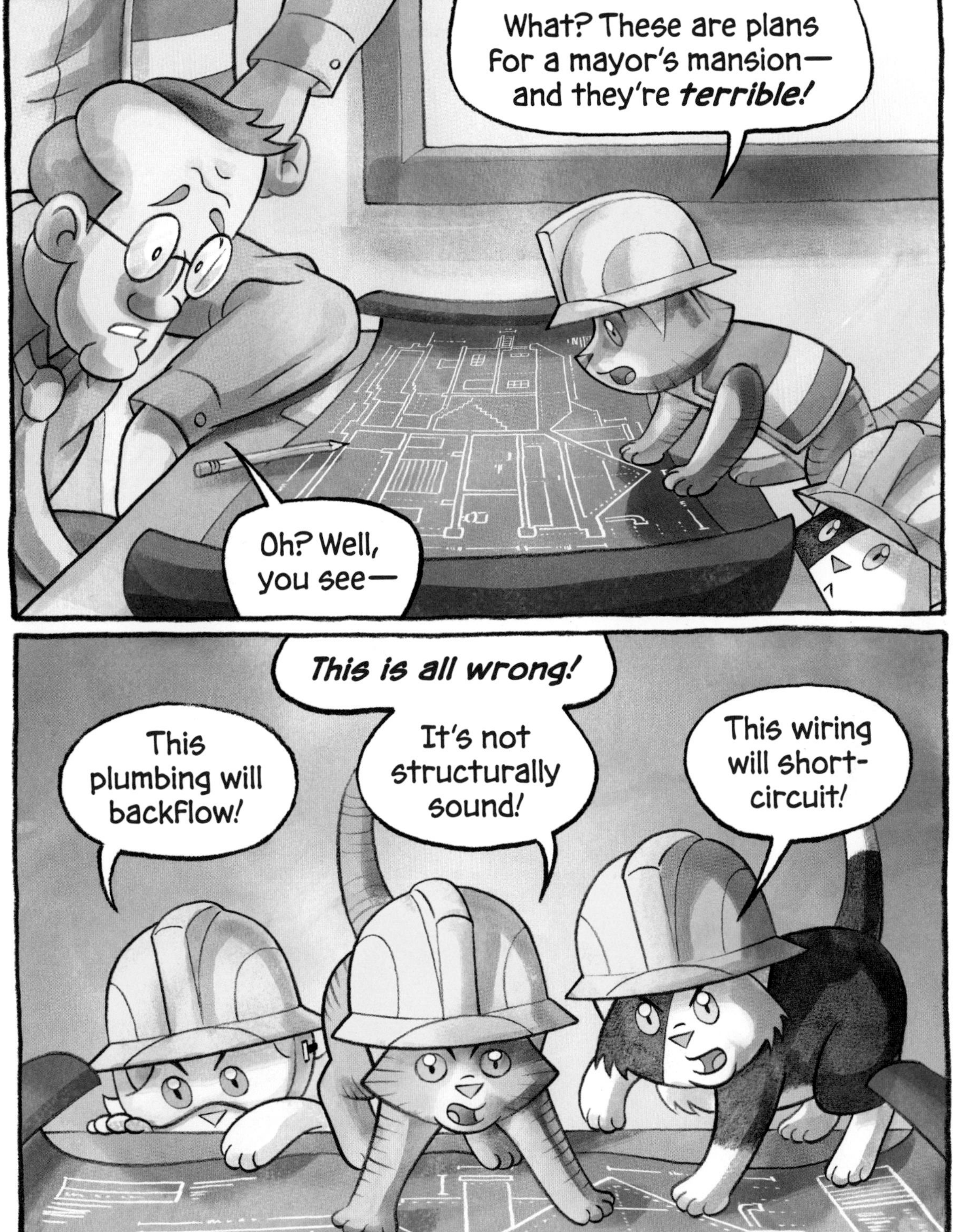
What? These are plans for a mayor's mansion—and they're *terrible!*
Oh? Well, you see—
This is all wrong!
This plumbing will backflow!
It's not structurally sound!
This wiring will short-circuit!

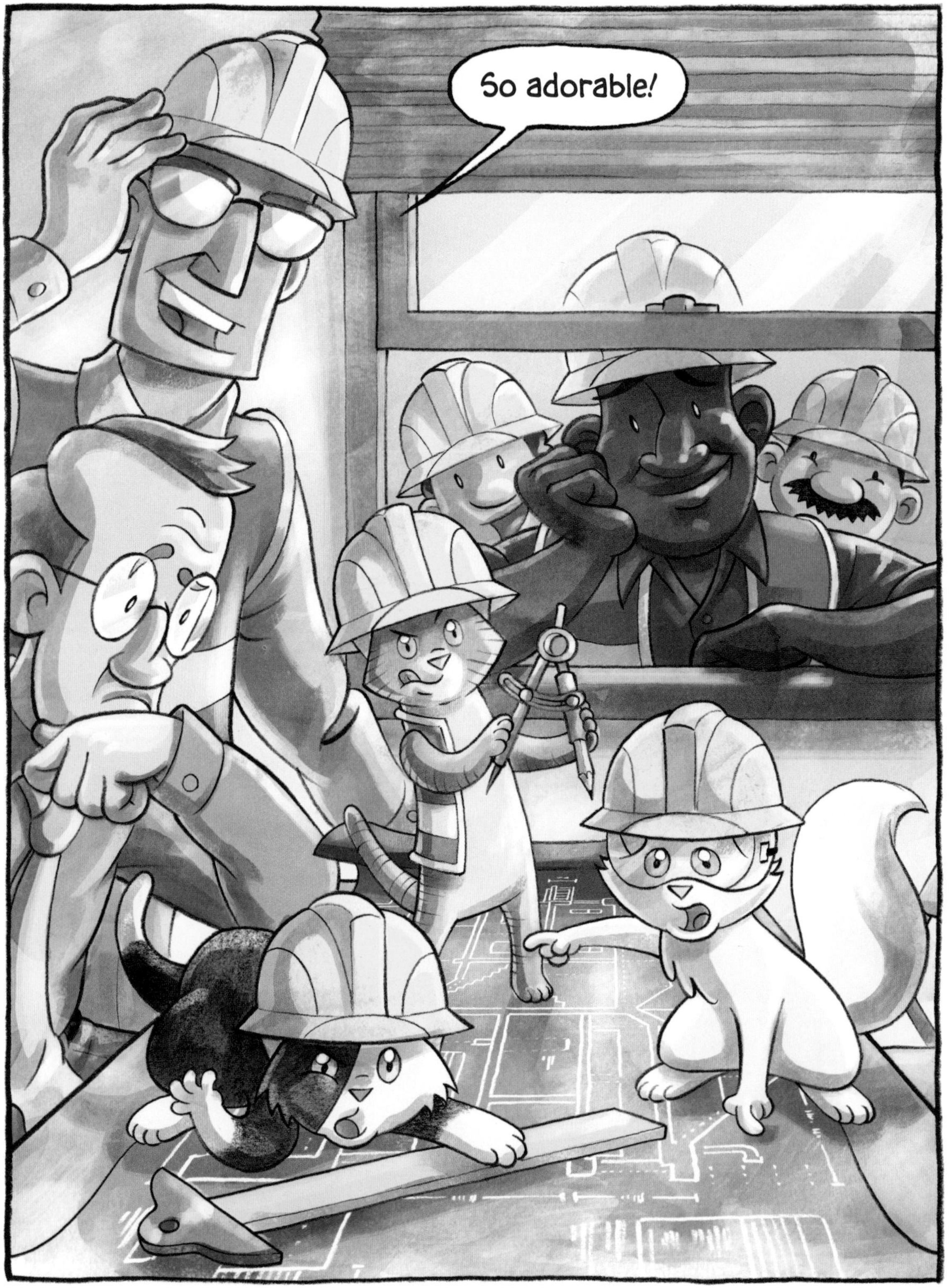
So adorable!

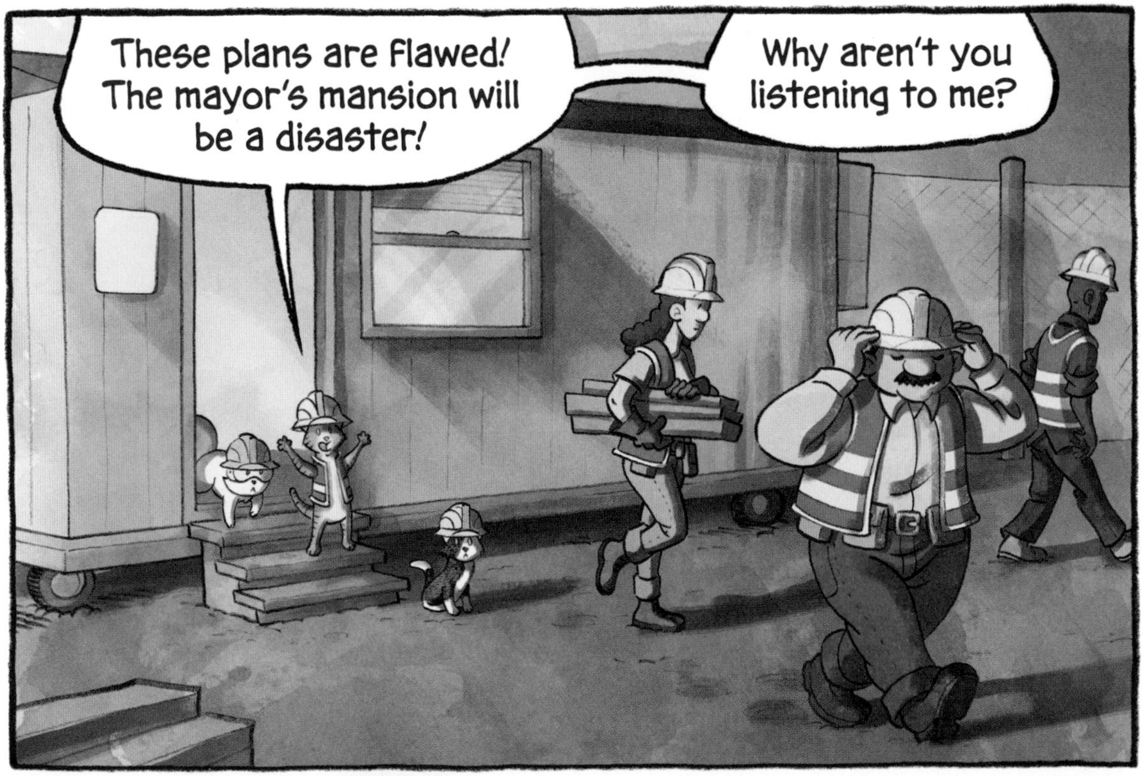
These plans are flawed! The mayor's mansion will be a disaster!
Why aren't you listening to me?

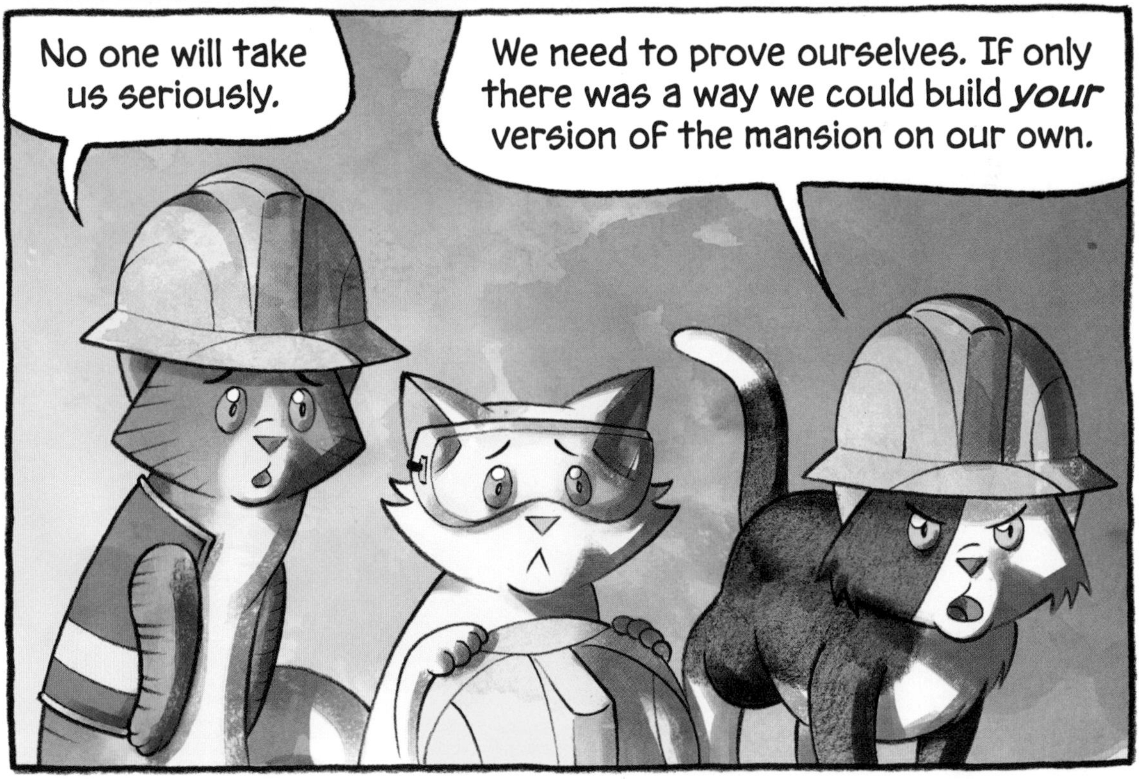
No one will take us seriously.
We need to prove ourselves. If only there was a way we could build *your* version of the mansion on our own.

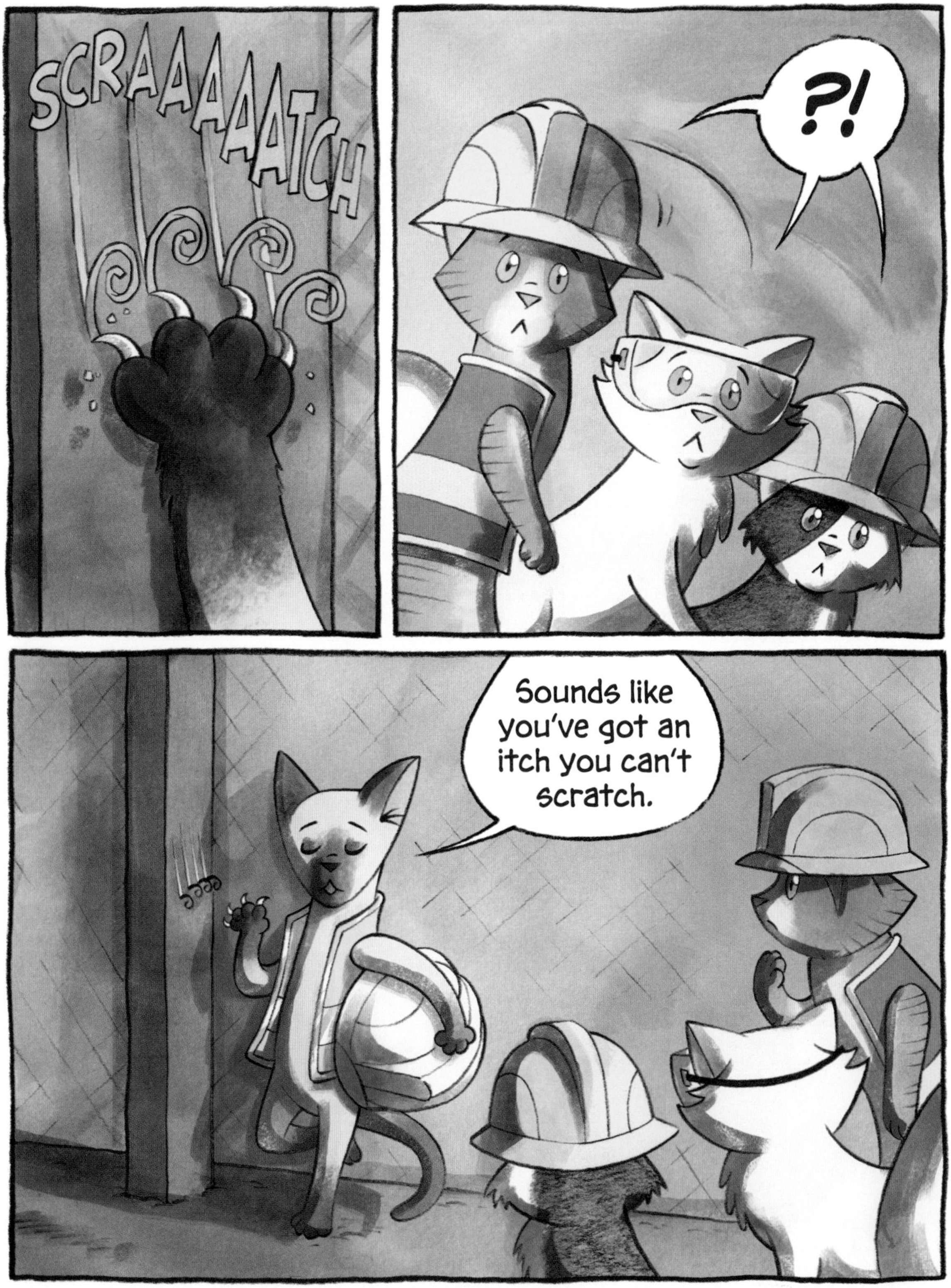
SCRAAAAAATCH
?!
Sounds like you've got an itch you can't scratch.

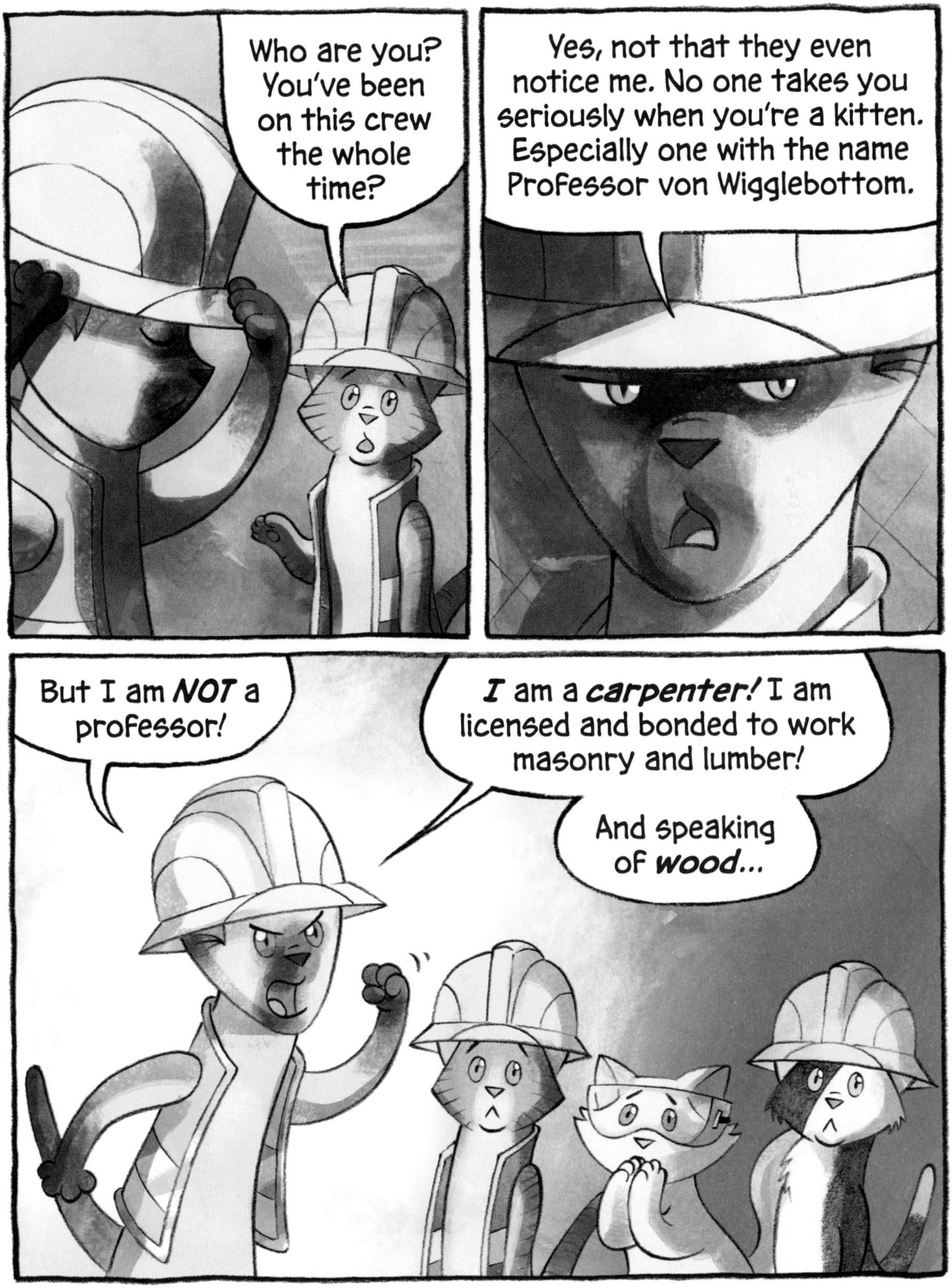
Who are you? You've been on this crew the whole time?
Yes, not that they even notice me. No one takes you seriously when you're a kitten. Especially one with the name Professor von Wigglebottom.
But I am *NOT* a professor!
I am a *carpenter!* I am licensed and bonded to work masonry and lumber!
And speaking of *wood*...

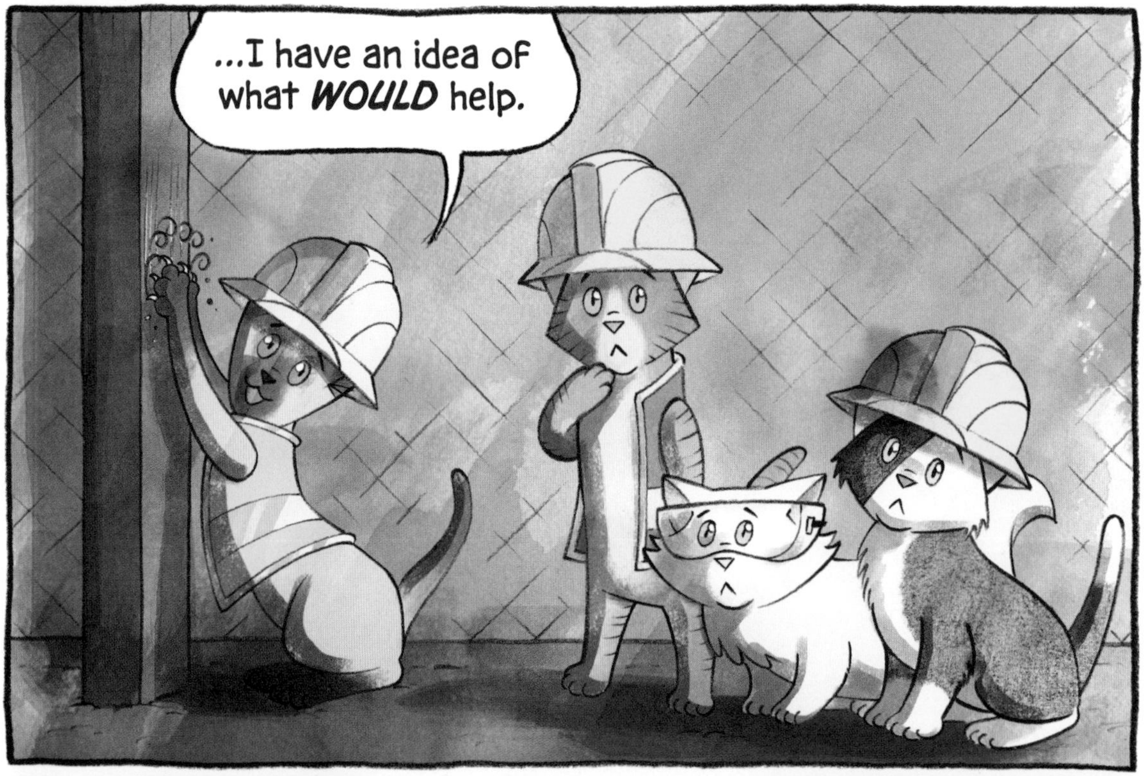
...I have an idea of what **WOULD** help.

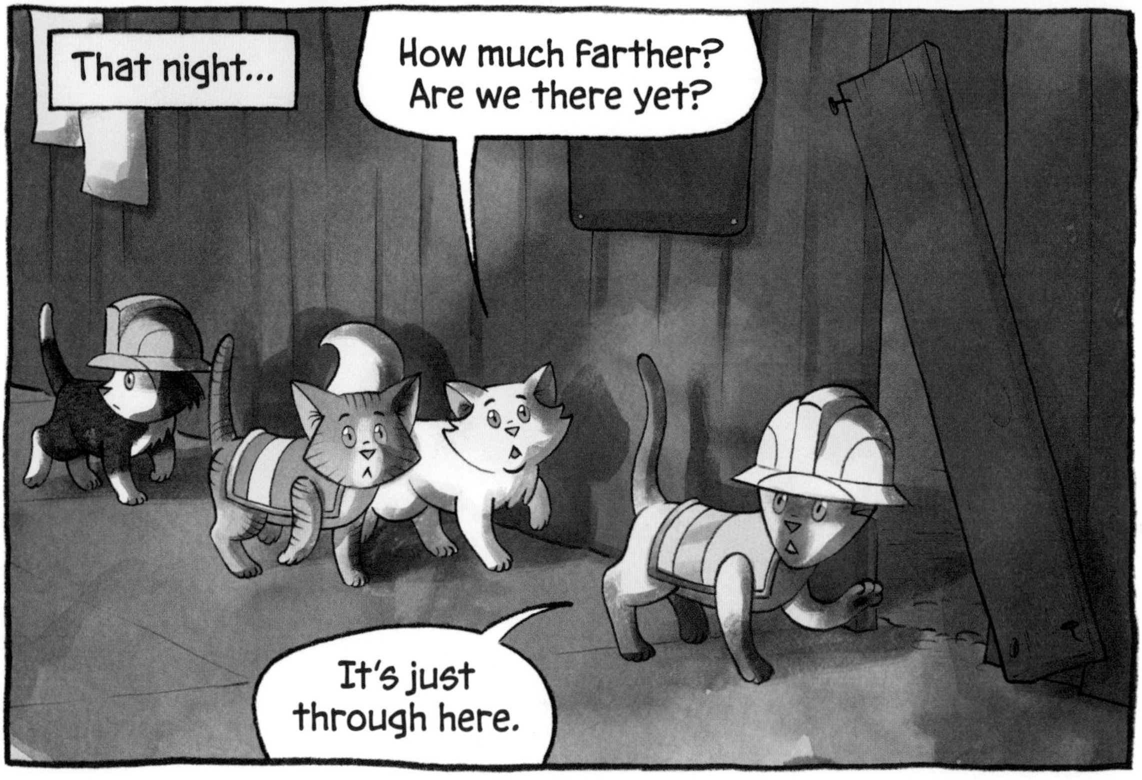
That night...
How much farther? Are we there yet?
It's just through here.

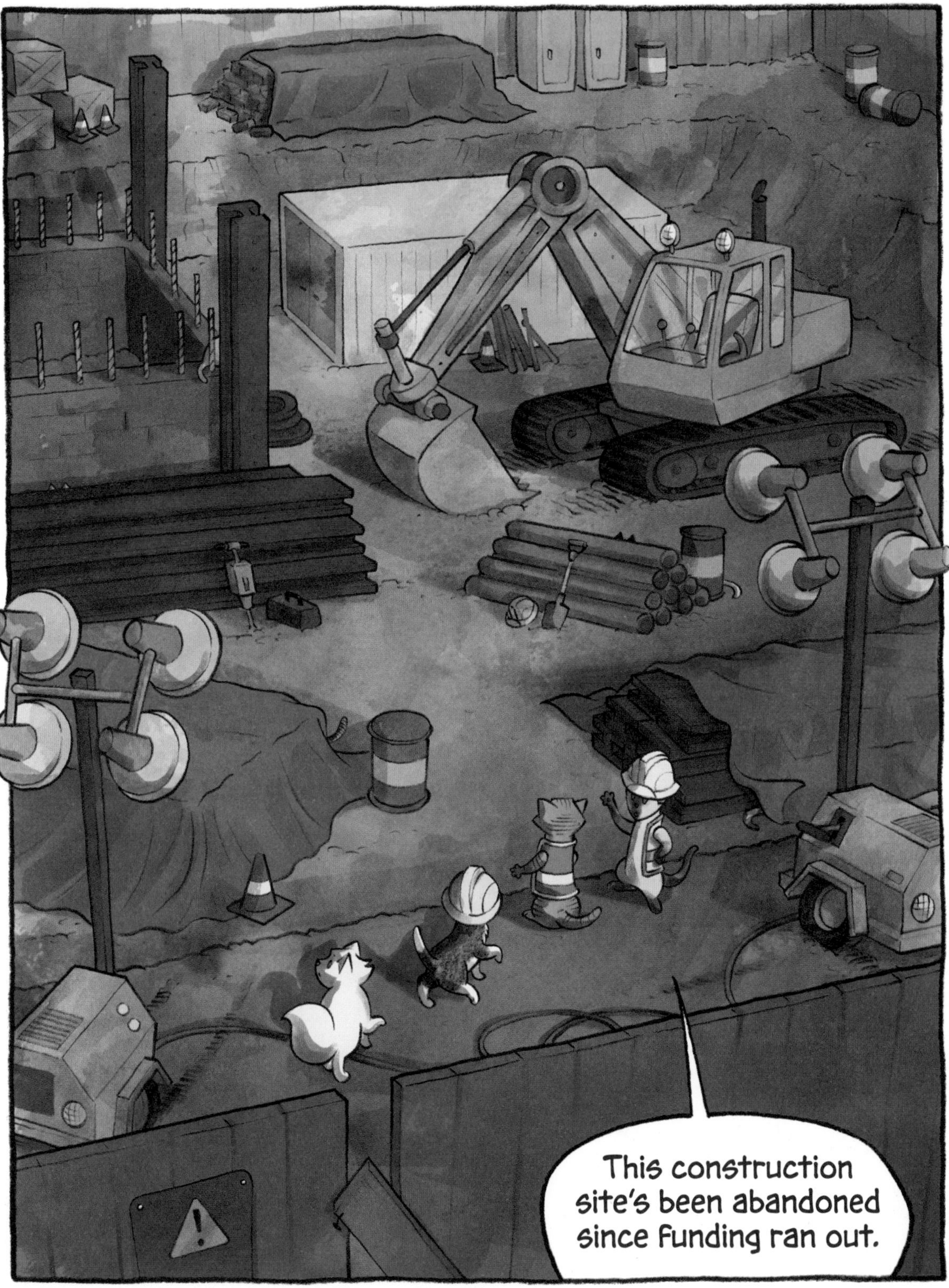
This construction site's been abandoned since funding ran out.

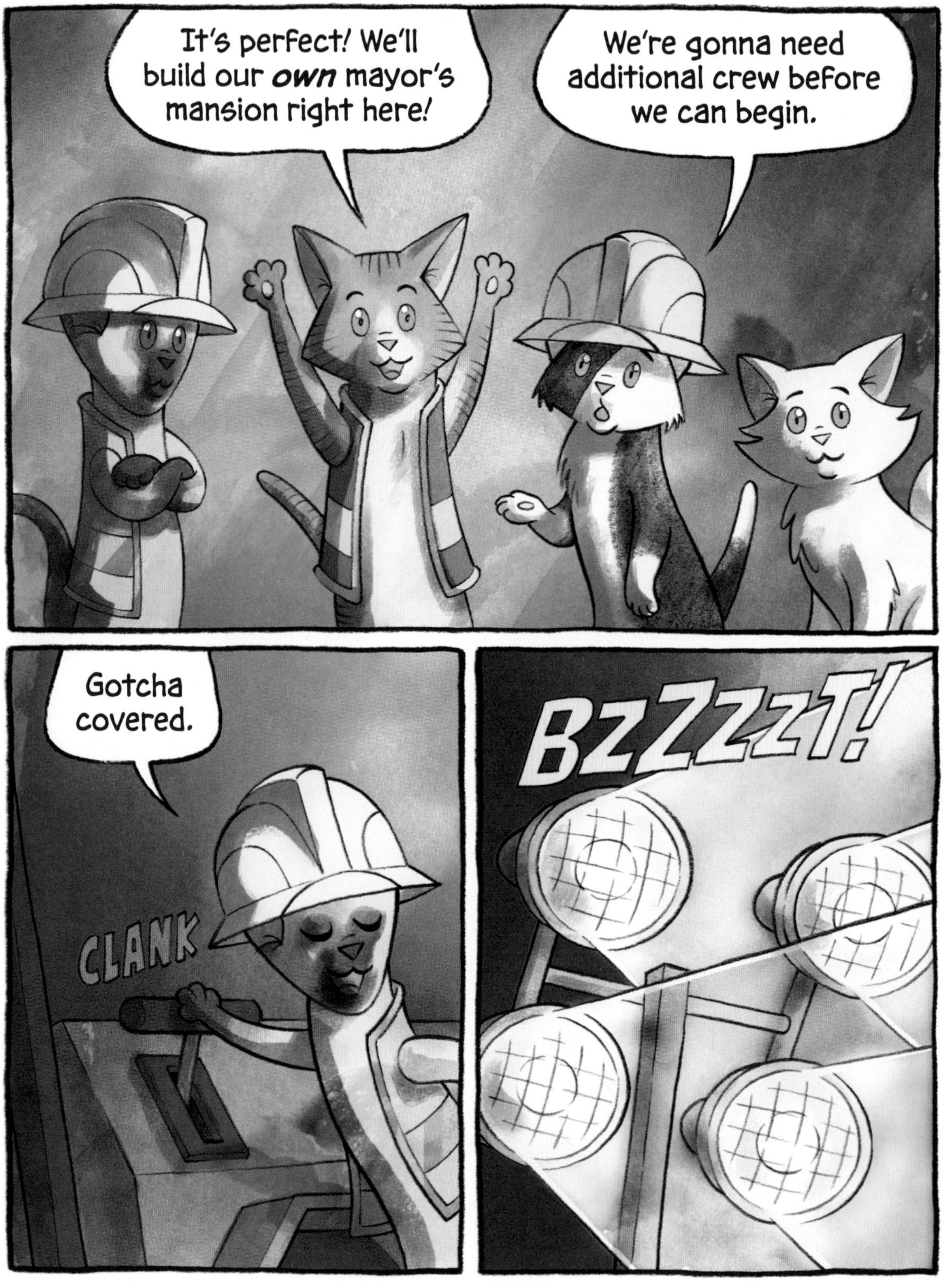
It's perfect! We'll build our ***own*** mayor's mansion right here!
We're gonna need additional crew before we can begin.
Gotcha covered.
CLANK
BZZZZT!

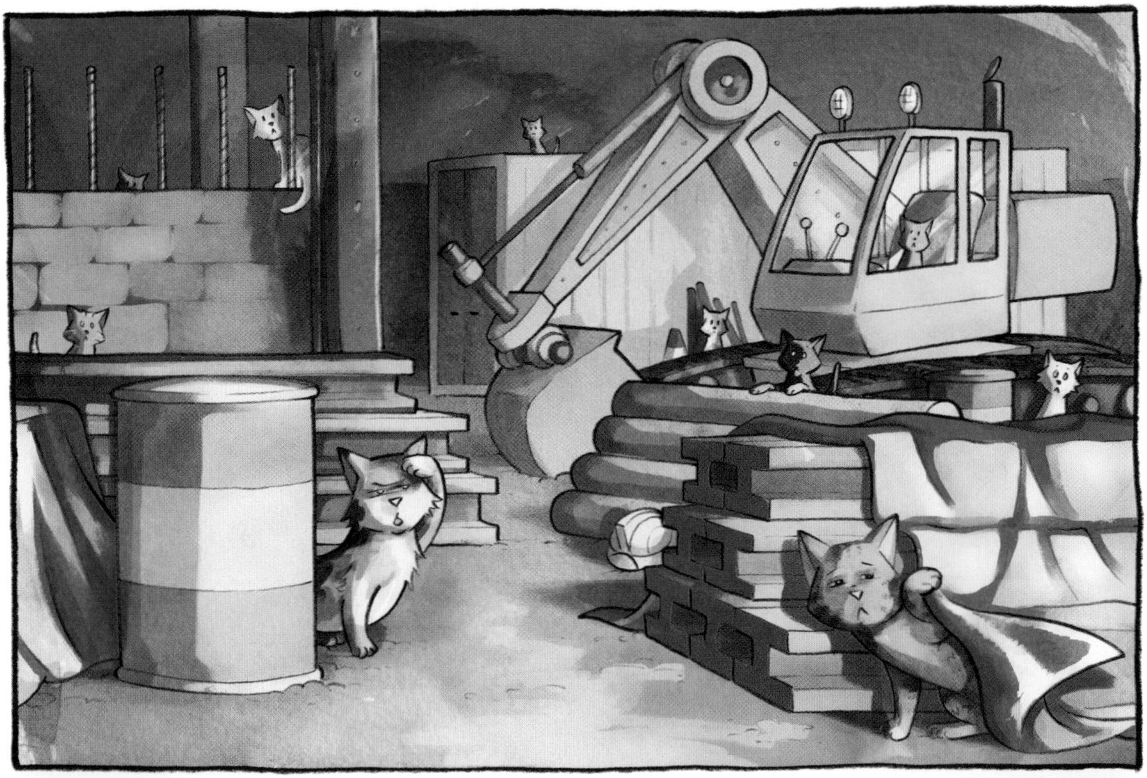

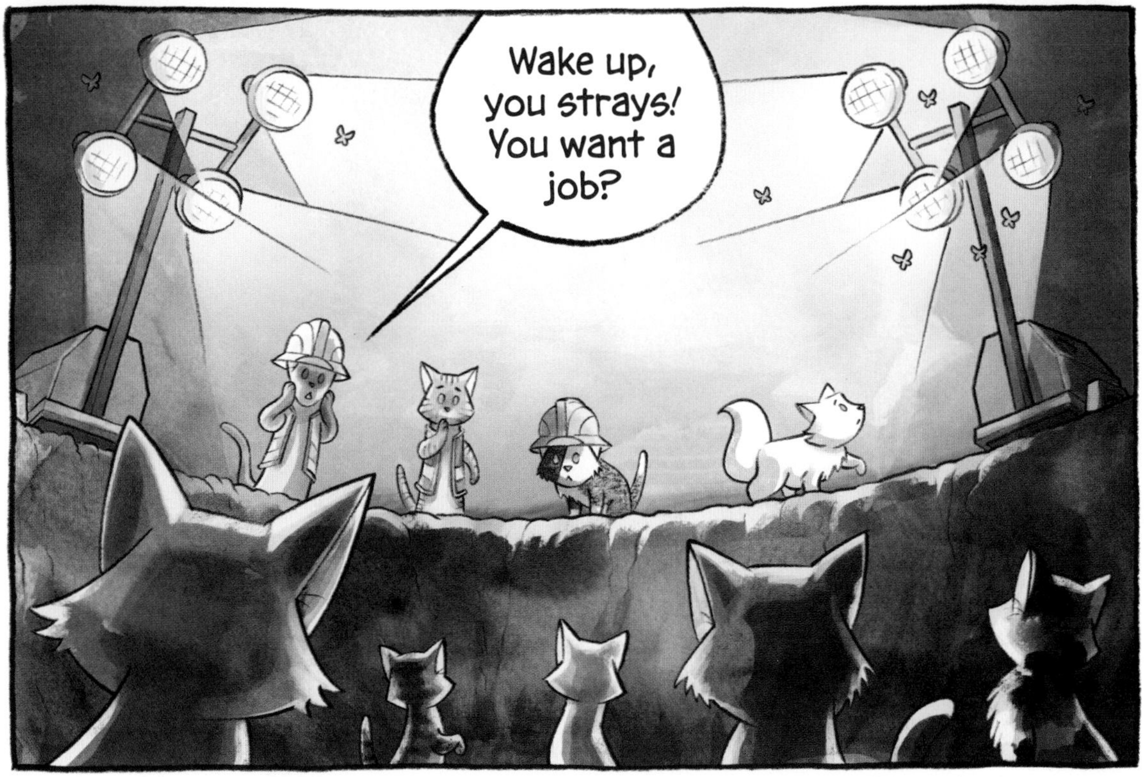
Wake up, you strays! You want a job?

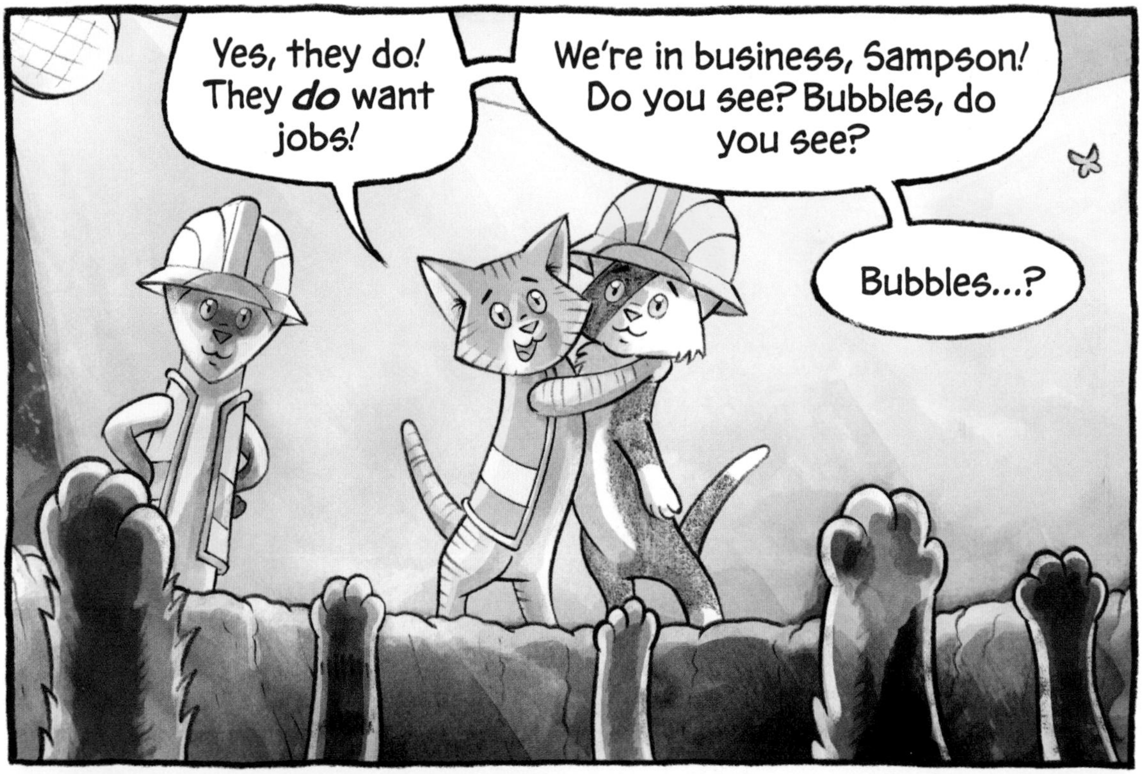
Yes, they do! They *do* want jobs!
We're in business, Sampson! Do you see? Bubbles, do you see?
Bubbles...?

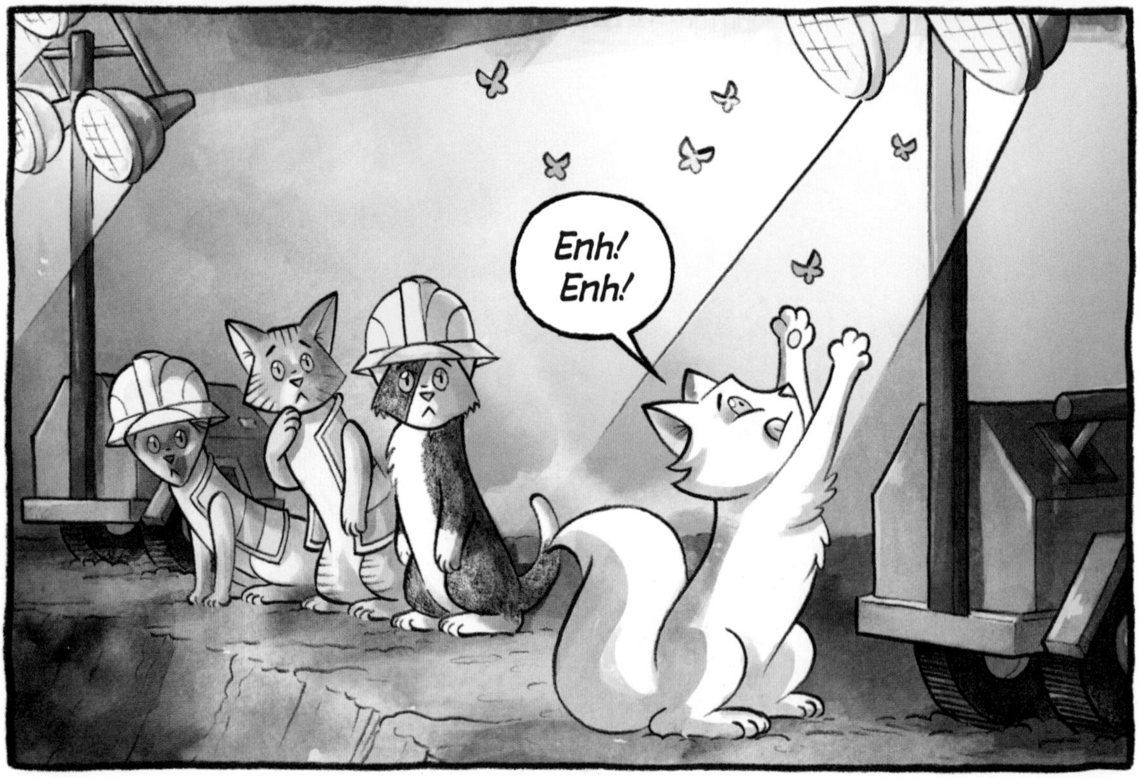
Enh! Enh!

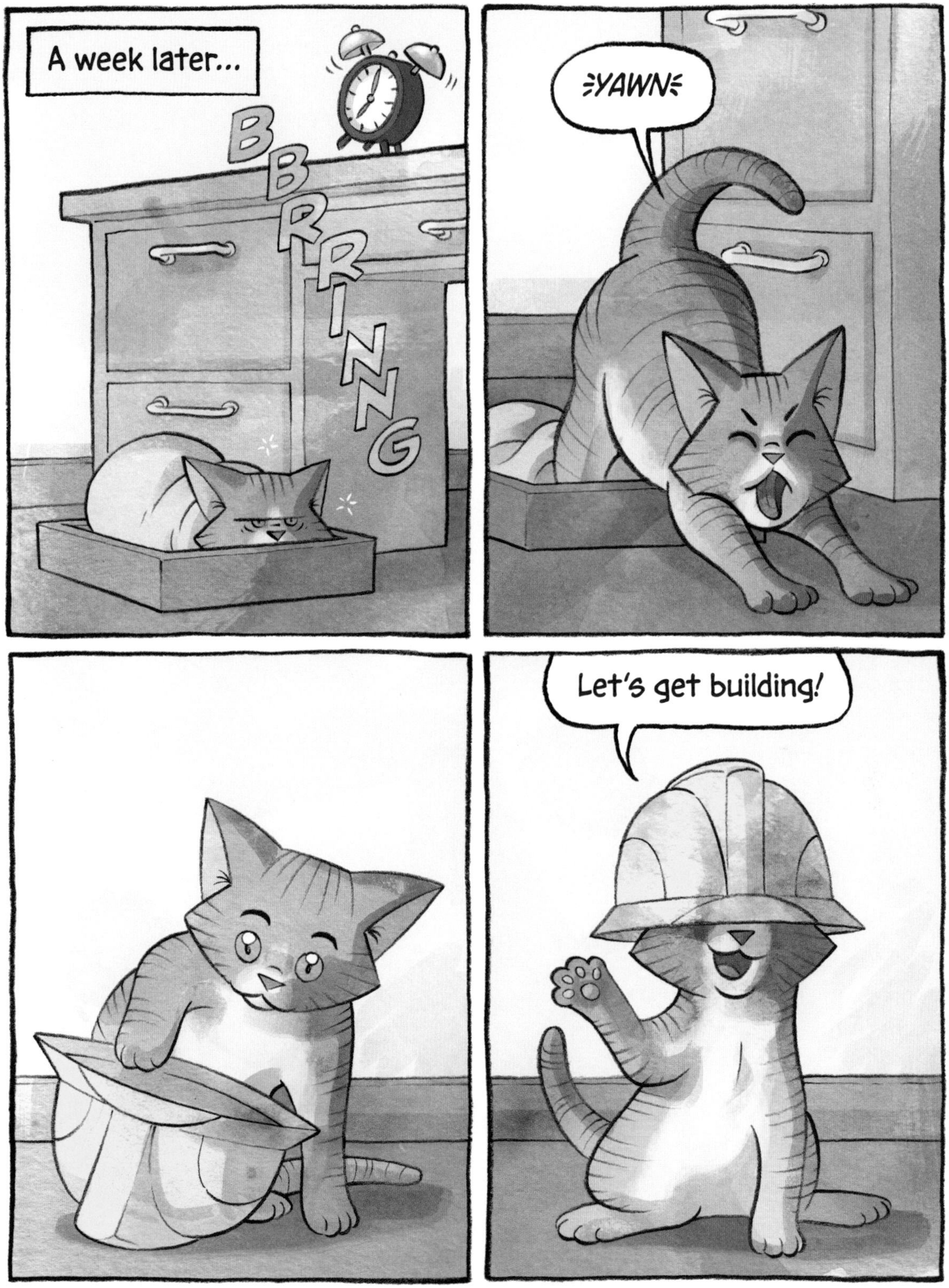
A week later...
BBRRRINNG
YAWN
Let's get building!

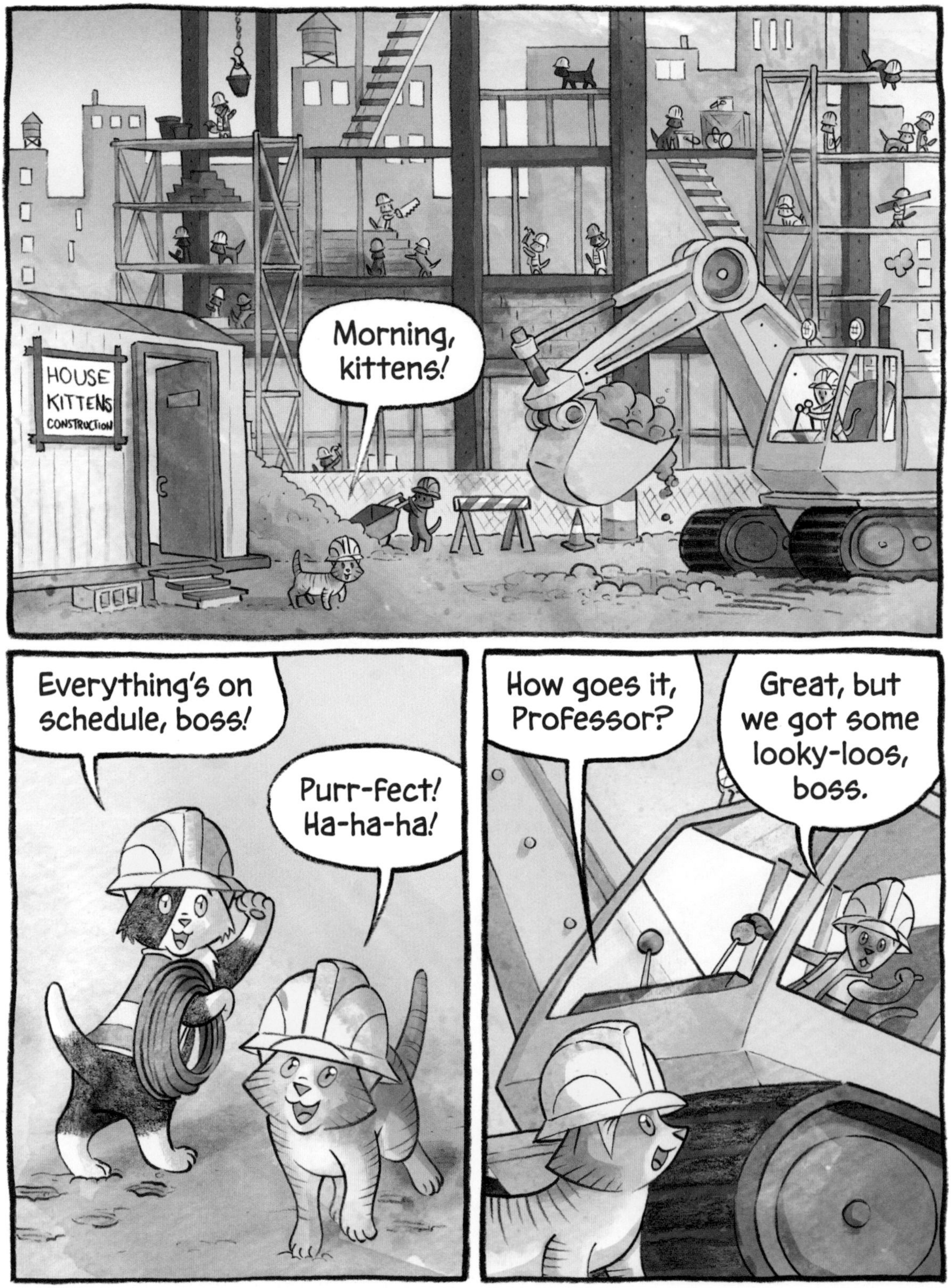
HOUSE KITTENS CONSTRUCTION
Morning, kittens!
Everything's on schedule, boss!
Purr-fect! Ha-ha-ha!
How goes it, Professor?
Great, but we got some looky-loos, boss.

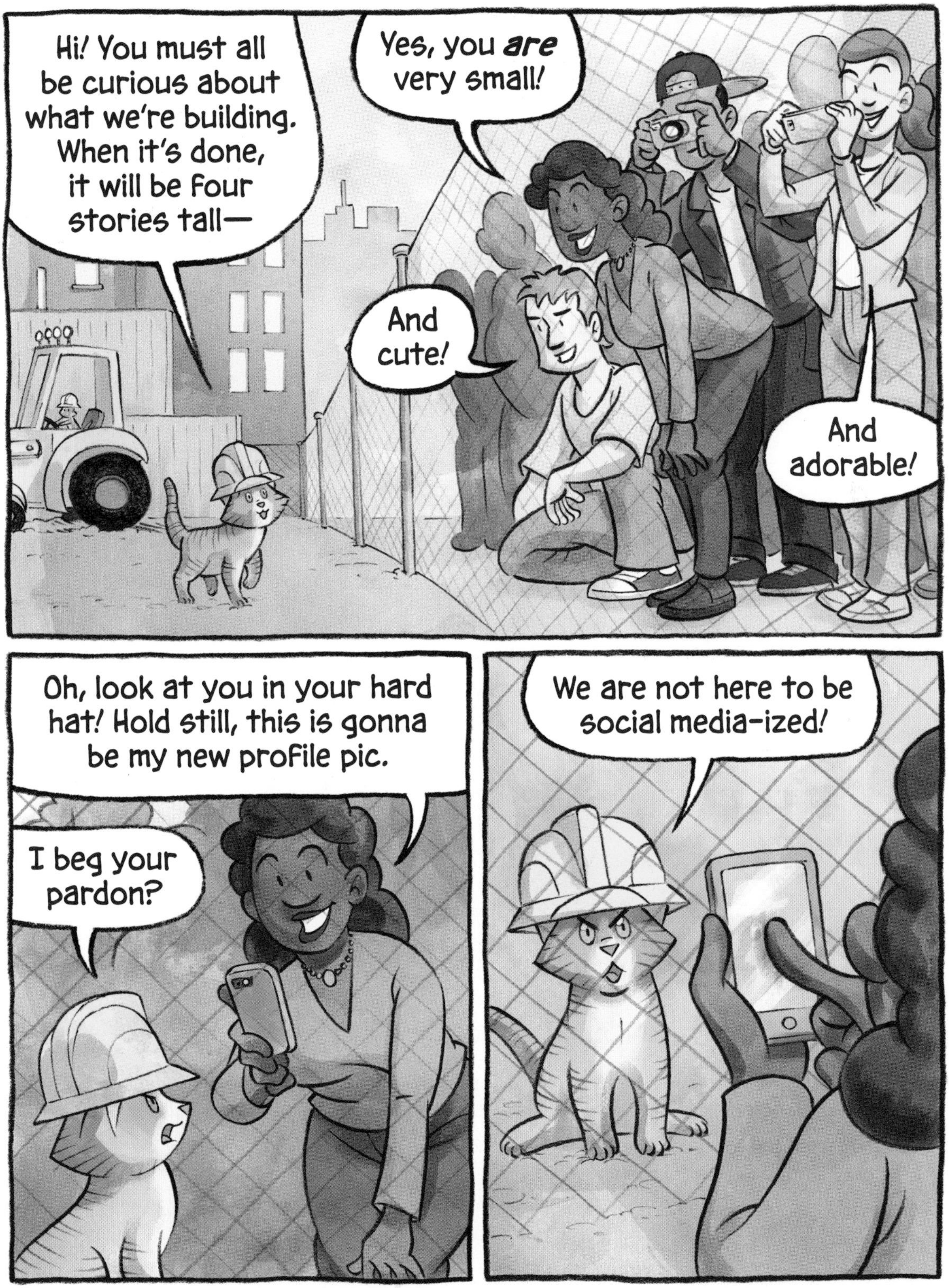
Hi! You must all be curious about what we're building. When it's done, it will be four stories tall—
Yes, you **are** very small!
And cute!
And adorable!
Oh, look at you in your hard hat! Hold still, this is gonna be my new profile pic.
I beg your pardon?
We are not here to be social media-ized!

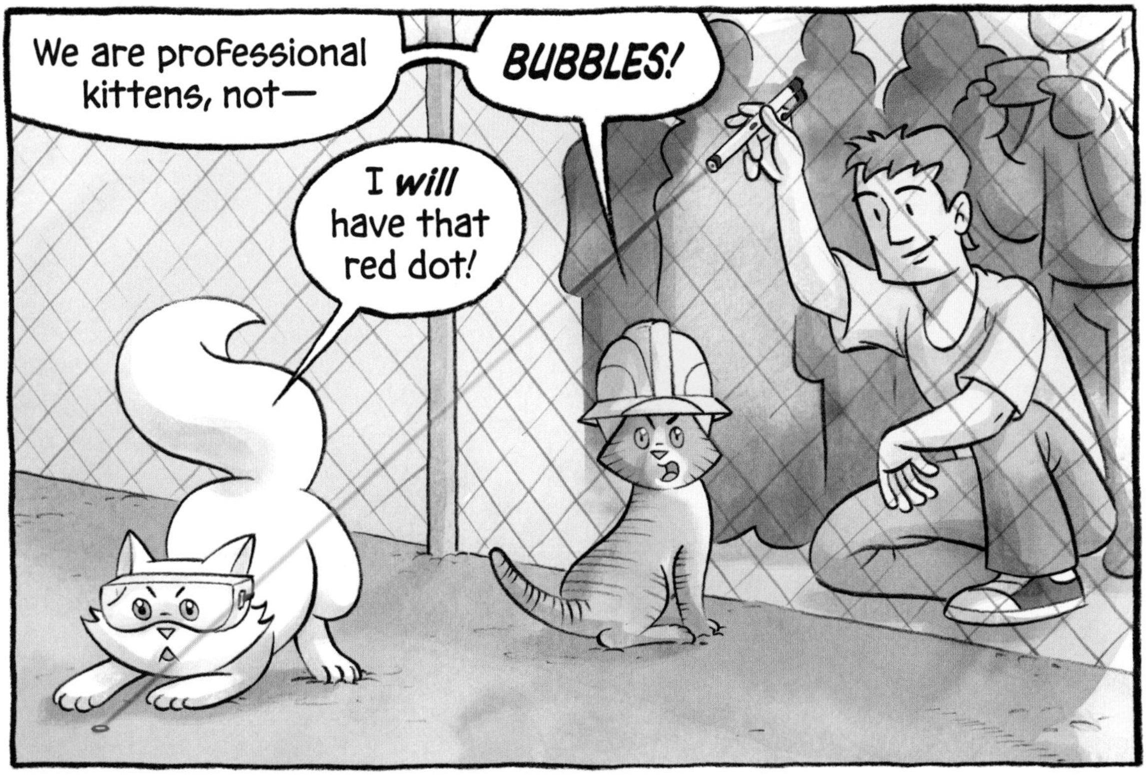
We are professional kittens, not—
BUBBLES!
I *will* have that red dot!

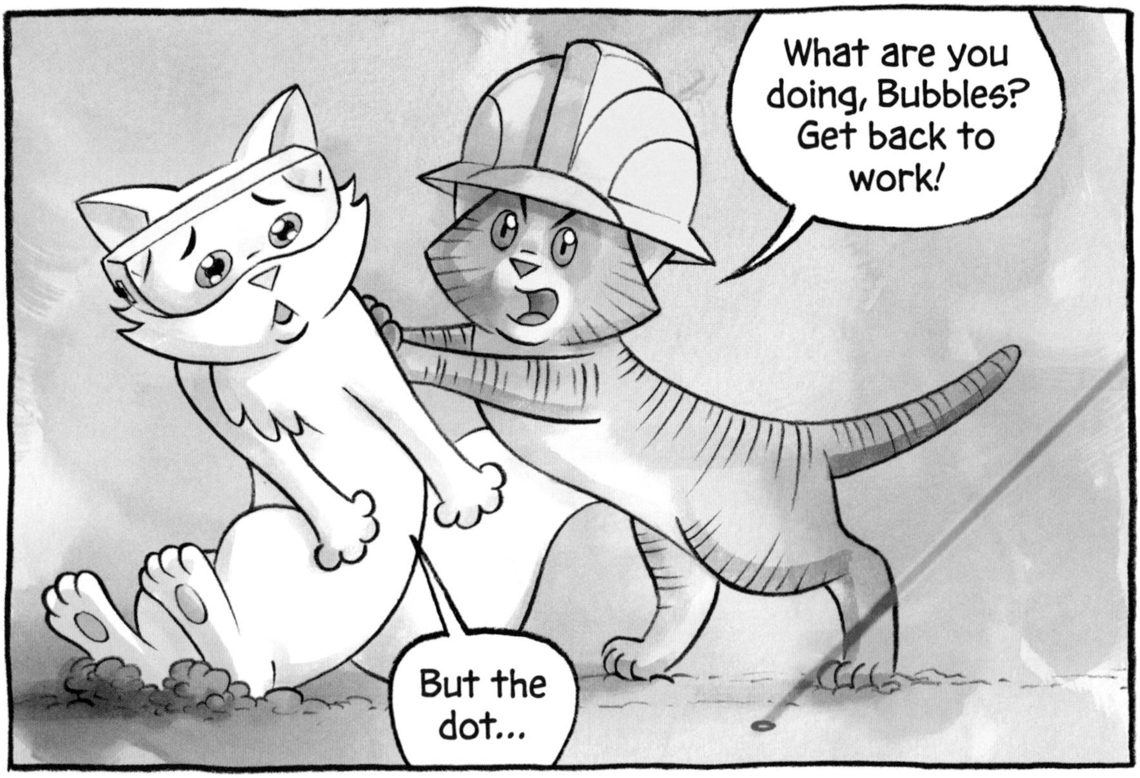
What are you doing, Bubbles? Get back to work!
But the dot...

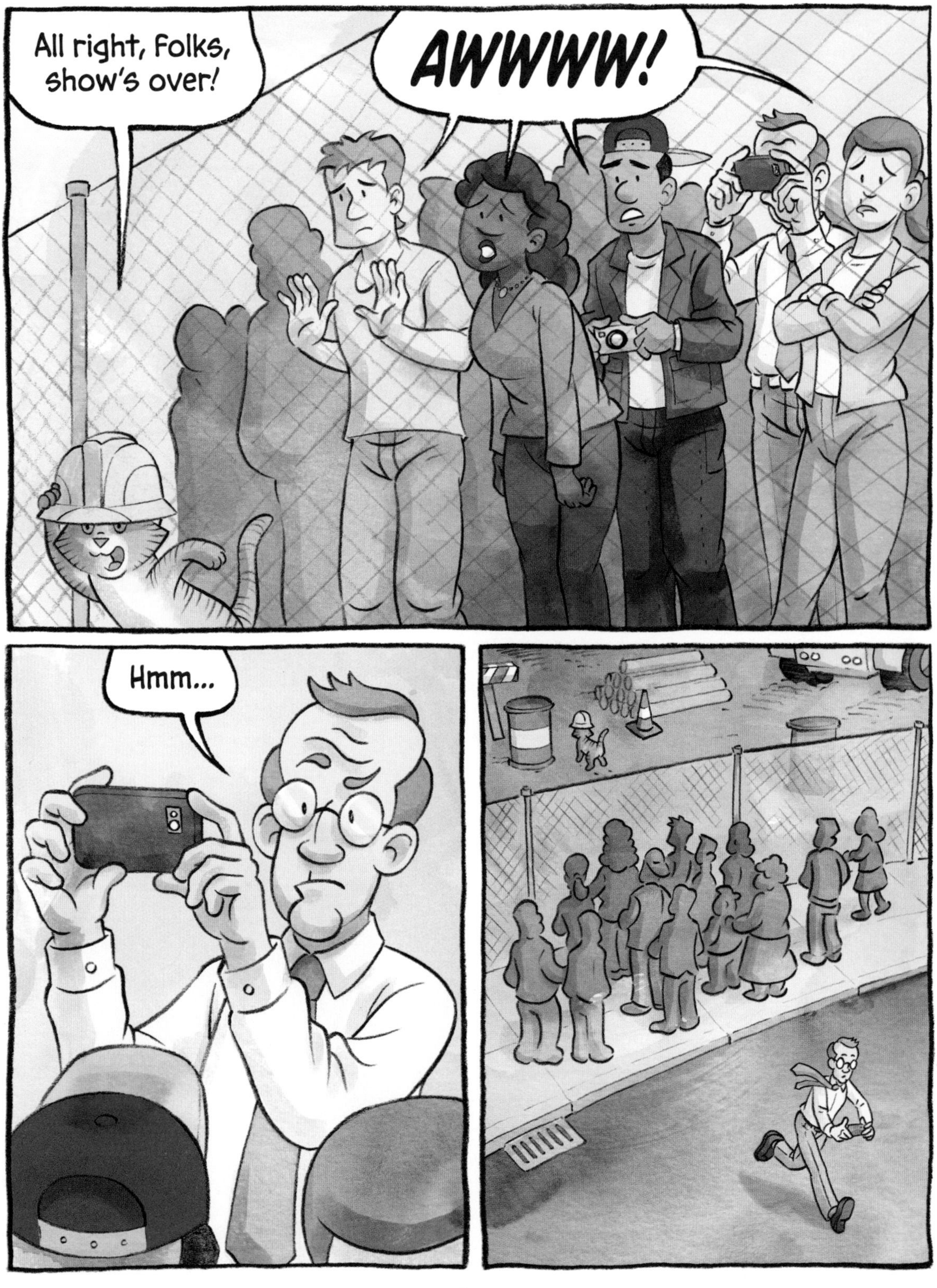
All right, folks, show's over!
AWWWW!
Hmm...

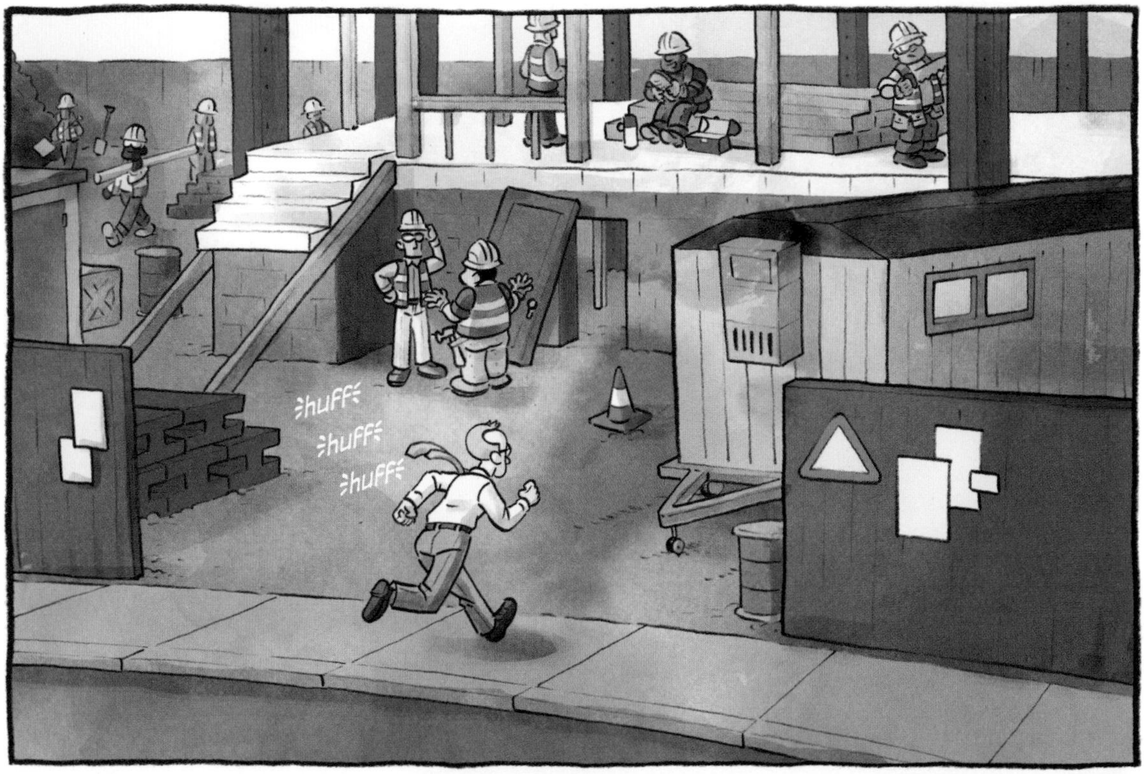
huff
huff
huff

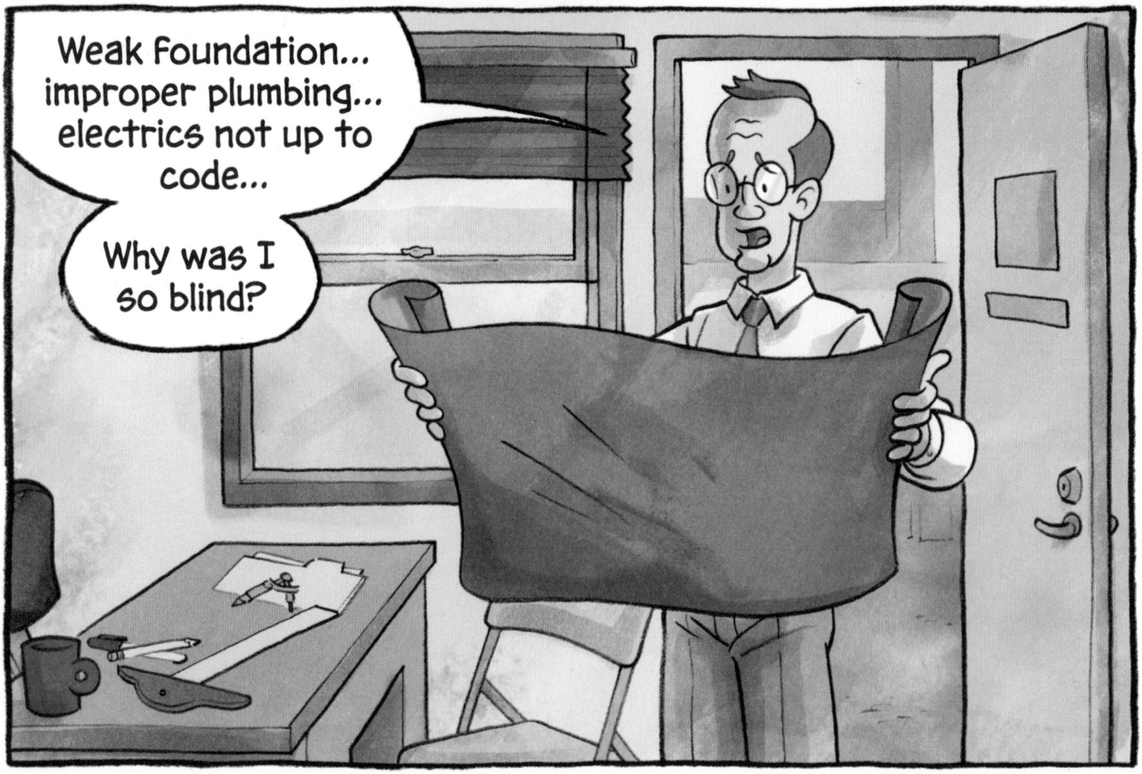
Weak foundation... improper plumbing... electrics not up to code...
Why was I so blind?

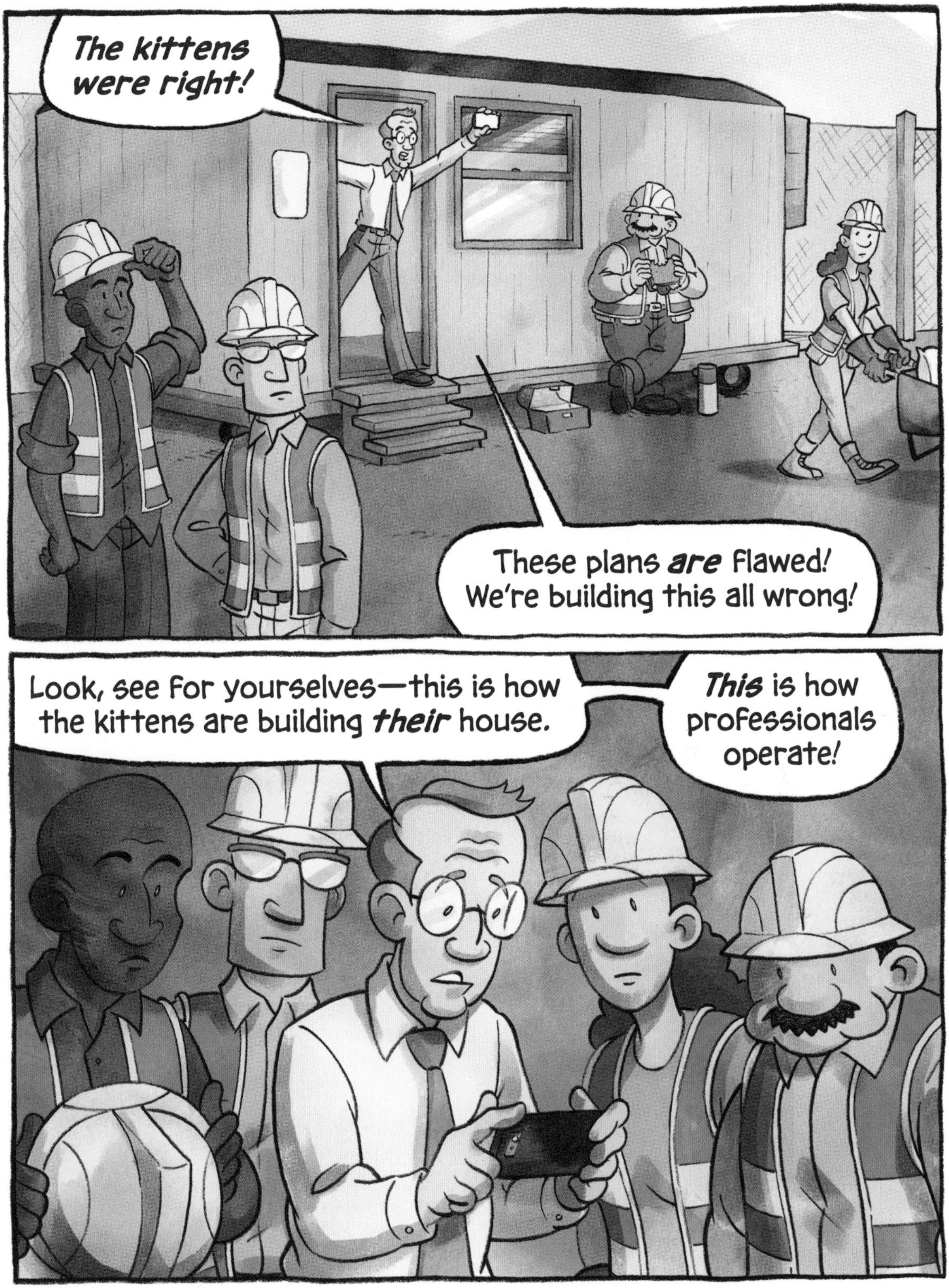
The kittens were right!
These plans are flawed! We're building this all wrong!
Look, see for yourselves—this is how the kittens are building their house.
This is how professionals operate!

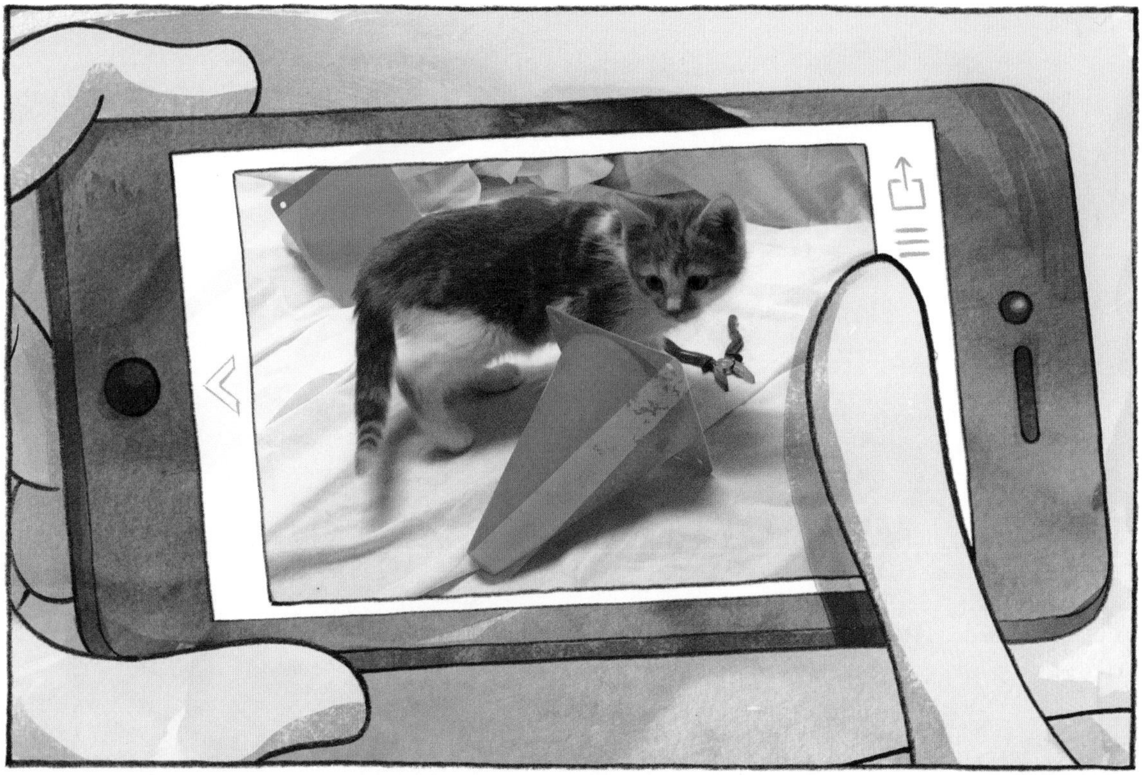

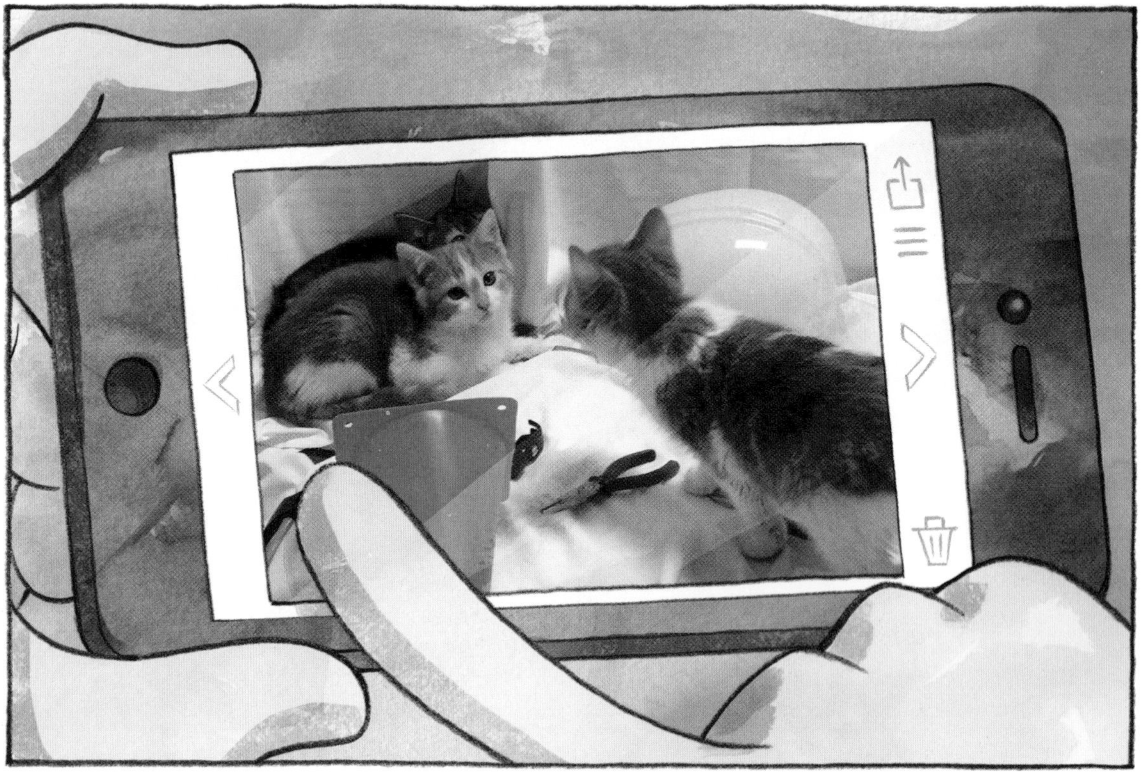

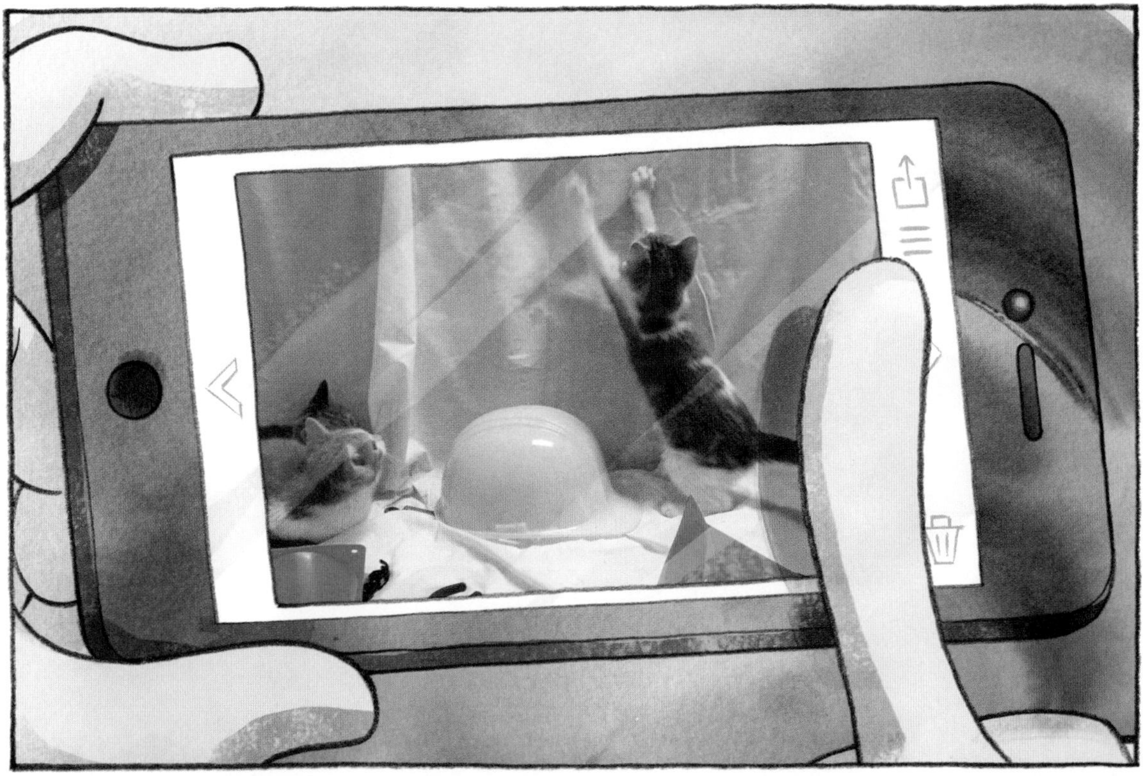

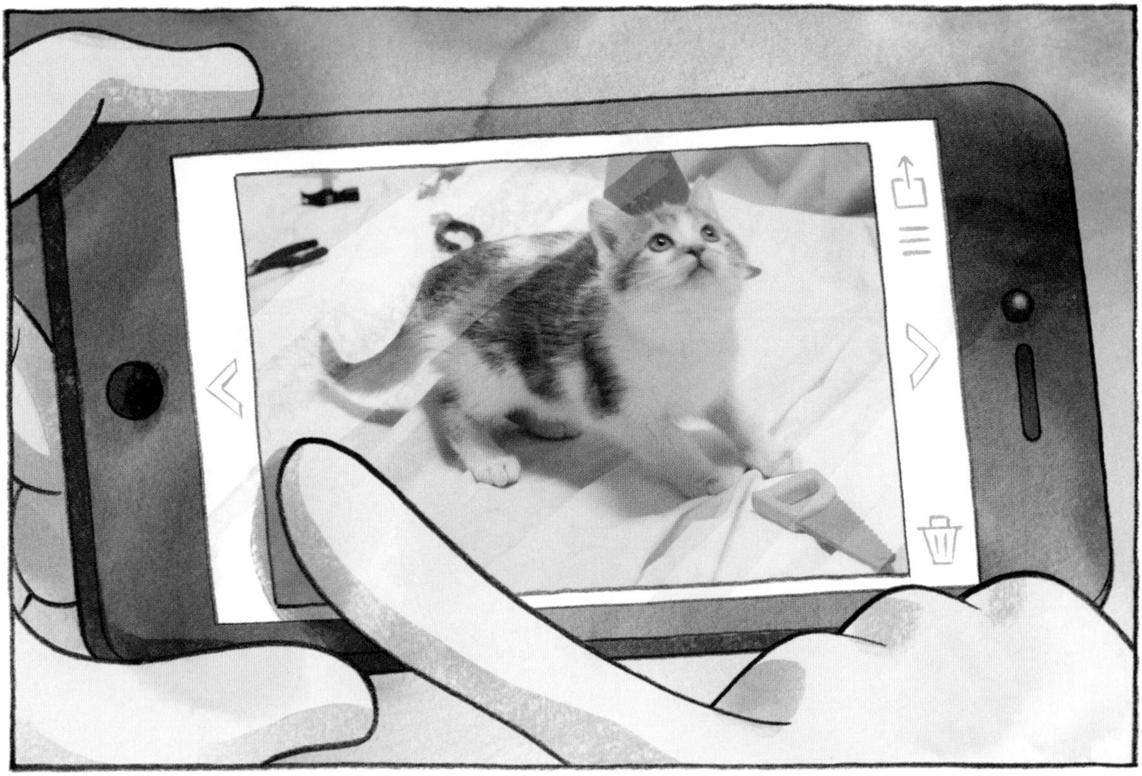

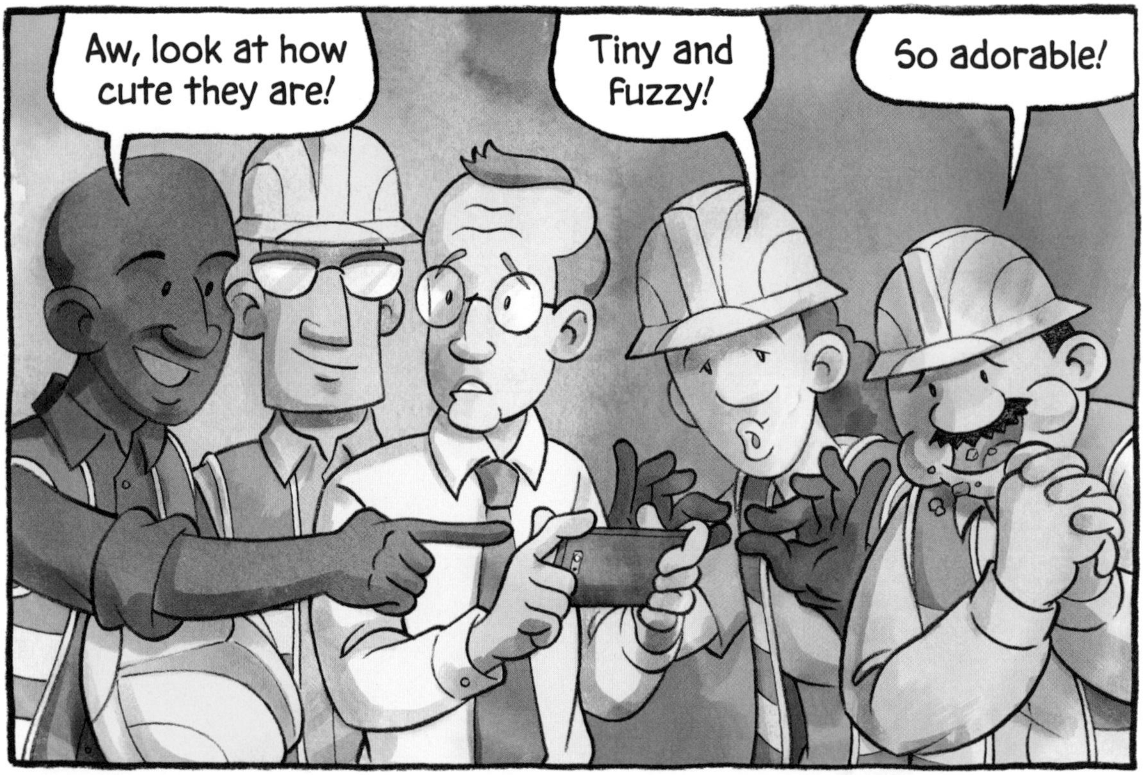
Aw, look at how cute they are!
Tiny and fuzzy!
So adorable!

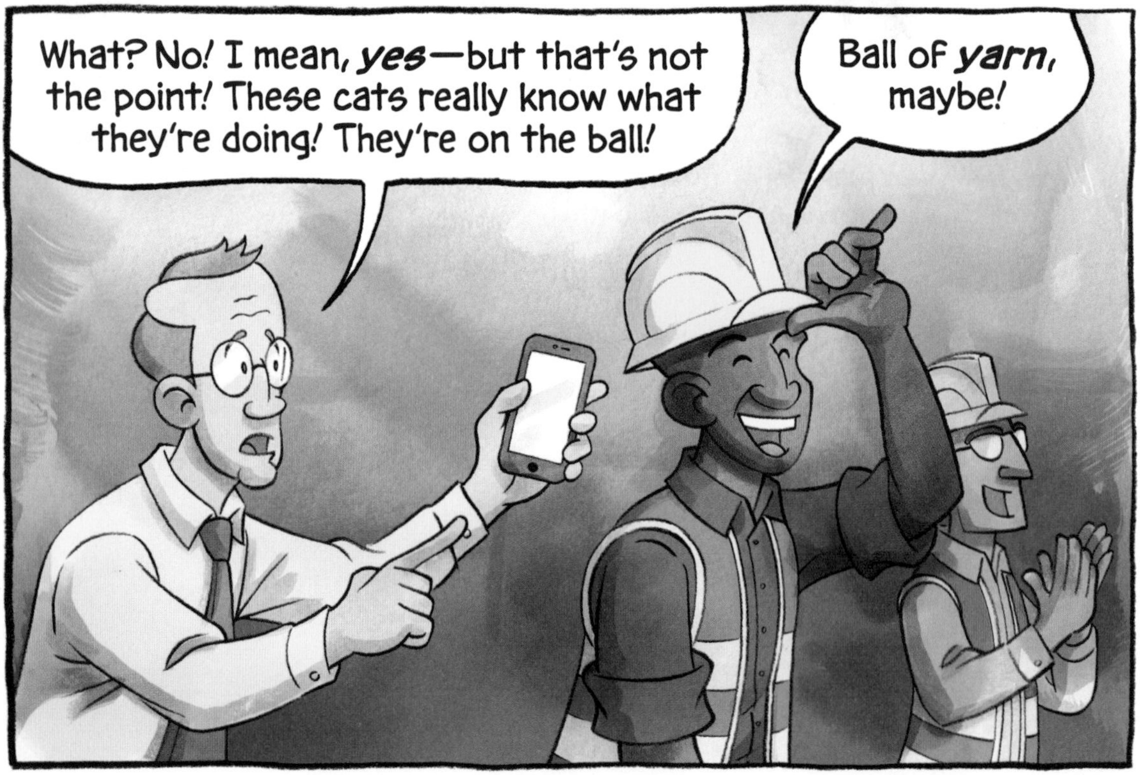
What? No! I mean, ***yes***—but that's not the point! These cats really know what they're doing! They're on the ball!
Ball of ***yarn***, maybe!

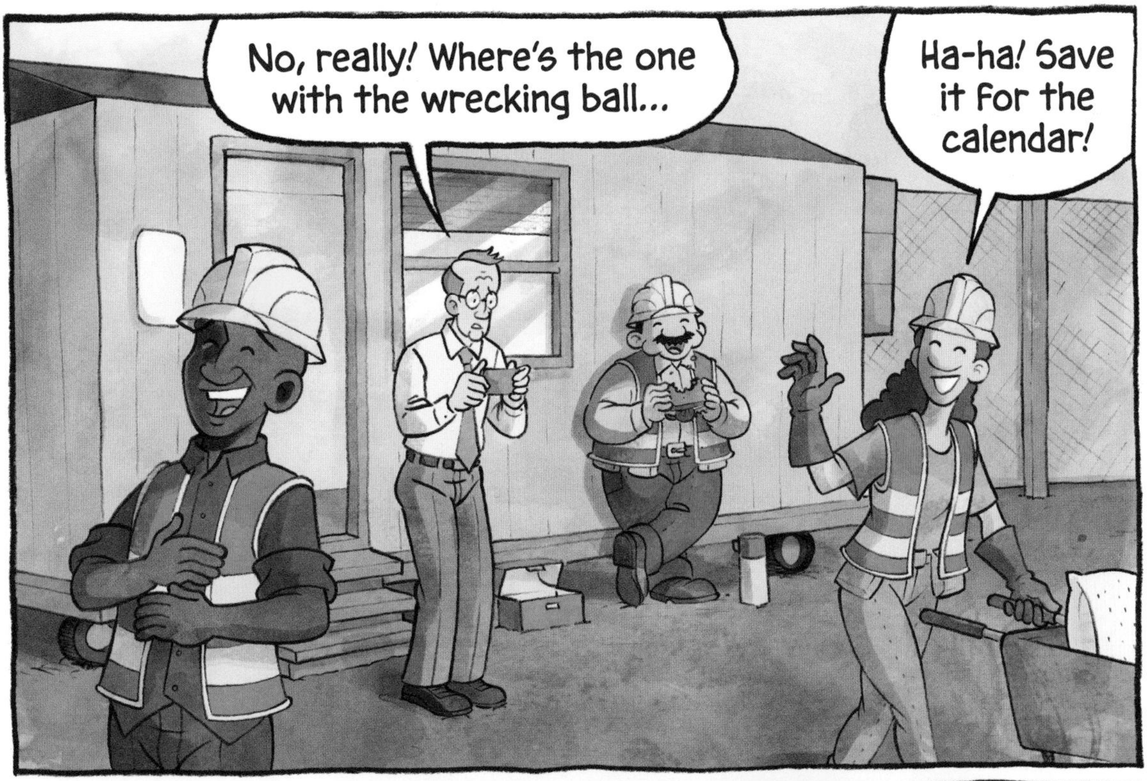
No, really! Where's the one with the wrecking ball...
Ha-ha! Save it for the calendar!

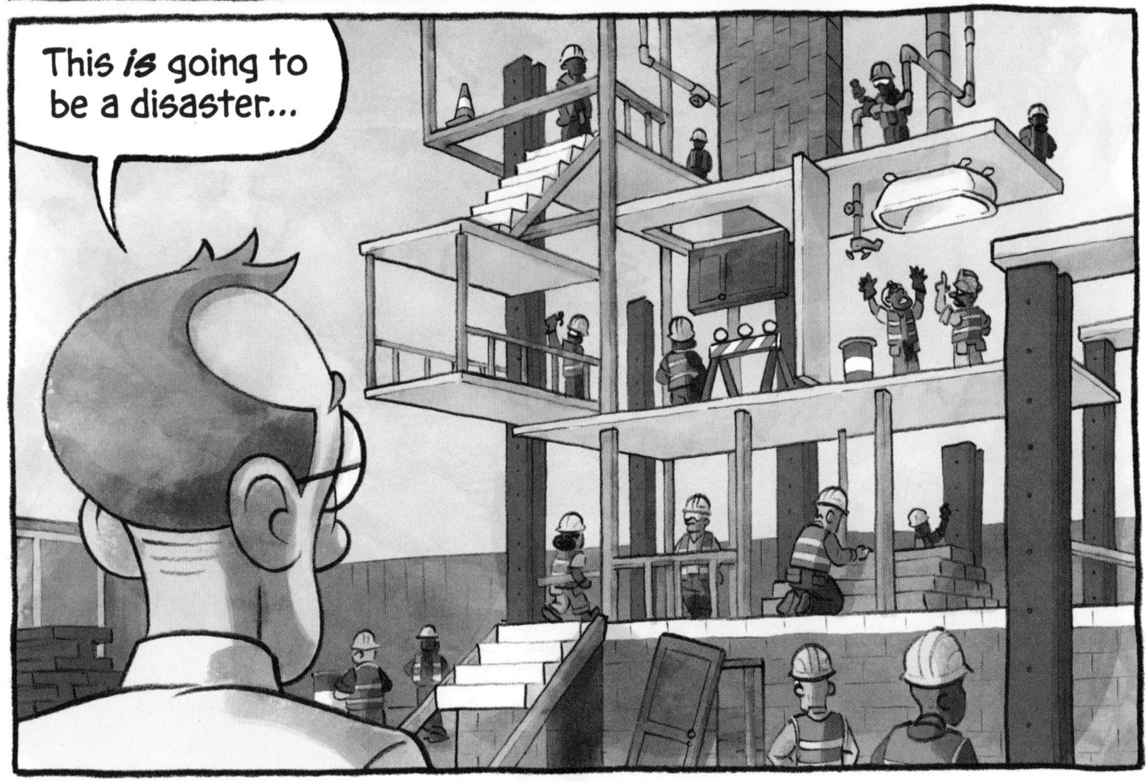
This *is* going to be a disaster...

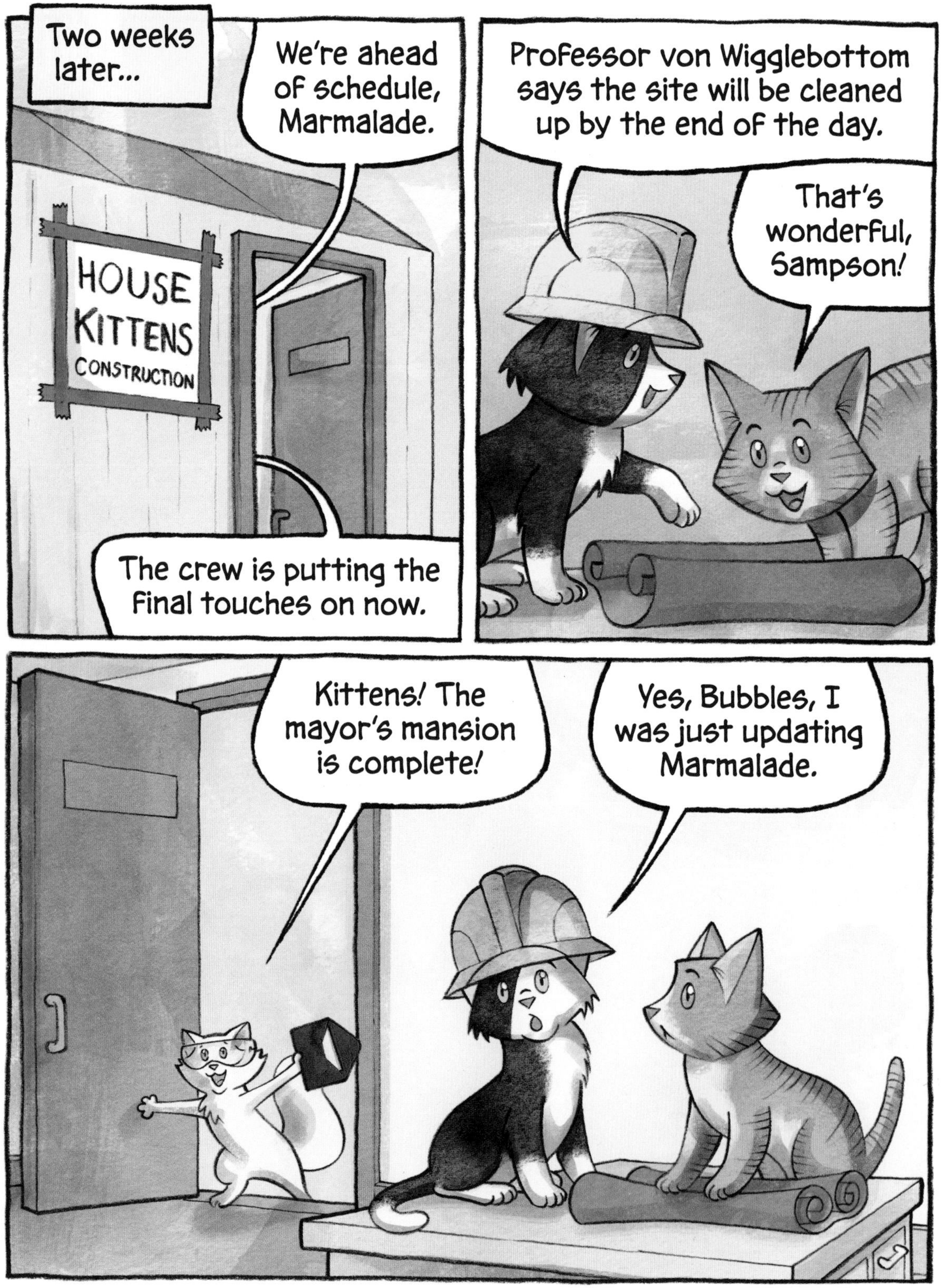
Two weeks later...
We're ahead of schedule, Marmalade.
HOUSE KITTENS CONSTRUCTION
The crew is putting the final touches on now.
Professor von Wigglebottom says the site will be cleaned up by the end of the day.
That's wonderful, Sampson!
Kittens! The mayor's mansion is complete!
Yes, Bubbles, I was just updating Marmalade.

No, no, the *real* mayor's mansion. It's being unveiled today, and we've been invited!

We all saw *their* blueprints. It's going to be a disaster!

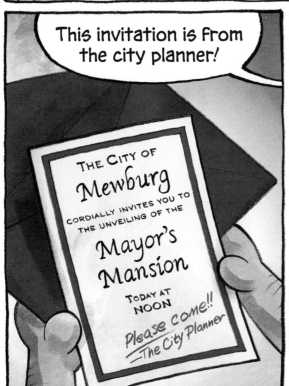

This invitation is from the city planner!

THE CITY OF
Mewburg
CORDIALLY INVITES YOU TO THE UNVEILING OF THE
Mayor's Mansion
TODAY AT NOON
Please Come!!
—The City Planner

What's he up to, inviting us?

There's only one way to find out. Let's go!

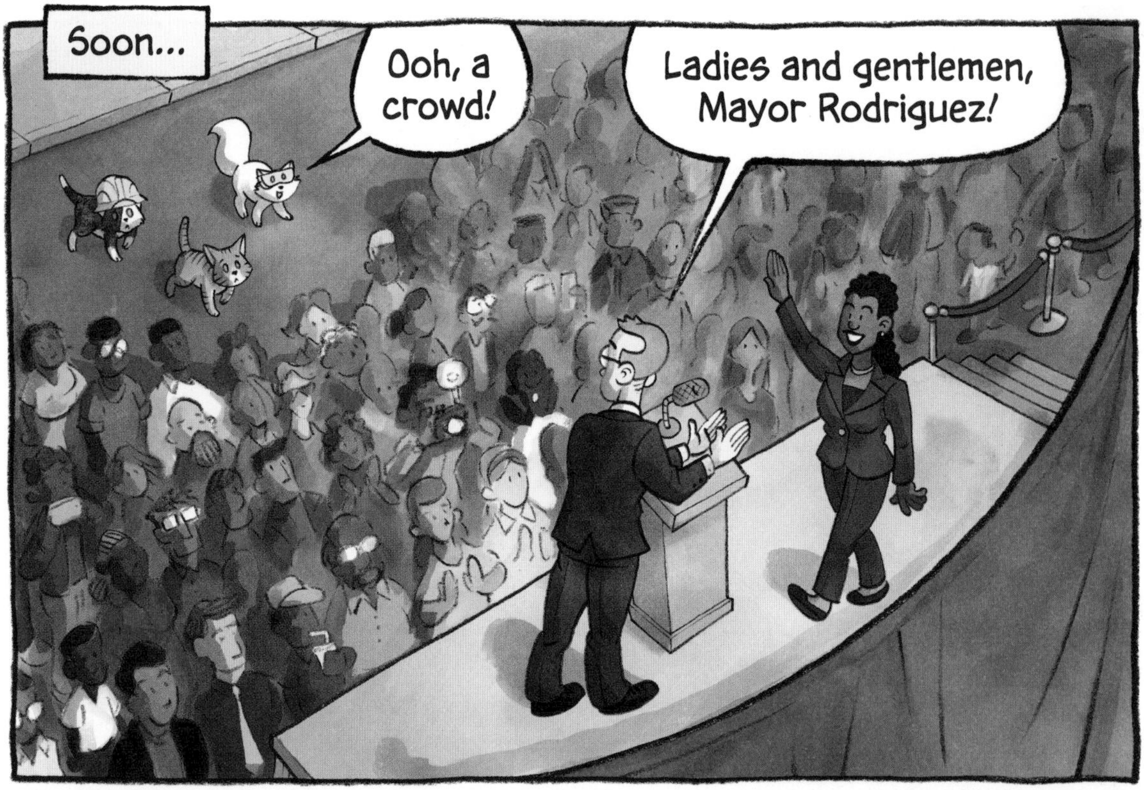
Soon...
Ooh, a crowd!
Ladies and gentlemen, Mayor Rodriguez!

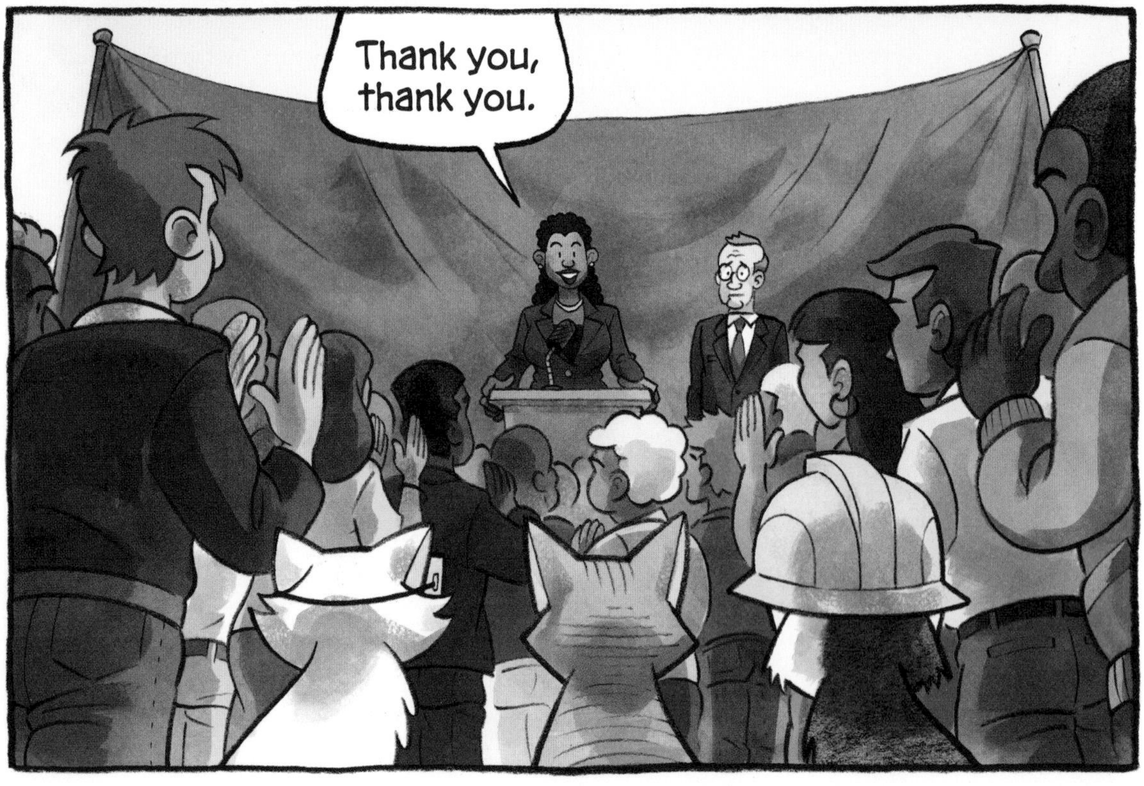
Thank you, thank you.

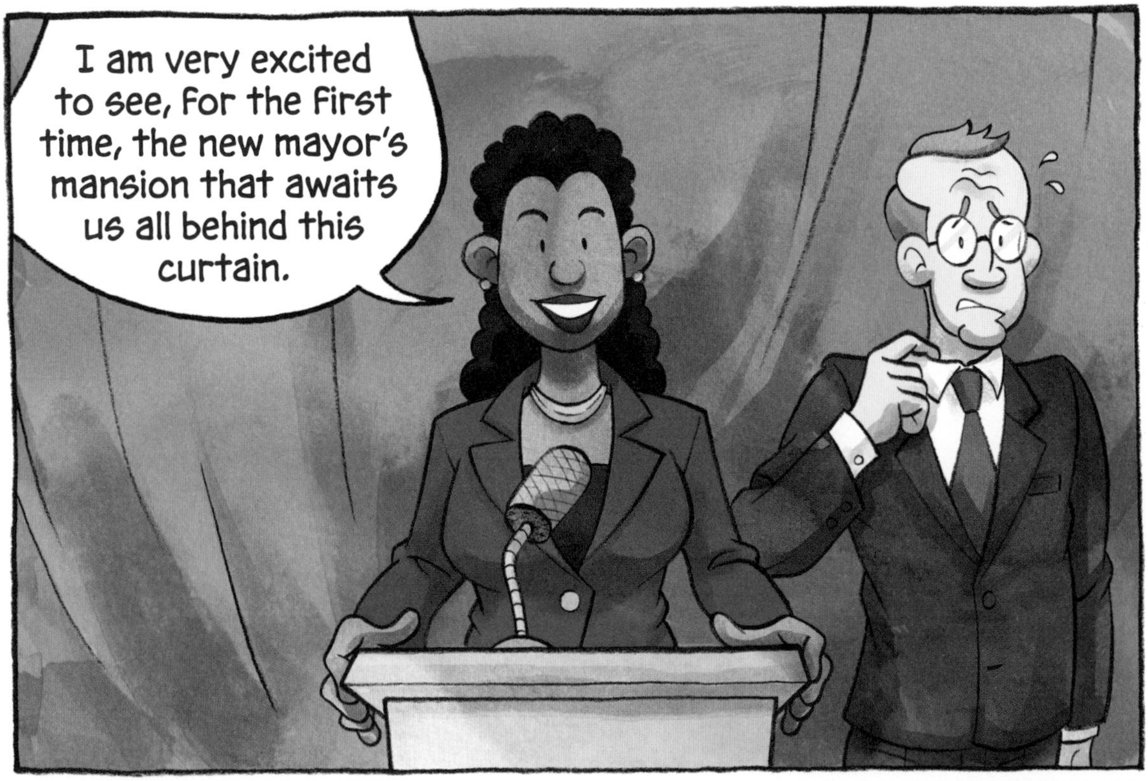
I am very excited to see, for the first time, the new mayor's mansion that awaits us all behind this curtain.

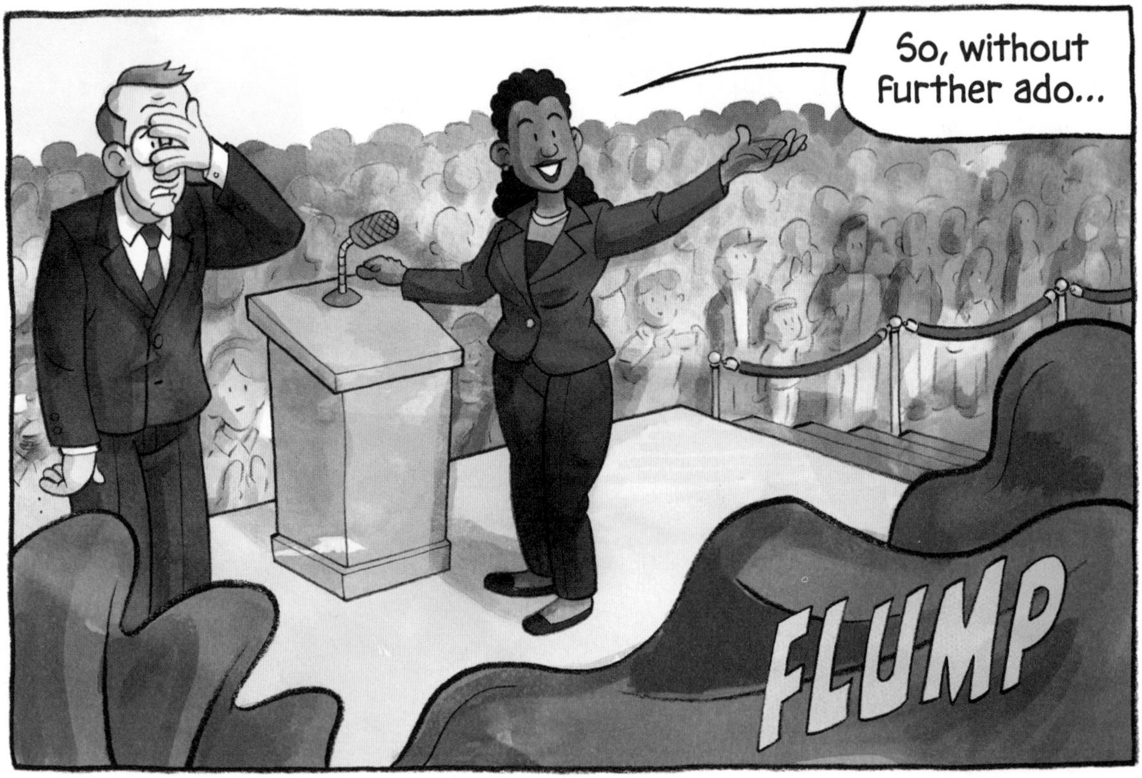
So, without further ado...
FLUMP

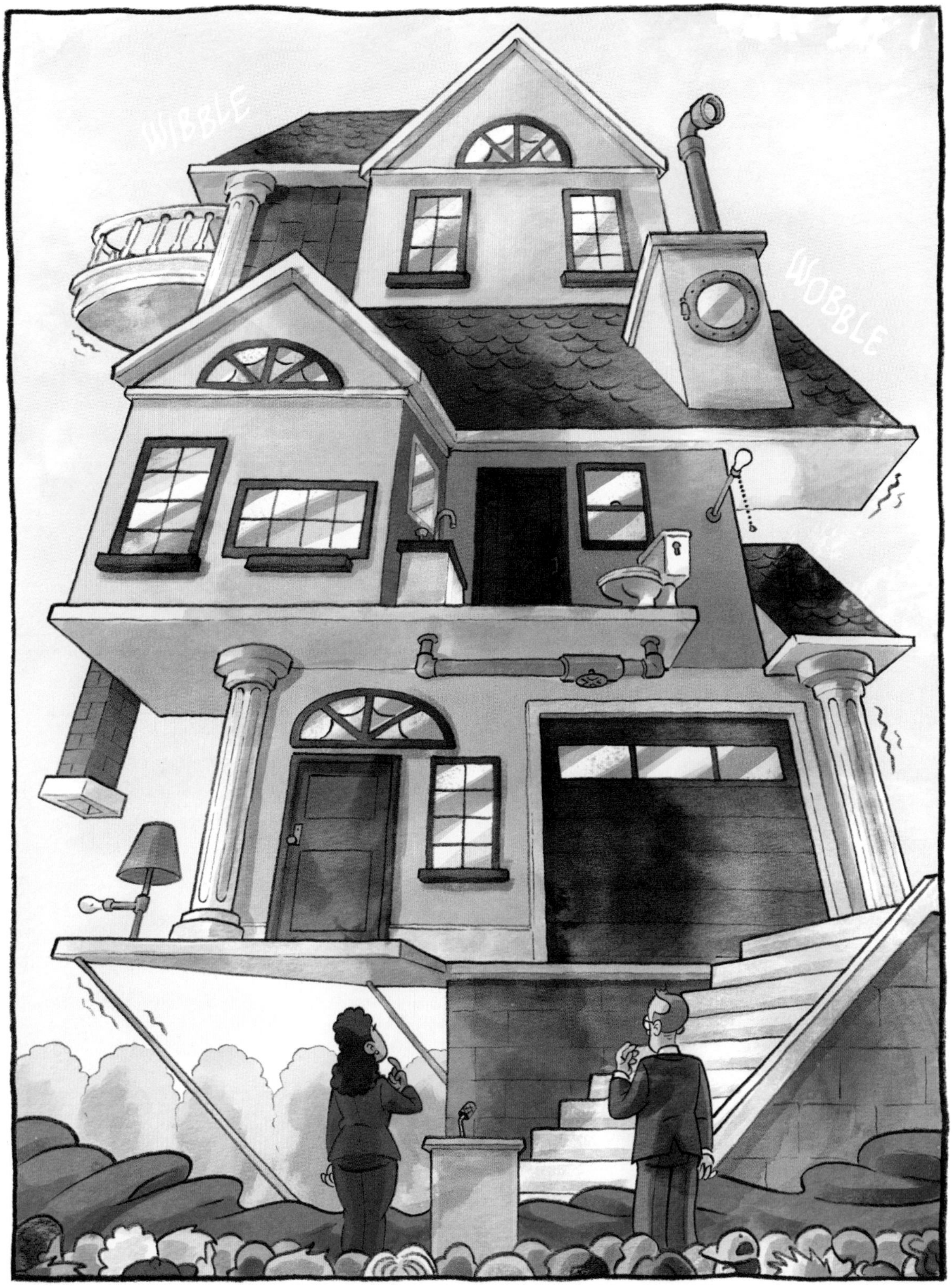
WIBBLE
WOBBLE

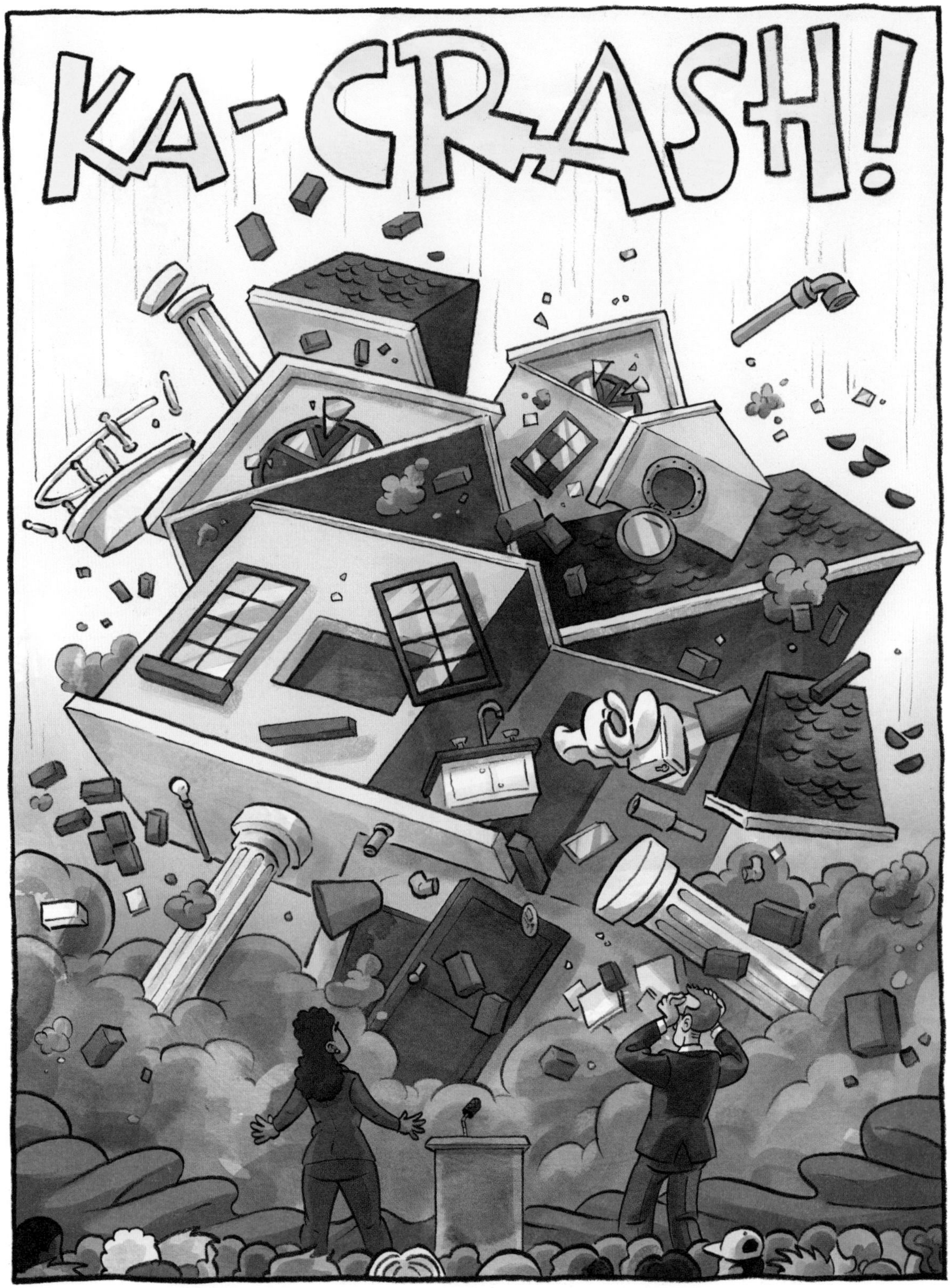
KA-CRASH!

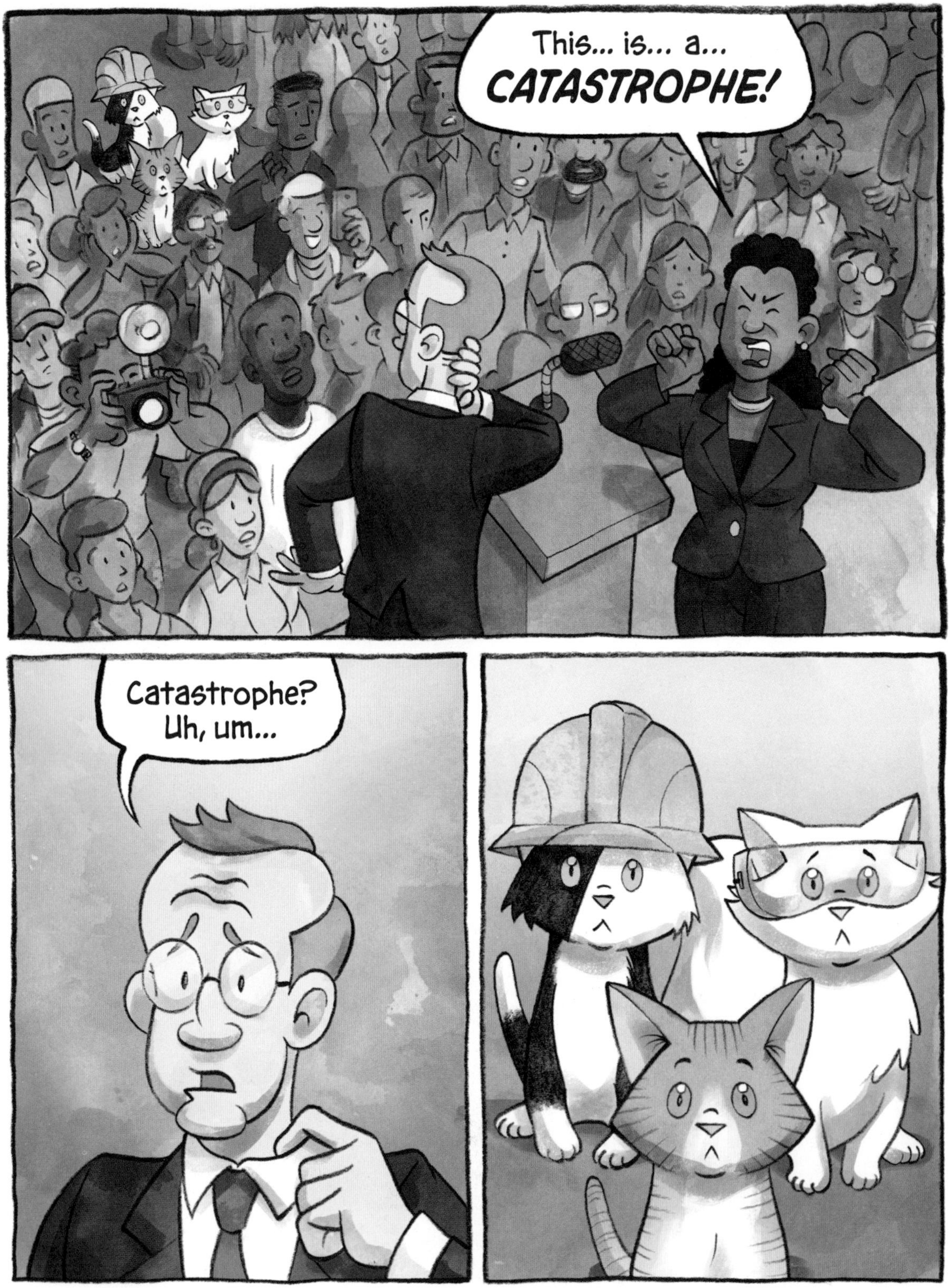
This... is... a... CATASTROPHE!
Catastrophe? Uh, um...

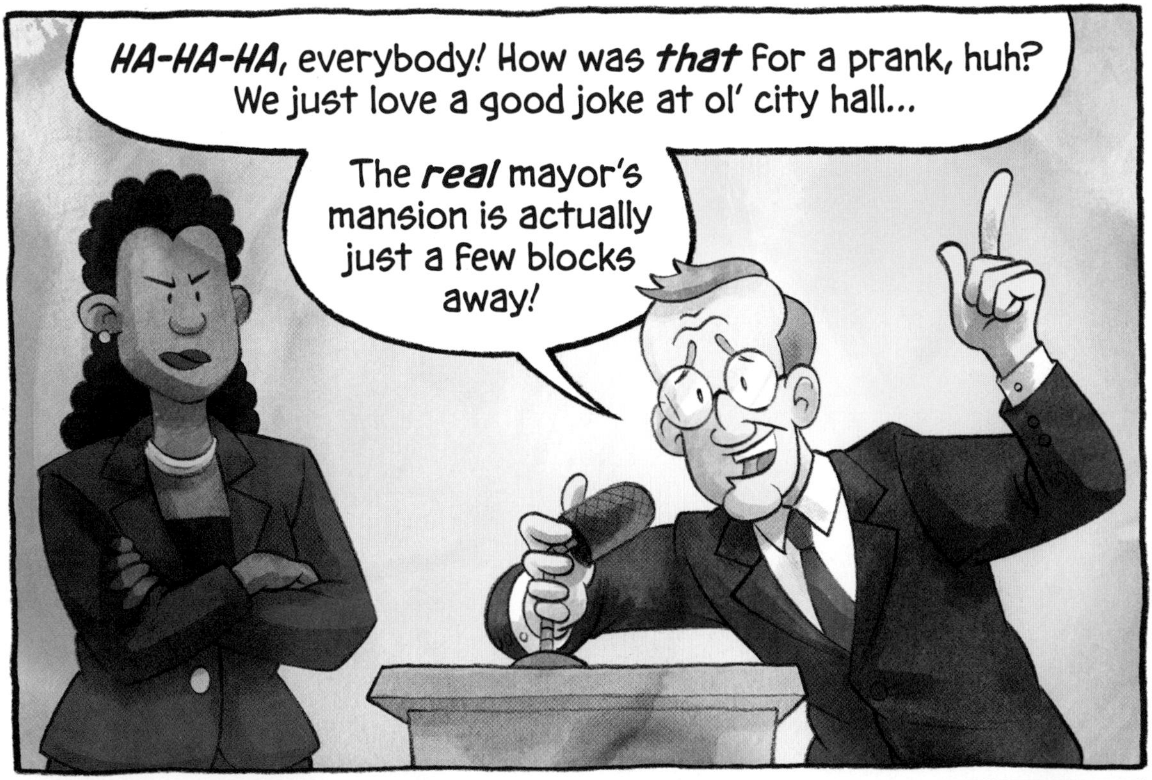
HA-HA-HA, everybody! How was ***that*** for a prank, huh? We just love a good joke at ol' city hall...
The ***real*** mayor's mansion is actually just a few blocks away!

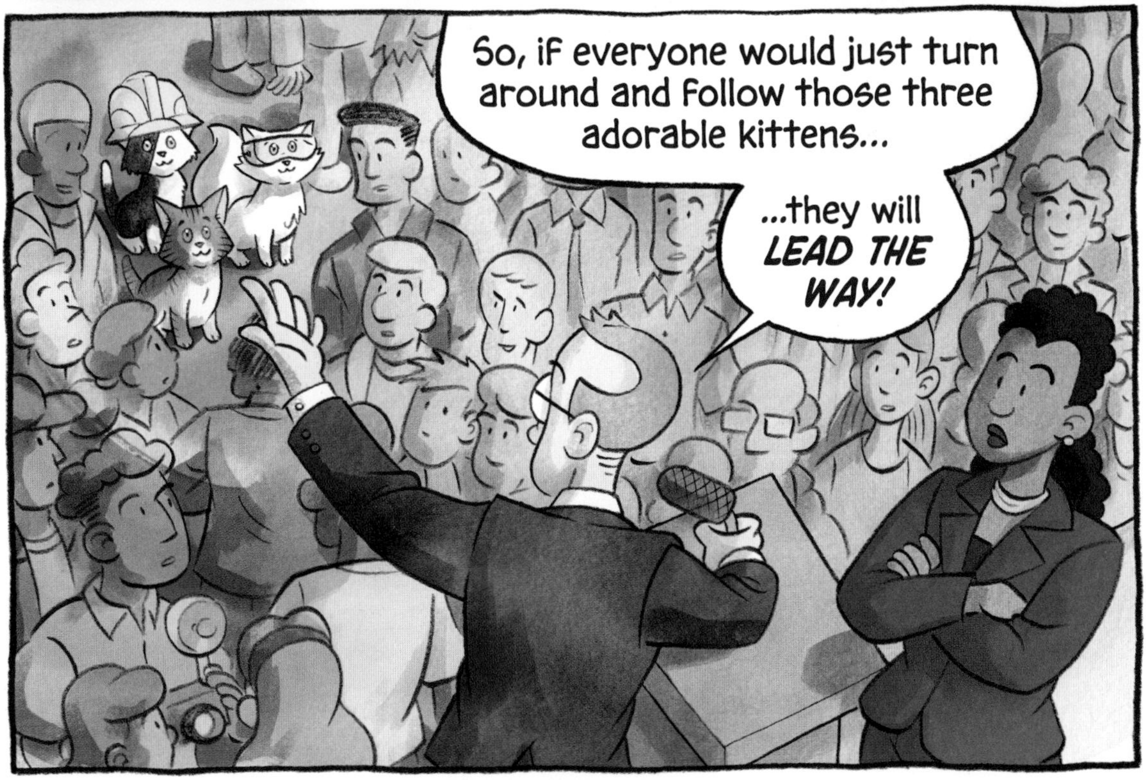
So, if everyone would just turn around and follow those three adorable kittens...
...they will ***LEAD THE WAY!***

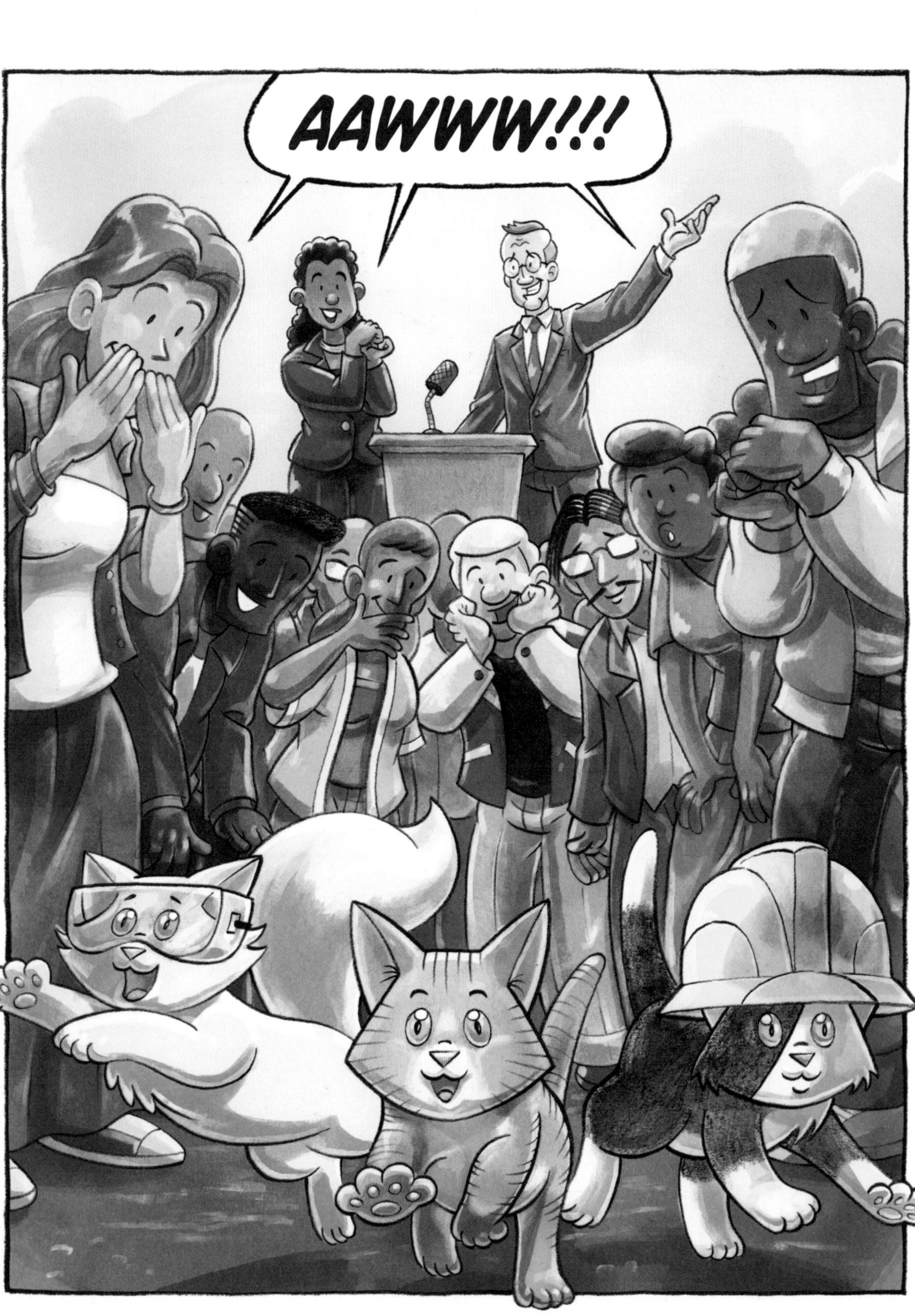
AAWWW!!!

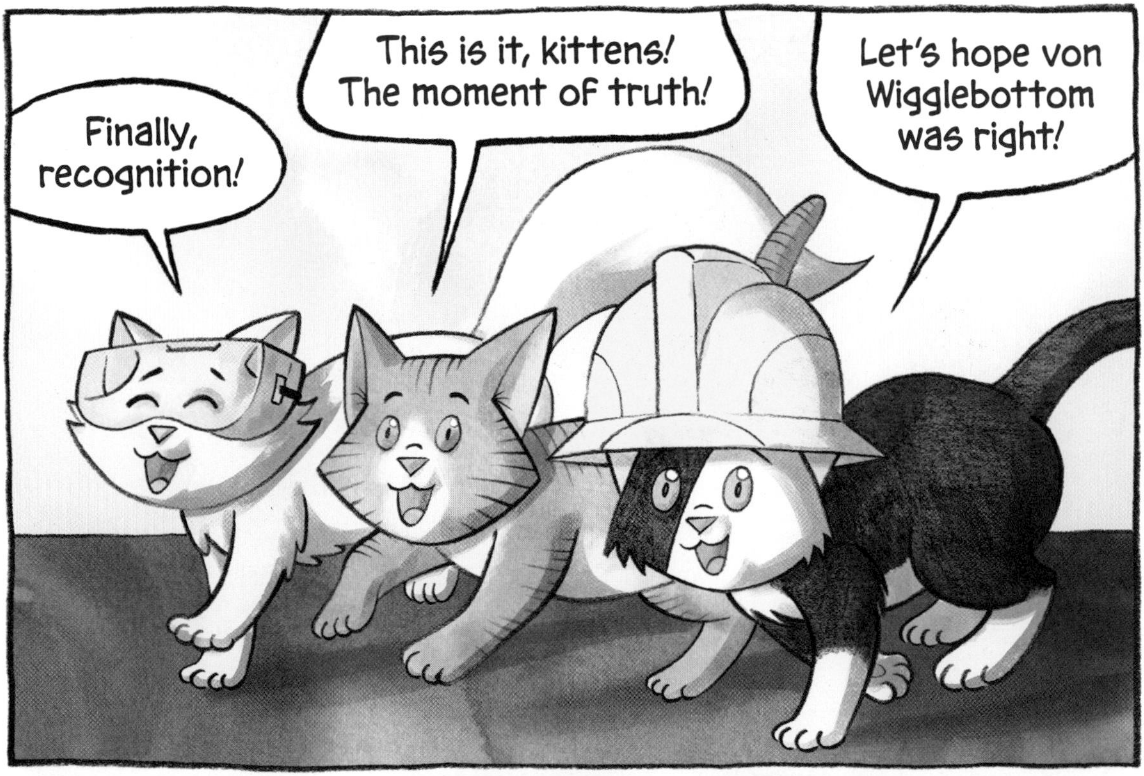
Finally, recognition!
This is it, kittens! The moment of truth!
Let's hope von Wigglebottom was right!

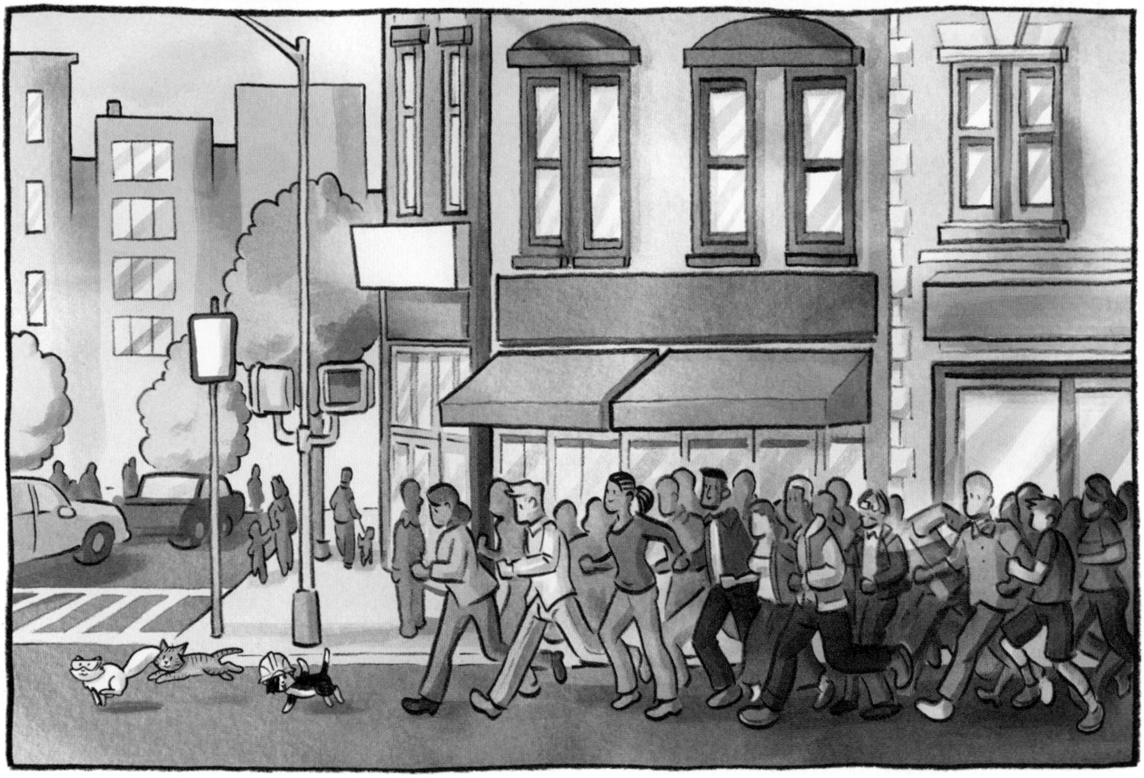

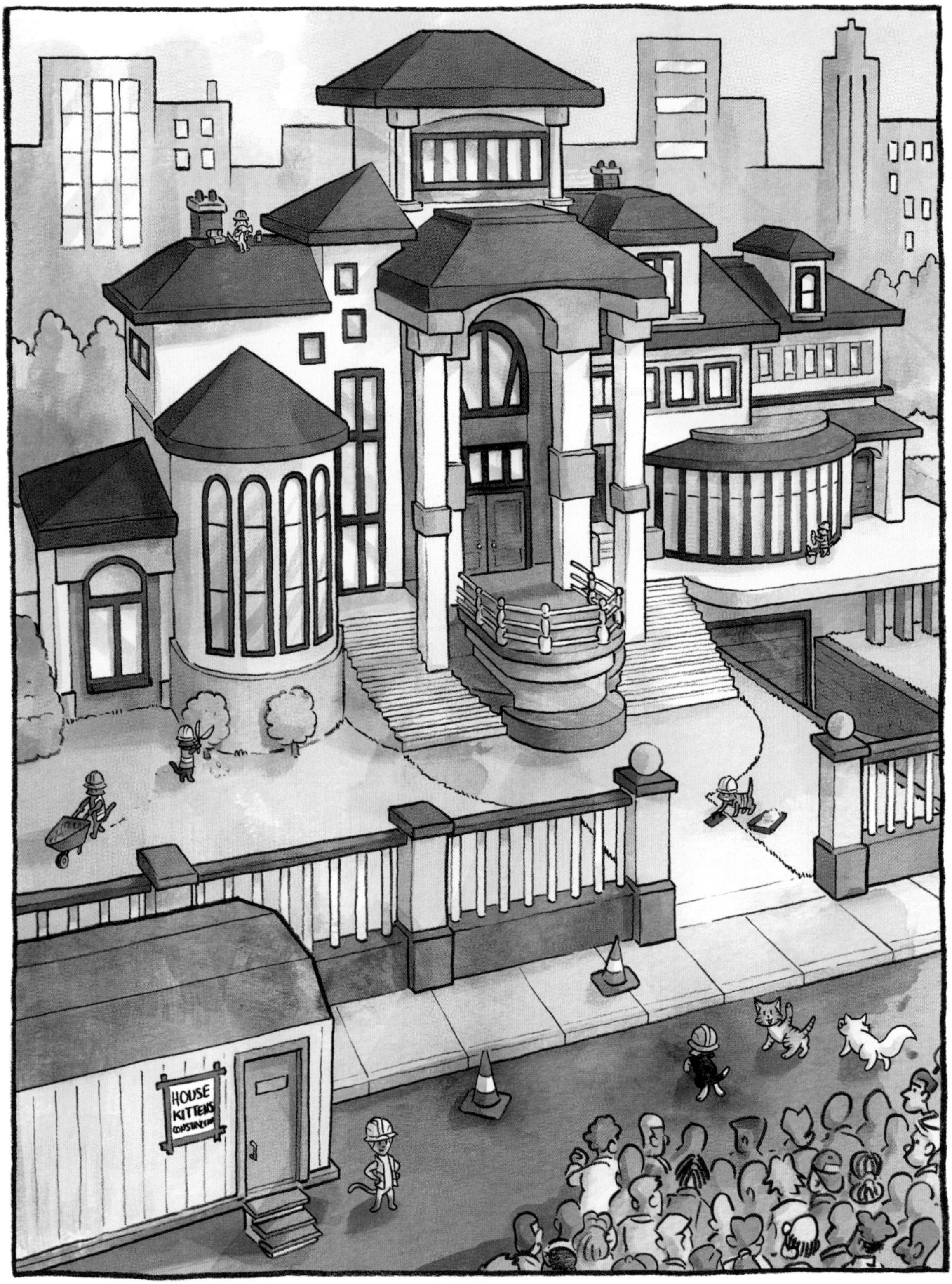
HOUSE
KITTENS

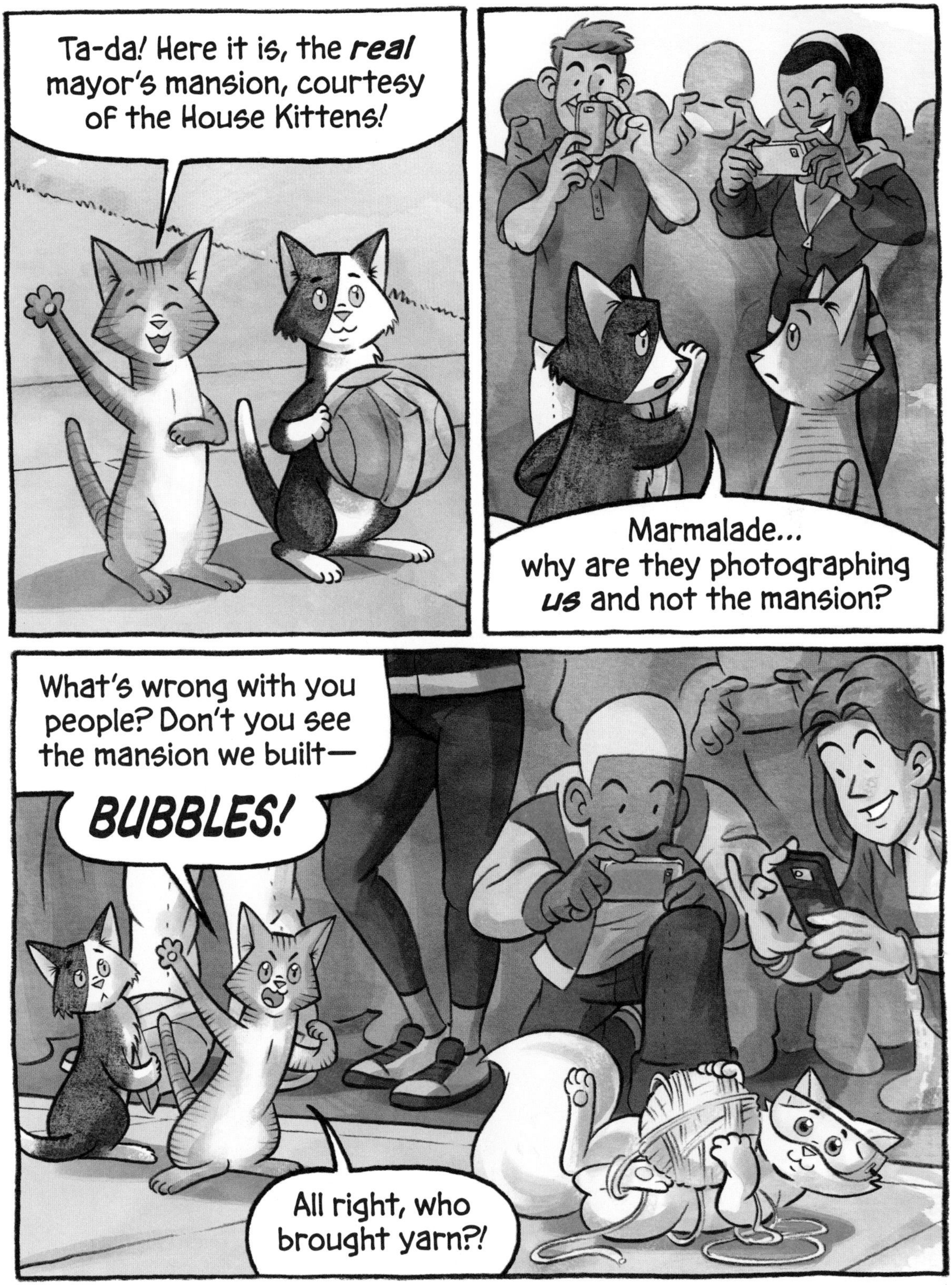
Ta-da! Here it is, the *real* mayor's mansion, courtesy of the House Kittens!
Marmalade... why are they photographing *us* and not the mansion?
What's wrong with you people? Don't you see the mansion we built—
BUBBLES!
All right, who brought yarn?!

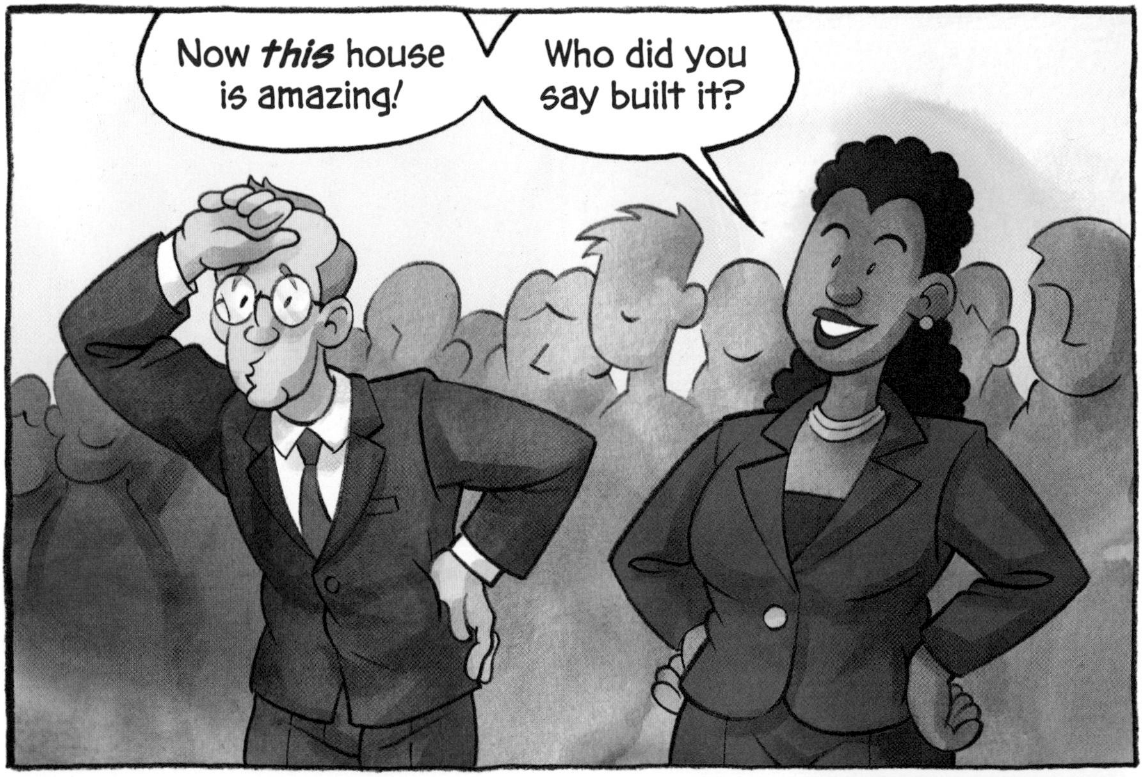
Now *this* house is amazing!
Who did you say built it?

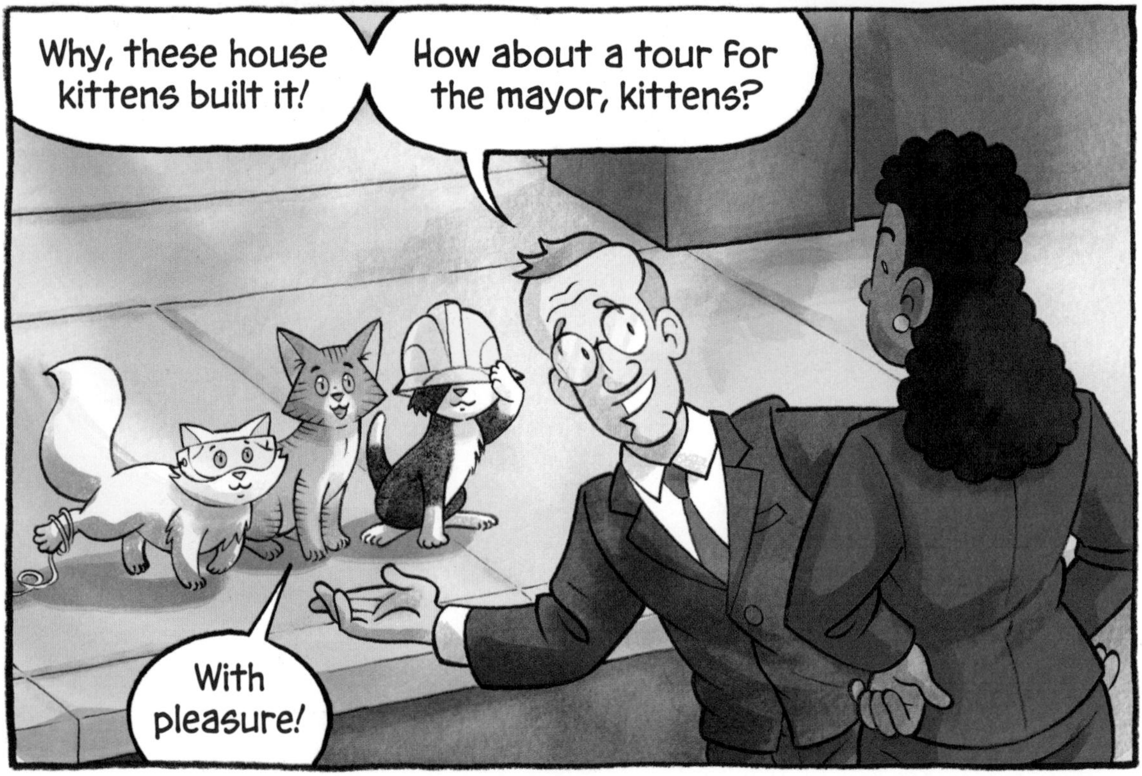
Why, these house kittens built it!
How about a tour for the mayor, kittens?
With pleasure!

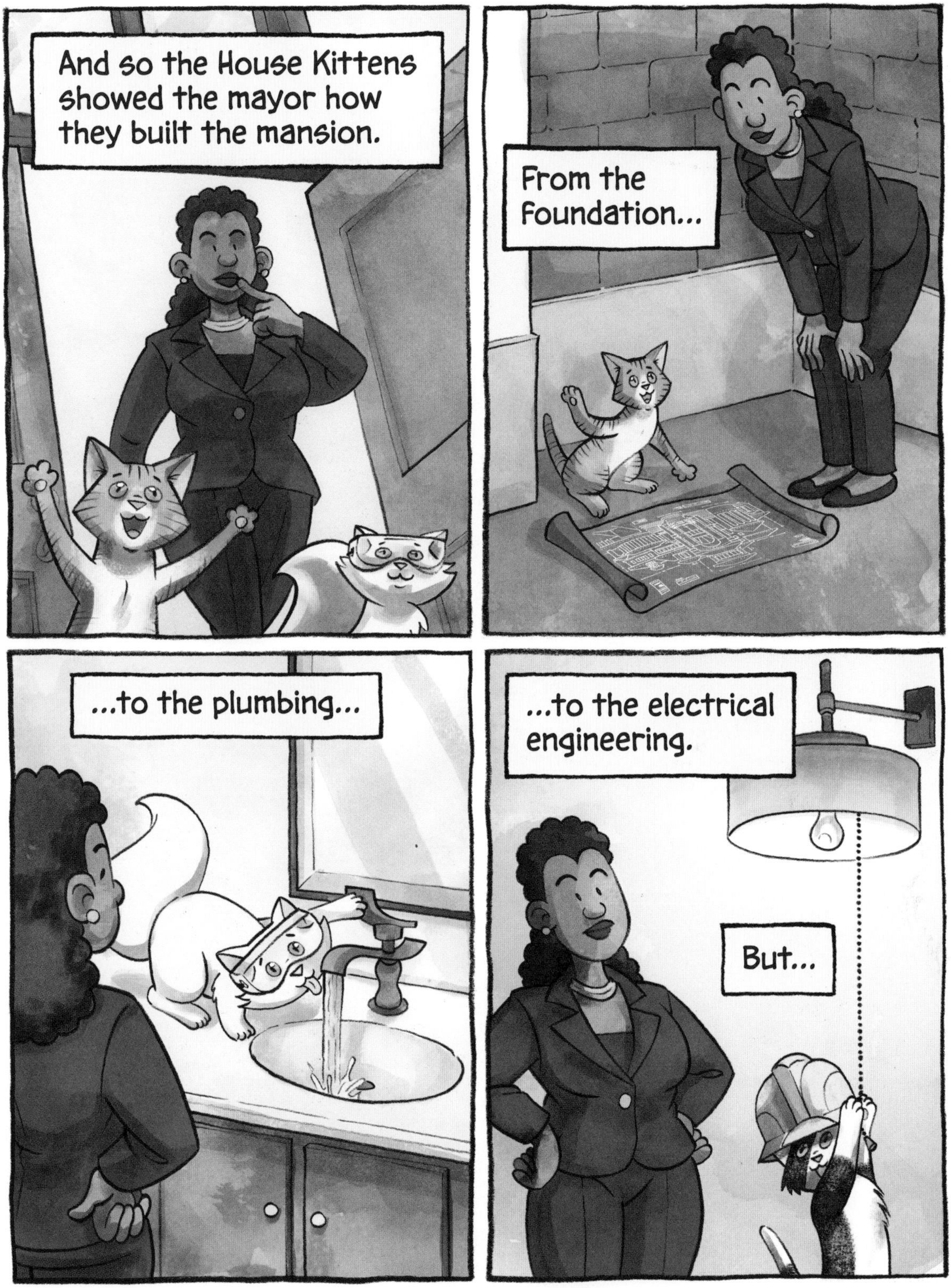
And so the House Kittens showed the mayor how they built the mansion.
From the foundation...
...to the plumbing...
...to the electrical engineering.
But...

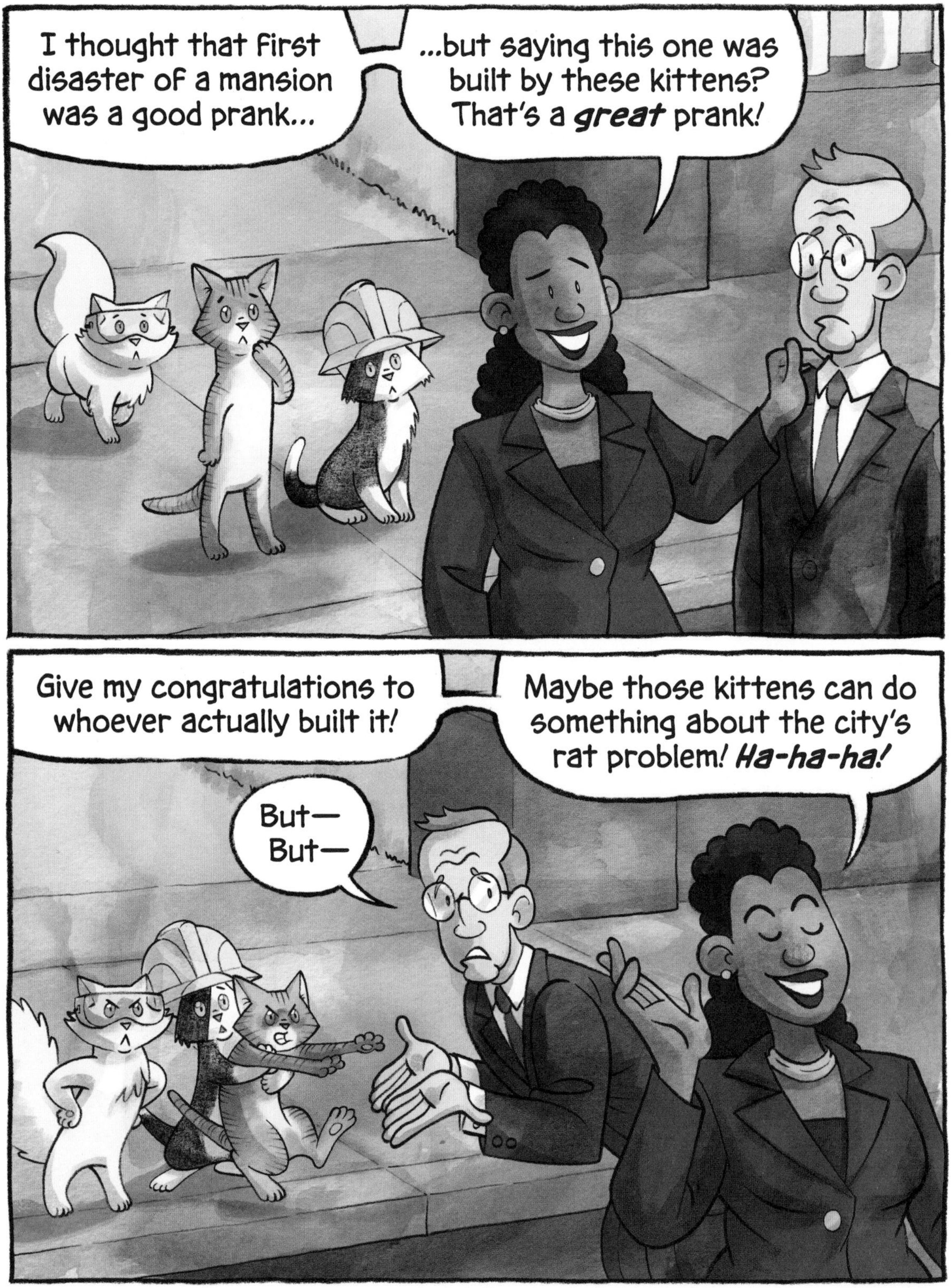
I thought that first disaster of a mansion was a good prank...
...but saying this one was built by these kittens? That's a *great* prank!
Give my congratulations to whoever actually built it!
Maybe those kittens can do something about the city's rat problem! *Ha-ha-ha!*
But— But—

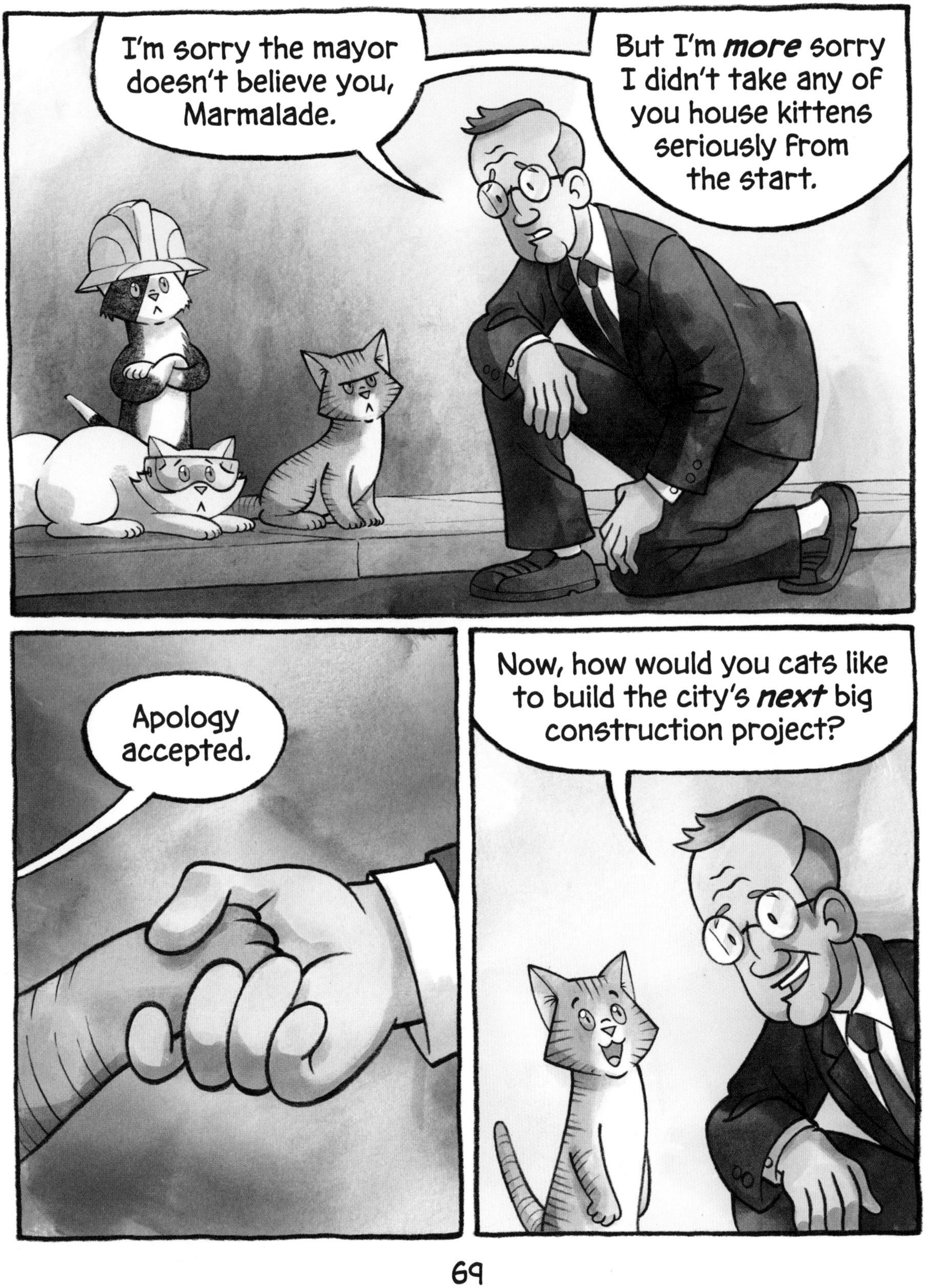
I'm sorry the mayor doesn't believe you, Marmalade.
But I'm *more* sorry I didn't take any of you house kittens seriously from the start.
Apology accepted.
Now, how would you cats like to build the city's *next* big construction project?

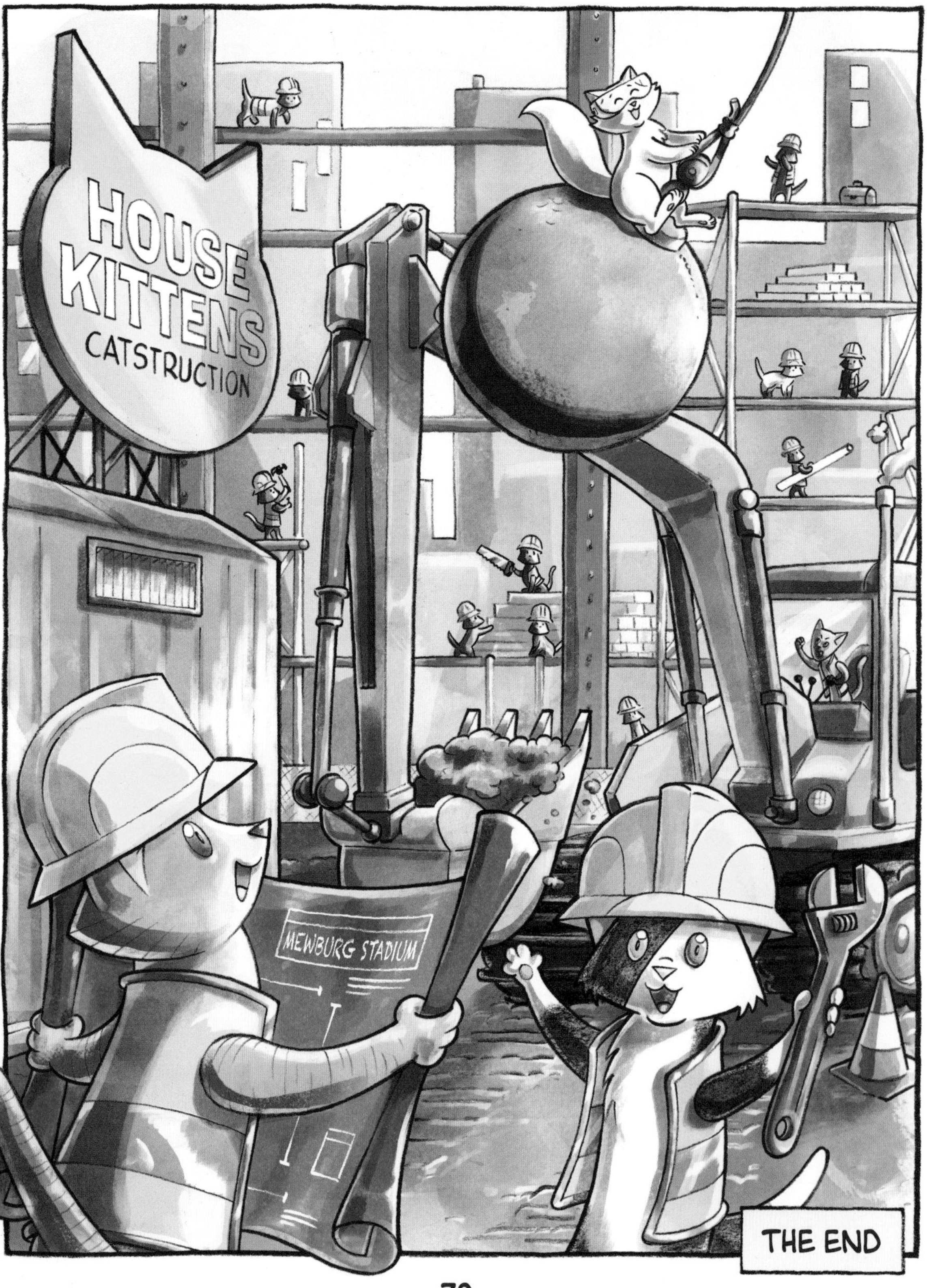
HOUSE KITTENS
CATSTRUCTION
MEWBURG STADIUM
THE END

KITTEN CONSTRUCTION COMPANY

ORIGINAL CHARACTER DESIGNS

The final designs of the House Kittens look a lot like the first versions I drew, with a few minor differences.

Marmalade was originally named Mittens. But since Sampson actually has mittens, it seemed odd that it wasn't his name instead.

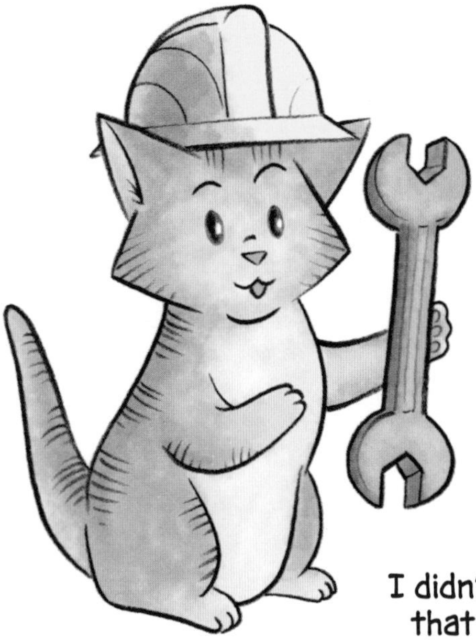

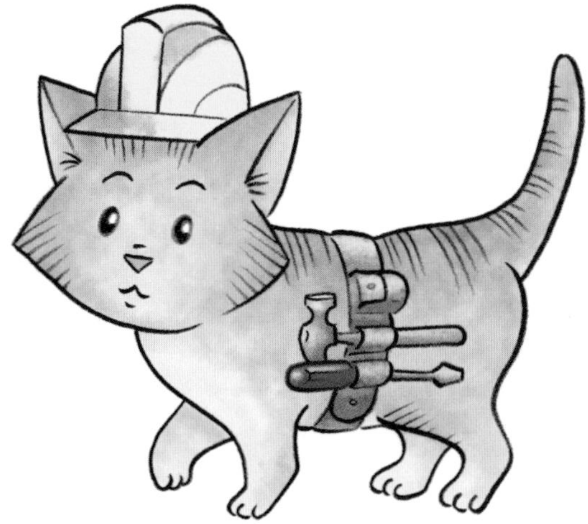

I didn't want two names that started with the letter M, though. The name Sampson seemed like a good fit for his personality.

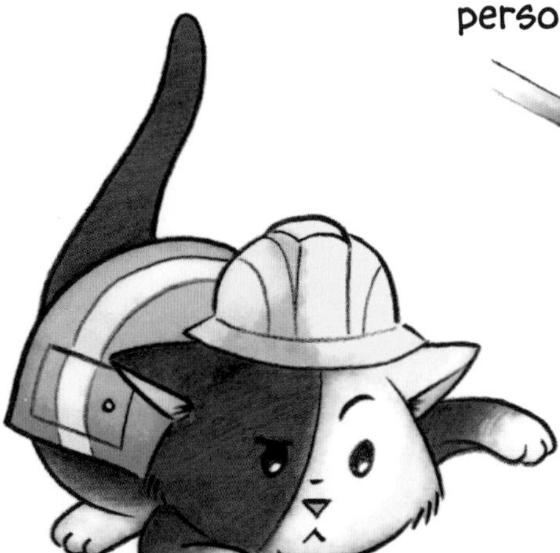

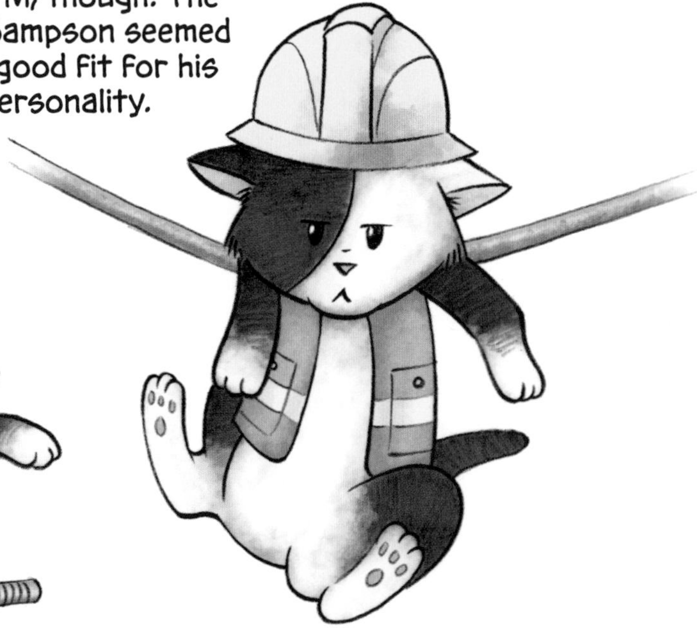

The Professor was always going to be a Siamese cat, but he started out as the office assistant. Maybe when the kittens' construction company expands they'll need someone to man the phones!

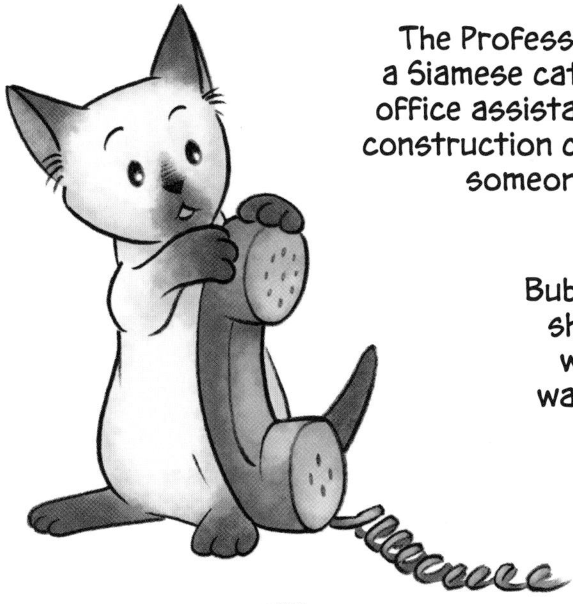

Bubbles's name came about because she likes water. She was always a white cat, but her big fluffy tail wasn't added until I drew the first page she appears on!

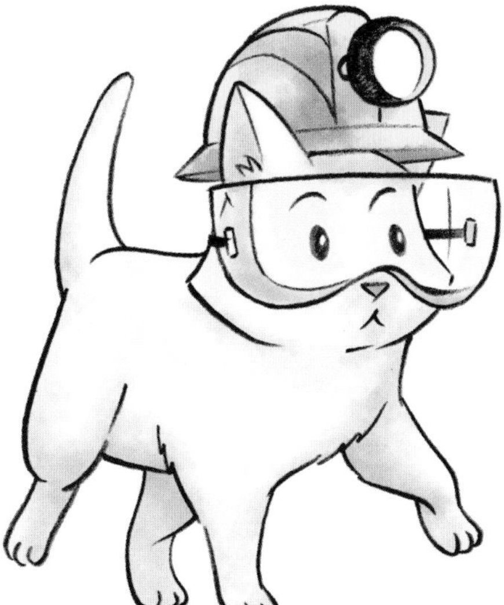

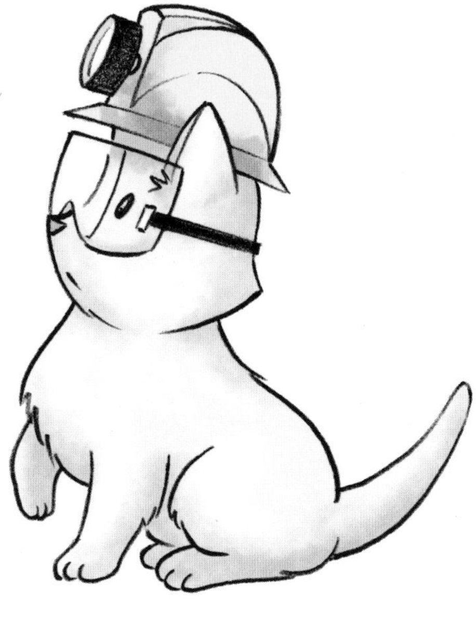

A few cats I designed didn't make it into the story. But maybe you'll see them in the next book!

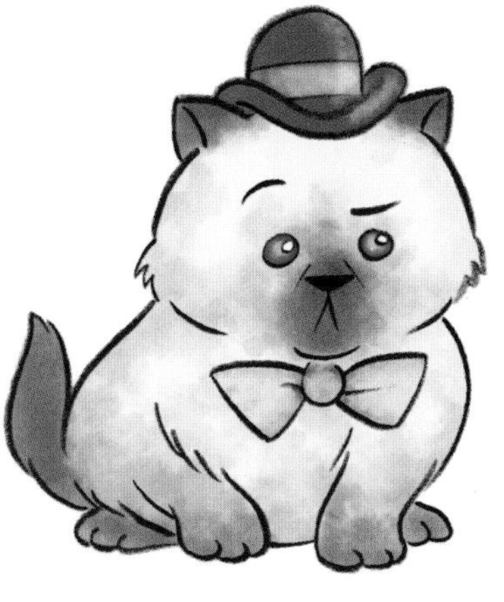

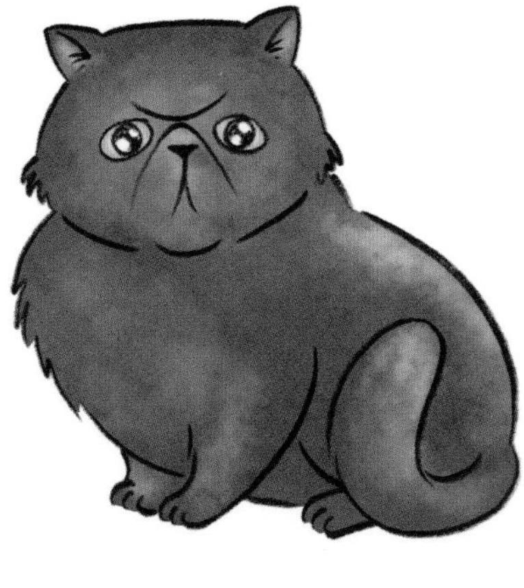

Special thanks—
to Janelle Asselin for her fabulous feline photo skills;
to Cat, again for her amazing colors; to the entire First Second crew;
to Tory Woollcott, Kean Soo, and Reginald Barkley;
to LEGO, erector sets, Robotix, Doozers, Garfield, and Jim Davis;
to kittens everywhere; and NO THANKS to my allergies.

First Second

Copyright © 2018 by John Patrick Green

Drawn on Strathmore Bristol vellum with Staedtler 2B, 3B, and 6B pencils,
and digitally colored in Photoshop.

Published by First Second
First Second is an imprint of Roaring Brook Press,
a division of Holtzbrinck Publishing Holdings Limited Partnership
175 Fifth Avenue, New York, New York 10010
All rights reserved

Library of Congress control number: 2017957144
ISBN 978-1-62672-830-1

Our books may be purchased in bulk for promotional, educational, or business use. Please
contact your local bookseller or the Macmillan Corporate and Premium Sales Department
at (800) 221-7945 ext. 5442 or by e-mail at MacmillanSpecialSales@macmillan.com.

FIRST
EDITION

First edition 2018
Book design by John Patrick Green
Printed in China by RR Donnelley Asia Printing Solutions Ltd., Dongguan City, Guangdong Province

1 3 5 7 9 10 8 6 4 2

BY ART
WE LIVE

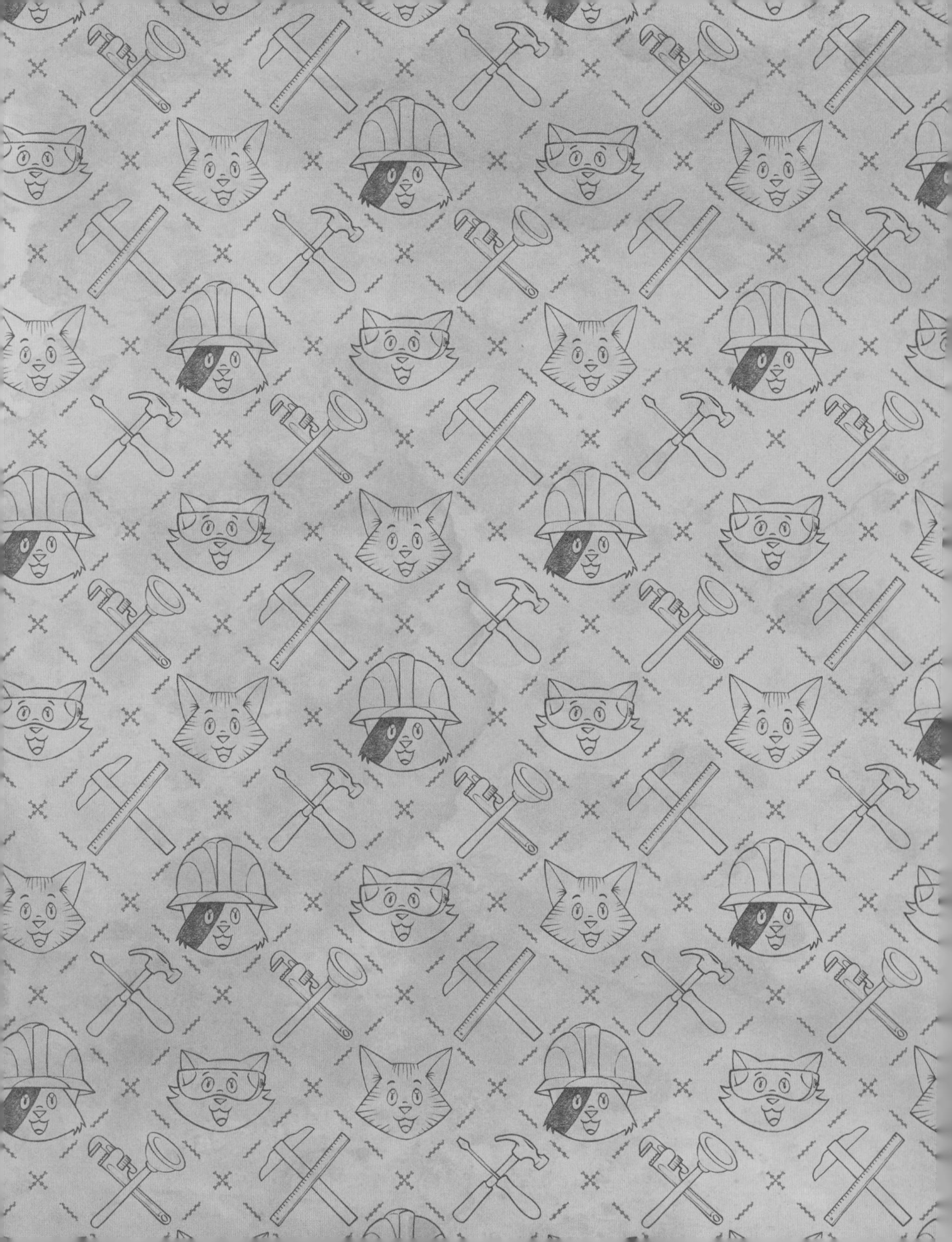